She had a fleeting, transient beauty to her—but her eyes emitted a wicked shine, and the edges of her lips were twisted upward in what seemed to be an expression of utter joy at the carnage she had seen.

That Time I Got Reincarnated as a SLIME

1

FUSE

Illustration by **Mitz Vah**

YEN ON

NEW YORK

That Time I Got Reincarnated as a SLIME ①

FUSE

Translation by Kevin Gifford
Cover art by Mitz Vah

TENSEI SHITARA SLIME DATTA KEN volume 1
© Fuse / Mitz Vah
All rights reserved.
First published in Japan in 2014 by MICROMAGAZINE PUBLISHING Co.
English translation rights arranged with MICROMAGAZINE PUBLISHING Co.
through Tuttle-Mori Agency, Inc., Tokyo.

English translation © 2017 by Yen Press, LLC

Yen On
1290 Avenue of the Americas
New York, NY 10104

Visit us at yenpress.com
facebook.com/yenpress
twitter.com/yenpress
yenpress.tumblr.com
instagram.com/yenpress

First Yen On Edition: December 2017

Yen On is an imprint of Yen Press, LLC.
The Yen On name and logo are trademarks of Yen Press, LLC.

The publisher is not responsible for websites (or their content) that are not owned by the publisher.

Library of Congress Cataloging-in-Publication Data

Names: Fuse, author. | Mitz Vah, illustrator. | Gifford, Kevin, translator.
Title: That time I got reincarnated as a slime / Fuse ; illustration by Mitz Vah ; translation by Kevin Gifford.
Other titles: Tensei Shitara Slime datta ken. English
Description: First Yen On edition. | New York : Yen ON, 2017–
Identifiers: LCCN 2017043646 | ISBN 9780316414203 (v. 1 : paperback)
Subjects: GSAFD: Fantasy fiction.
Classification: LCC PL870.S4 T4613 2017 | DDC 895.63/6—dc23
LC record available at https://lccn.loc.gov/2017043646

ISBNs: 978-0-316-41420-3 (paperback)
        978-1-9753-0110-1 (ebook)

10 9 8 7

LSC-C

Printed in the United States of America

That Time I Got Reincarnated as a SLIME

1

It was just your typical kind of life. I graduated from college, landed a job at a sort-of-big general contractor outfit, and with my older brother taking care of our parents for me, I was currently enjoying all the myriad benefits of the bachelor-pad life. Age thirty-seven. No significant other.

I wasn't exactly short or frumpy or hideous or anything. But when it came to the opposite sex, apparently I had nothing to offer. I'd made efforts along those lines, with varying degrees of dedication, but by the third rejection, something fizzled out within me. Besides—really, at this age, I was kinda past the point where a girlfriend needed to be my main focus. Work kept me busy enough. Plus, it wasn't like I was gonna die without one.

...I'm *not* making excuses, all right? It's just that I started thinking...

"Oh, hello, sir! Sorry we're late!"

There he was, walking toward me, bursting with all that youthful energy of his. He and the beautiful woman next to him. His name was Tamura, one of the guys who worked under me, and she was Sawatari, the front-desk lady and pretty much the "it" girl around the office.

These bums asked to see me because they were getting married and wanted my advice. In other words, this meeting was the whole reason I was brooding over why I was such a failure at personal relationships. I was leaning against a telephone pole at the intersection where we'd agreed to meet after work, thinking to myself.

"Nah." I nodded a greeting at Sawatari and asked, "What'd you want to talk about?"

"Oh, good to meet you. My name's Miho Sawatari. I've seen you at work a lot, but...um, I guess this is the first time I've spoken to you, huh? It makes me kind of nervous, somehow."

I'm the one who should be nervous, lady! my mind griped to itself. *It's not like I'm any good at speaking to women. How about a little sympathy here?*

Any way you looked at it, I was the wrong person to ask. I knew nothing about love. They were doing this just to spite me—I was sure of it. Pretty sure, anyway.

"Oh, there's nothing to be nervous about," I replied. "Satoru Mikami. It's good to meet you, Ms. Sawatari...although you're famous enough around the office that you hardly need to even introduce yourself, huh? Tamura and I went to the same college, and we kinda hit it off during his training period, so that's how we know each other."

"Famous? Oof! Not famous in a weird way, I hope?"

"Oh, y'know. I hear stories about you dating Kameyama or messin' around with Mr. Kihara in management..."

Somehow, I decided that picking on her would be a good idea. I just meant it as a passing joke, but it made Sawatari's face turn a bright shade of red, her eyes watering up a bit. It was cute, in a way. People were always telling me to tone that stuff down—that I needed to consider people's feelings more or, if not that, at least make it funnier—but I couldn't help myself. So mark that down as another failure. Maybe I really *do* have a crap personality.

Tamura took that chance to intervene, giving Sawatari a pat on the shoulder. *Dammit, Tamura! So blessed with the natural charm you need to live a decent life... I wish people like you would just explode!*

"Aw, stop being mean to her," he admonished with an effortless smile. "And don't worry, Miho, he's just having a little fun with you."

Cool, refreshing, and completely guileless—Tamura was impossible to hate. He was still just twenty-eight, quite a bit younger than I was, but we got on well nonetheless. I probably owed him at least a few congratulations...

"Hah, sorry," I said, figuring there was no reason to let my jealousy devour me. "I can't help but needle people like that sometimes. But no point standing here on the sidewalk. Wanna get something to eat while we talk?"

"Aaaahhh!!"

Screams. Chaos. *What is— What's going on?!*

"Move! I'll kill you!!"

I turned around to find a man sprinting toward me, a backpack in one hand and a kitchen knife in the other. I could hear shrieking. He was coming my way. With a knife. A knife? And at the other end of it...

"Tamuraaaa!"

The moment I shoved Tamura aside, I felt a burning pain run across my back. My body balled up as it collapsed to the ground, trying to withstand the shock. I couldn't tell what had happened. I wanted to move, but I couldn't.

"Get the hell outta my way!" the man shouted as he ran off. I watched him go and then checked to see how my companions were. The suddenness of it all had reduced Tamura to a stupor, but he was unhurt. That was good. But, *man*, was my back burning. So hot. Beyond anything I'd describe as pain.

What's up with that? It's too hot... Gimme a break.

Confirmed. Resist Heat...successfully acquired.

Did I... Did I just get stabbed?
So I'm gonna die from a stabbing? Holy crap...

Confirmed. Resist Piercing Weapon...successfully acquired.
Following up with Resist Melee Attack... Successfully acquired.

"M-Mr. Mikami, you're bleeding... You won't stop bleeding!"

I really didn't need to hear that right now. Was that Tamura? I thought I heard some kind of weird voice. If it was Tamura, then so be it.

I'm bleeding? Well, duh. I'm only human. If you stab me, I'll probably bleed all over you, yes.

Damn, this was starting to hurt, though...

Confirmed. Cancel Pain...successfully acquired.

Um... Well, shit. All this pain and panic was starting to screw around with my consciousness.

"T-Tamura... Shut up. It... It's nothing big, all right? Quit worrying..."

"Mr. Mikami, you're... The blood..." Tamura tried to hold me up, face drained of color and looking about ready to break into sobs. So much for that bravado from two minutes ago. I tried to see how Sawatari was doing, but my vision was too fogged up to manage it.

Now the burning feeling on my back was starting to fizzle out. Instead, an intense, frigid cold was attacking me from head to toe. *That... That's probably bad... People die once they bleed too much, don't they?*

Confirmed. Constructing a blood-free body... Successful.

Hey, what're you talking about? I can't hear you too well...

I tried to speak. And failed.

Shit. I think this might really be it... Like, the pain and the heat were pretty well gone by now. It was just cold. Cold as hell. I felt as if I was gonna freeze in place.

Who knew dying could keep you so damn busy?

Confirmed. Resist Cold...successfully acquired. Combined with the previously acquired Resist Heat, the skill has progressed to Resist Temperature.

Just then, what remained of my increasingly oxygen-deprived brain cells chanced upon a flash of brilliance.

Oh, craaaaap, the files on my hard drive!

I summoned up my remaining wells of strength, striving to relay the final regret I had left in life.

"Tamuraaa! If... If anything bad happens to me...take my computer, okay? Put it in the bathtub, turn it on, and just fry everything on the disk for me, man..."

Confirmed. Electricity-based deletion of data... Cannot execute. More information required. Substituting with Resist Electricity... Successfully acquired.

It took a moment for my plea to register with Tamura. He gave me a blank stare. Then he snickered.

"Ha-ha! That's just like you, isn't it?"

Even if it was just a snicker, it beat having to depart this plane of existence with a grown man blubbering on top of me. I'd take it.

"All I wanted was to show Sawatari off to you, too...," he continued. "Pfft..."

Hah. I knew it. That bastard.

"It's fine, okay? Make her a happy woman."

I wrung out the last bit of strength my body had to offer.

"Just kill my PC for me..."

∗

It was just your typical kind of life. I graduated from college, landed a job at a sort-of-big general contractor outfit, and with my older brother taking care of our parents for me, I was currently enjoying all the myriad benefits of the bachelor-pad life.

And I was a virgin.

Imagine that. Floating off to meet my maker in completely unused condition... My manhood was probably crying its single eye out right then. *Sorry I couldn't make you a real grown-up. If there's such a thing as reincarnation, I'm gonna go on the attack next time—I promise. I'll hit up everyone I see, stalking my prey before I go in for the kill... Okay, not like that, but...*

Confirmed. Unique skill "Predator"...successfully acquired.

I mean, here I was, lookin' at forty without ever losing my virginity. Like an old sage meditating in the mountains. Another few years, and I probably could've been the great sage of celibacy. Not the road I wanted to take in life, but there you go.

Confirmed. Extra skill "Sage"...successfully acquired. Evolving extra skill "Sage" into unique skill "Great Sage"... Successful.

...Hey, someone mind telling me who's talking? What do you mean, "unique skill 'Great Sage'"? Someone tryin' to start something with me? There's nothing "unique" about that! If you think I'm finding that funny, I'm not! That's just mean, man...

Before I could continue down that train of thought, however, I fell asleep.

Weird how death's nowhere near as lonely as I thought it'd be.

That was the last thought I had on the mortal plane.

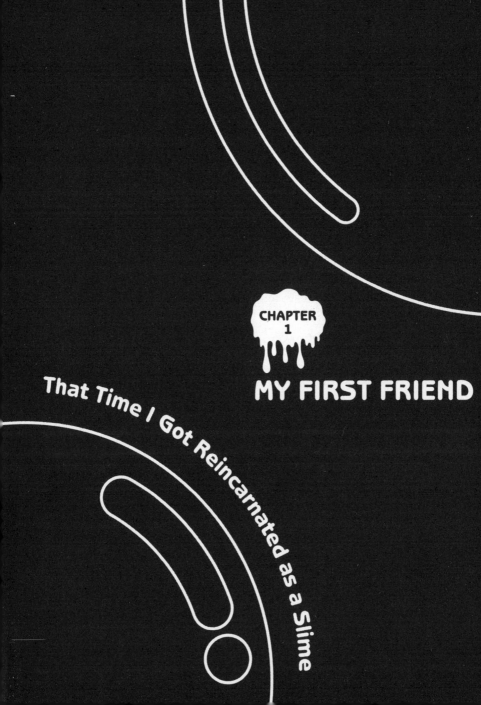

CHAPTER
1

MY FIRST FRIEND

That Time I Got Reincarnated as a Slime

It was dark. Too dark to see anything. Where was I? What even happened, for that matter? Someone was picking on me for being a celibate sage or something, and then...

That was enough to jump-start my mind again.

My name was Satoru Mikami. Just another thirty-seven-year-old in a suit. And when I shoved my coworker aside on the street, some random maniac stabbed me. Good. I remembered all of that. Which meant I must be fine. No need for panic. That wasn't like me anyway. I was known for having a cool head. The last time I panicked, it was grade school and all I did was wet my pants, just a little bit.

I tried looking at my surroundings. Then I noticed—I couldn't open my eyes. *Odd*, I thought as I tried to rub them and my arms didn't respond. And more to the point, *Where's my head, anyway?*

This was getting confusing. Like, whoa. Wait a sec. I needed some time to deal with this.

Whenever I start freaking out, I always find it helpful to sit still and start counting prime numbers until I calm down. Let's try that. *One, two, three—*

Wait, one doesn't count as a prime number, does it?

Ugh... Now wasn't the time for this. I couldn't let myself think about this stupid crap. This was *bad*, wasn't it? Like, what's going on, here?! Was I...like, past the point of no return, unless I did something?

Panicking, I checked to see whether I was hurt anywhere. I didn't seem to be. Physically, I felt terrific. No cold, no heat—perfectly comfortable. That, at least, came as a relief. Now for my hands and legs... Oop. Not so hot there. No response from any of my limbs. What's up with that? Getting stabbed in the back wouldn't force the doctors to amputate all my extremities, would it? I'd kind of like those back.

Then there was the whole "can't open my eyes" thing. I was in a world of darkness, where I couldn't see a thing. An anxiety like none I'd ever felt before began welling up in my mind.

Am I...in a coma or something?

I was conscious, certainly, but had I gotten detached from my central nervous system, maybe?

Oh, man, anything but that! I mean, think about it. When you throw a guy into a dark, enclosed space, it takes practically no time at all for him to go insane. And that was exactly where I was—and I couldn't even die in peace any longer, it looked like. If insanity was all that waited for me here, that was enough to take the wind out of anybody's sails.

Just then, I felt something brush against my body. *Hmm? What's that?* I focused all of my senses on this unknown sensation. It felt like grass against what might have been the side of my stomach. Concentrating on the sensations, I slowly began sussing out what was around me. I could feel the pointy edges of some nearby leaves prick against my body.

It made me a little happy, really. I was in total darkness a moment ago, but now I had my sense of touch back, at least. It made me so overjoyed that I made a beeline for the grass, and—

Creep.

I could feel my body sliding flat against the ground. *I... I moved?!*

This, at least, was clear evidence that I was not on any kind of hospital bed. The feeling beneath my stomach (?) took the form of hard, jagged rock. Hmm. It still didn't make much sense to me, but I appeared to be outdoors.

So I headed toward the grass, keeping my senses keen against what I touched, although I still wasn't quite clear on where my head was. There was nothing to smell; I wasn't sure whether I had that sense or not.

Really, I had no idea what I was shaped like. I felt...flowing. Jellylike. Kind of like a certain fantasy monster I was well familiar with. In fact, the idea had been running through my head for a while now.

...No. Come on. That's just silly. Anything but that. I decided to leave that anxiety-inducing prospect behind for the time being and instead try out the final, untested one of my five human senses. Not that I knew where my mouth was. So...now what?

Suddenly, a voice ran across my mind.

Use unique skill "Predator"?
    Yes
    No

Huh? Wh-what? Unique skill "Predator"?

And what was up with that voice? I thought I heard something weird when I was talking with Tamura earlier. That wasn't just me imagining things? Was someone there? Something didn't seem quite right with it. It wasn't that I thought I had a visitor, so much as...well, as I just had words floating into my mind. Cold, unfeeling words, like a computer-generated voice.

Let's go with no for now.

No response. I waited a while for one, but no further voices came. It appeared there wouldn't be a second question. Did I make the wrong choice? Was this the kind of game where you got stuck if you didn't start giving "yes" answers? I was assuming the question would just repeat forever until I said yes, like any normal RPG. *Guess not.*

Kind of rude of that voice, though. Showing up, asking a simple question, then disappearing forever. It was nice hearing someone for a change, but...the hell, man?

Oh well. Let's go on with what I was trying before. My sense of taste.

I moved toward the grass I felt earlier. As it brushed up against me, I leaned forward, feeling the whole of my weight settle over the field. It was definitely grass of some sort.

Once I was sure of that, I suddenly realized that the area where the plants met my body was starting to melt. I thought it was myself melting at first, but apparently it was only the grass. And with that, I could now tell that the components of the plant life beneath me were being taken into my body.

So that was how it worked? Instead of having a mouth to eat with, I just ingested plant matter with my whole body? It sure didn't taste like anything.

From this, there were a few conclusions I could sensibly make.

First, I was no longer human. That was a given by now. So did I really get stabbed to death? It didn't seem like much of an open question at this point. It'd also explain why I was resting on a rocky patch of grass instead of in a hospital room.

What happened to Tamura? To Sawatari? Did he scramble my hard drive for me, like he promised? I was full of questions—but also a suspicion that, by this point, none of them really mattered anymore. I had to think about what came next.

So...is this it? Am I really a... You know... With the kind of tactile feedback I'm getting at the moment...

I trained my senses back inside my body. It responded with a rhythmic motion. *Boing. Sproing.* Slowly, inside the total darkness, I took the time to ascertain the exact boundaries of my form.

...Heavens! I used to be such a handsome, attractive man, and now I'm so...*fluid*! So aerodynamic!

...Yeah, right! You think I'd accept this just like that?!

As far as I could feel, there was no longer any doubting it. I could picture it in my mind.

I mean...what else could it be? Not like I had a prejudice against it. Hell, it was kinda cute, if anything!

But was it for *me*, though? If you took a poll, I think at least nine out of ten people would have the same answer.

I would just have to accept it, though. Accept the fact that my

"soul," or whatever you want to call it, had been reborn inside a monster from another world. The odds of such a thing seemed astronomically low to me, but...

But I'd been reborn. As a slime.

✳

Munch, munch.
Munch, munch, munch, munch.
I just snacked on some grass.
Why did I do that? Well, why not?
Not like I had anything else to do!

It had been a few days or so since I was pretty much forced to accept the fact that I was now a slime. How many, I wasn't exactly clear on. The passage of time is tough to pick up on when all you can see is total darkness.

One discovery I had stumbled upon over the past few days was that a slime's body could be way more useful than at first sniff. I never got hungry, for one, nor did I get tired. Food and sleep, for me, were wholly unnecessary. And I had divined something else, too. I couldn't be completely sure, but there didn't seem to be anything else living around here. In terms of danger, I wasn't sure there was any to speak of. My days were blissfully free of worry.

Or anything else, really.

The whole time, I never heard that voice again. By this point, I wouldn't have minded a little companionship. But no. It was just me, the grass, and me eating it for lack of much else to do. It was simply a way to kill time. And by this point, I could sense the entire process—my body absorbing the blades, dismantling them internally, sorting through all the components, and storing them away.

What it all meant, I couldn't say. It was starting to frighten me a bit. I needed to do *something*, or I'd lose my mind. So I kept going through the cycle—absorb, break down, store up. But there was something odd about the process. Elimination never factored into it, somehow. Not even once. Maybe slimes didn't need to do that. Hell, not like *I'd* know either way. But where was all this stuff I was ingesting going, then? My senses told me that my form hadn't changed in any appreciable manner from when I first arrived.

So what the hell?

Received. It is being stored in the stomach of the unique skill "Predator." Current physical space usage is less than one percent.

What? Whoa! It speaks!

But since when was I using any skills? I thought I answered no back there.

Received. The unique skill "Predator" is not being used. The matter being ingested into your body is set to automatically be stored in your stomach. This can be changed as needed.

Oh? Well, nice to see we're having a real back-and-forth, finally. But back to business. If I use this skill, what happens then?

Received. The unique skill "Predator" chiefly comprises the following five effects:

Predation: *Takes the target into your body. Lesser chance of success if the target has its own consciousness. Can be targeted on organic and inorganic objects, as well as skills and magic.*

Analysis: *Analyzes and researches targets taken into your body. Lets you create craftable items. If the required materials are present, allows you to make a copy of the item. Successful Analysis of the casting method allows you to learn the target's skills and magic.*

Stomach:	Stores the Predated target. Can also store materials created via Analysis. Items stored in your stomach are unaffected by time.
Mimicry:	Reproduces the form and skills of absorbed targets. Only available once the target has been Analyzed.
Isolate:	Stores harmful effects incapable of being analyzed, neutralizing them and breaking them down into magical force.

Um... What?

For the first time in a while, I was thrown. That sounded like kind of an incredible ability. Not exactly the kind of thing slimes were known for. At least not the ones I knew.

And...hang on. Who was this voice answering my questions, anyway? Was someone there?

Received. This is the effect of the unique skill "Great Sage." The skill has taken effect, making it more immediately available.

A sage, huh...? And here I thought that voice was just screwing with me. Now it was the best partner I had. *Hope that keeps up.*

Hell, *anything* would have been fine at that point. As long as it helped smooth out the endless solitude I was preparing myself for. For all I knew, this "voice" was something my mind had crafted to keep my marbles intact. It was fine by me. For the first time in ages, I could feel a burden lifting from my heart.

✳

By my count, it had been ninety days since I was reincarnated as a slime.

To be more precise, ninety days, seven hours, thirty-four minutes, and fifty-two seconds. How was I so sure about this? Turned out that was one of the many side effects of evoking that "Great Sage" skill.

Holy cats, was that thing helpful. Talk about your best friend in a pinch. Any question that popped to mind, it instantly provided the answer.

According to this Sage, it took ninety days for the skill to fully fuse itself with my soul. Normally, it would be unable to provide responses in the form of conversation, but in order to answer my questions, it apparently revamped itself, diverting part of its "World Language" powers to assist me. That's how it was explained to me, at least.

This useful ability—relaying words into my mind—isn't normally possible. As it explained to me, this "World Language" was heard only when there were great changes to the world or when you either earned or upgraded a skill—something that normally didn't happen all that often. These skills were obtained only rarely, when the world recognized that you had grown in one way or another.

Evolution, meanwhile, was something most people never got to experience in their lives. It was all Greek to me, but if that was how it was, I was willing to accept it.

So the Great Sage was answering my questions at the moment, but otherwise it was this totally passive thing. No real sentience or anything. Unless I spoke up, it would never talk to me of its own volition. That was the only real drawback, but tossing words around with someone again was a wonderful feeling, even if it was a one-way street.

Although, back in my home world, having a conversation with my own skill might have been considered strange...

So there I was, still locked in darkness, asking a barrage of questions.

One thing the replies confirmed was that yes, I was a slime now. I also found out why I never got hungry or sleepy. The slimes in this world, it turned out, never had to eat if they could keep absorbing the magic particles, or "magicules," in the air. In less magically abundant regions, I would be obliged to fill up by absorbing monsters or small creatures.

Most slimes shied away from areas with low magic presences, but the ones that didn't were apparently both quite strong and madly vicious. Usually it was the other way around, where a wealth of local magic meant especially strong monsters.

In other words, the area I took up residence in was so laden with magic that I didn't even have to eat.

As for the sleep question:

Received. The body of a slime consists of a mass of completely identical cells. Each individual cell may function as a brain cell, a nerve cell, or a muscle cell. Since the operational cells used for thought are rotated in and out at regular intervals, there is no need for you to sleep.

This raised the question of where my memories were being held, exactly. Maybe it was kind of like a RAID setup on a computer?

That would be close enough, came the response. Considering its lack of personality, the Sage certainly came up with some snappy replies.

Speaking of which, the "Great Sage" skill consisted of five effects:

Hasten Thought:	Boosts perception speed by a thousand times.
Analyze and Assess:	Analyzes and assesses the target.
Parallel Operation:	Operates on any matter you wish to analyze, separating it from the regular thought process.
Cast Cancel:	Annuls the casting period required when using magic, et cetera.
All of Creation:	Provides full coverage of all unsuppressed matter and phenomena in this world.

"All of Creation"? So I know about everything, everywhere, with no effort on my part? Score! Or so I thought.

It turned out that I could only be told information related to things I'd already heard about—in other words, I needed to recognize and understand a concept before I could grab a full Analysis of it.

And the spell thing—did that mean I could instantly use any magic once I learned it? And, like, there was *magic* in this world and stuff?!

The Great Sage replied with a big *Yes*.

Well, once I knew that, I just had to try to learn a few spells myself.

I checked with the Sage to see if it could help me cast magic, but that was a no-go. Eh, it was worth a shot.

Still, I had another great idea: Could I link the "Predator" Analysis skill with "Great Sage" Parallel Operation?

Received. It is possible to link "Predator" Analysis with "Great Sage" Parallel Operation. Do you wish to link them?
Yes
No

Uh, yeah? Not that I had anything to analyze yet... Wait. Or did I? That grass in my stomach. The stuff I had been eating to pass the time. What was that? Not like I had anything else to do. Let's give it a try.

Off you go, Sage.

....

......

...

Analysis complete.

Hipokute herbs: *A type of ingredient used in healing medication. Only thrives in areas blessed with high local magic densities. Fusing its juice with magicules produces recovery medicine. Grinding the blades and fusing them with magicules produces a salve that closes wounds.*

Wow! That was what I'd been snacking on? Talk about an unexpected windfall. I immediately set out to create some medicine of my very own. The process took place inside my body, so it didn't really feel much like crafting, but the Analysis took less than a second, and within another three-ish, I had my very first potion. Five minutes, and I could've had a hundred. And while I didn't have anything else to compare it to, using my Great Sage skills to assess them resulted in a "high quality" rating.

So there you go. I was happy enough with it, at least. It all went so fast, too. I asked the Sage about it, and it said the process usually took more time than that. Linking it with Parallel Operation must've been the right idea, I suppose.

To test that theory out, I unlinked it long enough to create a single potion. It took fifty minutes. Damn, that was slow. Looks like I had the foresight to stumble across some mega-compatible skills to combine. Not that I knew what I was doing at all.

Some of your garden-variety weeds were also sprouting here and there, but most of the local grasses were hipokute. How 'bout that? So I decided, as a little insurance, to Predate all the herbs I could in the area and turn my stomach into a little recovery-potion factory. I didn't have much else to occupy my time. It was still pitch black in here.

There was no doubt about it. I had put my guard down. I had a partner who granted me skills and the ability to engage in (kind of passive) conversation, and I let it get to my head.

I suppose that had a lot to do with how for ninety days in a row, I never ran into any other creatures. No danger to my life whatsoever. But either way, I had let my guard down.

For an instant, I was like, "Huh?"

I felt a sudden sensation that I had grown lighter or heavier or, like...unstable.

Did I...fall in some water?

In the past ninety days, I hadn't felt so much as a drop of water hit my body. I'd assumed I was in a rain-free cave or some other kind of shelter, so I had never even entertained the possibility before.

I had probably slipped into a river or something. Rivers don't exist indoors, so maybe it was some kind of underground creek in this cave I was in…? Up to now, I had been careful with every step I took, making sure everything remained steady in the darkness. But after learning about my skills, getting full of myself, and using Predation to eat a pasture's worth of grass, I had stopped paying attention to what was under me.

I was always like that. Getting cocky, then screwing it all up in the end. I'd proclaim to a customer, "Oh, absolutely! That won't be any problem at all!" and then have hell to pay. It had happened over and over. I still remember the spiteful looks the rest of my team gave me for it.

Too bad I didn't think to stop myself in time. What kind of idiot runs off into parts unknown when they can't even see? If I survived this, I was gonna give myself what for. Of course, given my personality, I doubted I'd learn anything from it.

It was funny how serenely I was handling this whole thing, though. Not like I had much in the form of arms or legs I could flail about in horrified panic…

Guess it's over, then. Pretty short lifetime—even by slime standards, maybe. I said my final prayers, awaiting my inevitable suffocation.

…………

……

…

Suffocation never came.

Why not? Did I *not* fall in the water? Time to call on the Sage, maybe.

Received. A slime's body operates exclusively on magicules. Oxygen is unnecessary, and therefore, so is breathing. That is why you have not been engaging in that behavior.

Oh… Right. I wasn't paying attention, but I guess there wasn't any breathing, was there? Made sense. Even after ninety days, I was still learning something new!

But now wasn't the time to celebrate. I *had* fallen into water, and even if I wouldn't die, it did still put me in kind of a bind. What now? I couldn't really tell whether I was floating or sinking. My lack of limbs precluded any attempt at swimming. Would I wind up at the bottom sooner or later and be able to creep my way back to the surface? Or was I doomed to bob around in the middle of the current, never reaching much of anywhere?

Though, if anything, it felt less like a violent torrent and more like I was being rocked in a cradle. Very gently rocked. It felt pretty good, even...

Something told me this wasn't flowing water after all. Maybe it was a lake, not a river. I didn't feel as though I was being taken anywhere. I was just kind of bobbing up and down, like a plastic bag, and it didn't feel as if I'd ever hit bottom. If things stayed this way, I was in big trouble.

What now?

Just then, my brain cells—or my slime body, I guess—came up with an ingenious plan. Maybe I could go all Predator on this water and then spit it out for some water-jet propulsion. Would that work? Only one way to find out. Not like I could do anything else.

So I started drinking, filling my Predator stomach up to approximately 10 percent of its capacity. Then, I expelled it like I was wringing out my stomach.

The sense of release was exhilarating.

Suddenly, I heard a voice in my mind:

Water Pressure Propulsion skill acquired.

It was the first time I recognized it. This had to be the so-called World Language. There was no mistaking it, since the Sage spoke only when spoken to, but the two voices did sound exactly the same.

But I didn't have a moment to ponder over this. The more pressure I applied on the water, the more pressure I felt on myself, and I was rocketing forward at astonishing speed, as if I was about to launch myself into the sky. The acceleration was intense. Honestly, maybe it was a good thing I couldn't see. Instead, I just basked in the sensation of my body zipping along through the darkness.

Well, let me clarify. If I could've seen my surroundings, I'm sure the fear would've been intense...but not being able to see was just as terrifying.

If you've ever been on a roller coaster in an amusement park in total darkness, perhaps you'd understand the feeling. My mind flashed back to my previous life and the single day I spent visiting a certain paradise under the rule of a certain rodent. At least *his* magical dreamland offered safety harnesses.

By this point, I wanted to punch myself for coming up with the idea. And trying it out right after thinking it up? Come on, man! What happened to some kind of, you know, preliminary safety check?

The terror was starting to affect my train of thought. How long would I keep accelerating? How much water did I spit out, anyway?

As that thought occurred to me, I felt my body crash headlong into something and bounce off it. I braced myself for a wave of paralyzing pain. Which never came.

Huh? Shouldn't that have, like, damaged me? Or did it damage me, and I just didn't feel it or whatever?

Received. You have acquired Cancel Pain, which interrupts the creation of pain. Your Resist Melee Attack has reduced the amount of damage taken. The amount of damage your body has incurred is ten percent. The intrinsic slime skill Self-Regeneration has taken effect. Would you like to support it with your Predator unique skill?
> *Yes*
> *No*

Oh, so I was hurt a little, then? Made sense. I wasn't sure whether this was a good or bad thing, but as long as I knew something was up, then maybe I didn't need to feel pain after all. It'd make certain things easier.

Predator support, though, huh? I don't really get it, but sure. "Yes."

At that moment, I was greeted with the feeling that I had suddenly lost some of my body mass. After a while, I felt it return. My damaged parts had been Predated, analyzed, and repaired. *Talk about a useful body to have. I should try testing later to see how much of it I can afford to lose before I'm KO'd.* It was way too dangerous to mess with in detail, but I guess I could afford to go without at least a bit of it at a time, so...

Something told me I was getting a little too careful, anyway. I had a stockpile of recovery potions, which I didn't even have to use. And I would've figured losing a tenth of my body would be a pretty serious issue, but now I knew I could just regenerate it in the space of ten seconds. Next time I was damaged, I'd try using those potions.

So where am I, I wonder? Making sure my body was back to normal, I checked out my surroundings. No telling what kind of dangerous monsters might be nearby. I was out of the water, but maybe there were scary, scaly things waiting for me on the other side.

Slowly, carefully, I started taking action.

It kind of seemed as if whenever I did something "carefully," it meant I was about to be exposed to a heap of danger. I was sure it was just my mind playing tricks on me, though.

And that thought probably did me no favors, because...

Can you hear me, little one?

I heard something.

*

Little one? It's probably not anyone besides me, is it?

It wasn't a voice, exactly, but something I could recognize more directly and instinctually in my mind. I didn't have any ears to listen with anyway.

Hello! You can hear me, can you not? Respond to me!

Well, no shit! But how was I supposed to reply without any mouth? As an experiment, I tried thinking *Shut up, baldy!* in my mind—not like this guy could hear it or anything. But how was I gonna get anywhere here if I couldn't even give a—

...Oh-ho! You dare to call me bald, do you...? Rather a lot of nerve packed into such a little body, no? I had hoped to give my first guest in quite a while a little kindness, but it would seem you are in rather a hurry to die!

Uh-oh. Geez, could've warned me that would work first. And I had no idea who I was dealing with, either. Well, that was it. My loss. Time for an apology.

I'm sorry! I didn't know how to reply to you, so I just tried saying the first thing that came to mind! I'm really sorry about that! I can't see anything right now, so I have no idea what you even look like!

Did that come across? Kind of rude to call this guy bald when I couldn't even see him, I supposed. If he was, I'd probably just pushed some very delicate buttons.

Heh-heh-heh... Eh-ha-ha. Ahh-ha-ha-ha-ha-ha-ha!

The resulting laugh came in three distinct levels. A masterpiece. So were we cool now, or—?

How fascinating. I had assumed you reacted as such upon seeing me, but you cannot, eh? Most slimes are low-level monsters, incapable of conscious thought as they run through the cycle of absorption, division, and regeneration. It is the rare one, indeed, that ever leaves its habitat.

Now what was he talking about? Was he more curious than angry, then, or...? Either way, this was my first contact with another intelligent being. The first conversation in my new, oozy life. I wanted to keep it a friendly one.

You had aroused my curiosity, slime, by the way you so eagerly slammed into my body. The regenerative powers you just showed astonish me. Are you a named monster, perhaps, or a unique?

A what? And a what? Say again? *I'm sorry, I don't get what you mean. I've only been alive here for ninety days...*

Hmm. I suppose, with your sentience, you were never destined to be merely a slime. Named monsters are those who have been assigned an exclusive name. But only ninety days? Ridiculous. Are you a unique, then?

"Unique" meaning...?

A unique monster is an individual who has suddenly attained unusual abilities, akin to mutation. They are occasionally born in areas with high magical concentrations... Perhaps you were born from the mass of magicules that leaked out from me, then?

Muh? What the heck?

Let's try using my previous-world knowledge to suss this out. This guy (I'll call him a guy for convenience's sake) had been leaking magic all over the local area. It was so thick, in fact, that it gave birth to a monster. A slime. Me. Was that it?

Hmm. No monster has ever come close to approaching my domain in the past three hundred years. If you were born from my magical force, then perhaps, indeed, that gave you the power to touch me and live to tell the tale!

Oh... So you're kind of, like, my dad, then?

No, not your parent by blood. I have no reproductive ability to speak of. Some monsters do, and some do not, you see.

Really? 'Cause I thought that kind of came with the package by default. But if I just spontaneously burst out from magic or whatever, maybe you don't need it, huh?

...Your intellectual abilities surprise me. Very few, indeed, are the monsters that possess anything of the sort. Among all the monsters, only magic-born have sentience in the way you or I would understand it.

The commentary went on for a while. But the most important thing to learn from it was that apparently humans existed in this world, too. Then there were nonhumans, species very close to mankind in nature and similarly gifted with reproductive abilities. These included races like elves, hobbits, dwarves, and other fairy types, and generally they were allied with the humans.

Alongside that, you had races like goblins, orcs, lizardmen, and so on, which were hostile toward mankind and treated like monsters as a result. This animosity wasn't inherent to their biology, however, so crossbreeding was entirely possible.

Next were the "magic-born people"—the catchall term for those who came into being from magic itself, monsters who experienced sudden mutation, and sentient beings evolved from animals or magical beasts. They had both intelligence and reproductive ability, but only within their own subspecies. In their upper social castes existed titans, vampires, devils, and other longer-lived species—all equally capable of having offspring, although they rarely did so, since their overwhelming magic force caused them to be nigh immortal, obviating the need to leave descendants.

These diverse intelligent, reproducing species were hostile to mankind and collectively referred to as the "magic-born race." And reading between the lines, the impression I got was that the magic-born weren't so much overtly hostile toward humans as the humans feared and coveted their powers. It remained true, though, that both sides were fighting for their own living spaces.

These sundry monsters had been classified by levels of danger. The upper ranks of the magic-born were packed with some pretty powerful buggers—all capable of leveling a human town solo if they felt like it. Not the kinds of guys you'd want to hang around.

So my new companion kept going for a while—about how he'd fought against the upper-level magic-born in the past and so on. Finally, the subject turned back to me.

As I told you, then, I lack the ability to produce offspring. The reason is simple… Because I do not need to. I am of the dragon race—one of only four in the world, both unique and the most perfect of my kind. You will hereby know me as Veldora, the Storm Dragon! My life span is infinite, my flesh unfathomable! As long as my will remains intact, I shall be ever alive! Ahhhhh-ha-ha-ha-ha-ha-ha-ha!!

He could've skipped the laughter. I got it. So he didn't need to have kids, because he was gonna live forever, right?

And while this guy took a while to get to the point, he did mention something I didn't want to overlook.

Veldora was the Storm…Dragon?

Plus, if he liked taking a good-natured swipe at upper-level magic-born now and then, he was…like, pretty tough, wasn't he?

Using my knowledge of Earth stuff, I tried to picture Veldora the Storm Dragon, no doubt seated in front of me right now. I didn't like what my mind came up with. He seemed to be acting polite with me, and that made it all the creepier.

So what now…?

W-wow, really? Well, thanks for all that handy guidance, sir! Guess I better be on my way, then!

I tried my best to flee.

Halt. I have told you all about myself. It is your turn now, would you not agree?

I probably shouldn't have expected any other treatment. Hmmmm. He wanted to know about me? If I told him about my miraculous journey from an alien planet, would he believe me? He seemed to marvel at how smart I was for a slime—if I tried to make something up, I doubted he'd fall for it. Such an attempt seemed like a good way to dig my own grave.

Well, whatever. If he didn't believe me, I'd deal with it then. Summoning my resolve, I told Veldora everything that had happened to me so far.

·········

······

···

So... Yeah. Here I am, I guess! It's been super rough, y'know?

While prudently keeping the topic of my skills unexplored, I regaled the dragon with my tale of being stabbed, waking up as a slime, and everything else that happened on the way to his domain.

It was a bit weird how...well, non-rough it all sounded when I put it into words. But it was rough for me all the same. And the worst part was how I was literally operating blind the entire way. If some cute lady passed me on the road later on, would I ever get to see her? The thought saddened me a little.

Hmm. So a transmigrant, then? Your origins are quite rare, indeed.

Huh? Are they? And you... "Transmigrant"? This isn't any big surprise to you?

What's with that reaction? So these "transmigrants" were common enough that he had a name for them? What was so rare about it, then?

Hmph. You do see transmigrants, on occasion. Their memories from the past are burned into their souls, due to a powerful will. There are some, indeed, who retain every memory of their past lives. But a transmigrant from another world... That is quite uncommon. A regular soul, by itself, would have no hope of surviving a journey across realms. It would dissolve midway, taking its memories with it. Someone retaining their full mind and becoming reborn as a monster out of pure magic... I cannot recall any past example of that. Quite... peculiar, indeed.

Transmigrants from other worlds, it seemed, kept only part of their memories at best. Someone like me, who still had them all, was pretty well unheard of—not that I cared too much.

He had just told me something I couldn't afford to ignore. A soul, "by itself"...? So you could travel to this world without getting reincarnated or anything?

Huh. Am I that unusual? 'Cause it sure doesn't feel that way... Are there people, then, who come here from other worlds without being trans-whatevered?

There are. None have succeeded in traveling to another world from here, but there are more than a few that have completed their travels here from elsewhere. They are known as "visitors," or "otherworlders," and they bear knowledge of things that do not exist in this world. They acquire, as I hear it, some manner of special power when they make the journey here. Beyond that, there are records of transmigrants, who—as I said—bear knowledge of other worlds. Not all of them choose to openly identify themselves as such, though, I imagine.

Interesting. I didn't know whether they came from the same planet I did, but it might be good to chat with them a bit. There might even be some from Japan, for all I knew. It was probably best for my sanity to have a goal while I was here, besides.

I see, I see! In that case, I think I'll try and track down some of these "otherworlders," as you called them. Maybe I'll find someone from my own land!

Well, one moment. You said you cannot see, yes?

Oh, uh, yeah. And? It was a pain in the ass, yes, but as long as I took my time and kept from getting myself killed, I was sure I'd run into some fellow visitors. Probably.

Let me help you see, then.

Um, what? Damn. This guy... I mean, Veldora the Storm Dragon... He was acting way too nice to me, wasn't he? Could I really trust him?

Uh, really?

Indeed. On one condition, however. What do you say?

I didn't like the sound of that, but...ah, what the hell.

What kind of condition?

A simple one. When I grant you the ability of sight, I beg of you not to fear me. That, and I bid you come visit and speak to me again. That is all. I trust my terms are agreeable to you?

That's all? Was he sure? What a lonely dragon. Guess there was no one else around at the top. No wonder he couldn't stop talking to me—I must've been his first conversational partner in ages.

If I'd had my druthers, I would have said this dragon was a total pushover. He might've been feeding me a line this whole time, even, saying he was a dragon. Maybe the dragons in this world weren't even all that powerful in the first place.

Heh. This was a pretty good deal.

Is that really all you need?

Yes. To be honest with you, I was sealed away in here three hundred years ago. Ever since then, I have had so much free time on my hands, I was practically out of my mind with boredom. What do you think?

Well, if that's all you need, you got yourself a deal!

Good. It is a promise, then...and I trust you will hold up your end of the bargain.

Of course! Maybe I don't look it, but you can count on me, man! Just ask anybody on Earth! They'll vouch for me!

Hopefully he wouldn't try to. That would be bad.

Very well. There is a skill known as Magic Sense. Can you use it?

Oh, here we go again. More walls for me to deal with. So unfair.

No, I can't. What kind of skill is that?

It allows you to perceive the particles of magic floating around you. It is not a very powerful skill, and all it offers is a visual reference, so it is not difficult to acquire.

Oh... Sounds easy enough.

Indeed. I can wield it as easily as I can breathe. I hardly even bother to think about it.

Really? So once I learn that, I'll be able to see again?

Precisely. This world is covered in sheer magic, although it is not spread evenly across its entire surface. Did you know, also, that light and sound both have the properties of a wave?

Yeah, I've heard about that. Light waves and sound waves.

Ah. How intelligent of you. Did you learn of that in your past world? You must have, I wager. But, indeed, you will be able to observe how these waves disturb the nearby particles of magic, then use that information to calculate how the area around you looks and sounds. Simple, yes?

Um? Not really? What kind of BS was that? I, um, I'm not really sure whether that sounds simple or not, actually...

No? But that is what allows one to continue fighting even after losing both their sight and hearing! It protects you from surprise attacks, and that is all but a requirement for survival here, is it not?

Y-yeah, but...can we skip all that fighting talk and just get me seeing again, maybe?

Mmm... Very well. Allow me to help you acquire this skill, then. This is the only method I am aware of.

W-wait, can you do that? I'm kind of a newborn here...

Worry not. You do have your memories from your past life, yes? And there, you gained knowledge about the nature of light and sound. Without that, not even I could help you, I wager. Luck is on your side, truly.

True. I supposed it *would* be hard to explain sight to someone who can't see at all. I certainly couldn't manage it. I read somewhere that Helen Keller learned how to speak only by following cues she learned before going deaf at age two. Maybe I could use my knowledge of Earth to harness this "Magic Sense" thing to figure out what the world around me was like...

Worth a shot, I guessed. This blindness was getting to be a massive pain. Plus, I had the Sage on my side. It could work this out.

I'm ready to learn, sir!

Now, now, no need for such ardor. It is quite simple. First, try moving the magic around you with the force in your body.

I had an inkling of what he meant. It was the skill I'd probably adapted to blow myself out of the water a moment ago.

Like this?

I tensed up, trying to imagine the strength circulating through my body. I could feel something moving within—the magicules my companion was talking about. I hadn't been conscious of it in the water, but it looked as though I could adjust the force by how much I tensed up. Before, I hadn't been controlling the water so much as I was controlling the magic dancing around in it. I was exercising my magical muscles, and the particles around me were reacting. It came to me surprisingly quickly.

Mmm. You are more gifted in this than I thought. Now, do you see the difference between the magic moving within you and that outside of your body?

Whoa. Maybe this actually *was* easy. Maybe I was more sensitive to the magic I absorbed now that I was conscious of the way I lived off it.

Well, sure! Like, that's the stuff I've been eating all along, right?

Heh-heh-heh! If you understand that much, the rest is child's play. All it takes is feeling the movements of the particles outside of you.

Yeah, *that* I didn't get. But I gave it a shot, doing as I was told and feeling out the particles surrounding me. And I found I could.

I could sense them hanging in the air, riding air currents, moving around—all sorts of sensations.

Let's ask the Sage about this.

Confirmed. Extra skill "Magic Sense"...successfully acquired. Use the extra skill Magic Sense?

> Yes
> No

Huh? It was that easy?

Well, sure—yes, then... Man, talk about a rock I can rely on!

The moment I invoked Magic Sense, my brain was filled with new information. A massive amount, something my human brain never could've processed—the waves of light and sound pushing every single tiny particle around—and I processed it all, converting it into perceptible data.

The thing about human eyesight is that it doesn't give you even a 180-degree view of what's in front of you. Now, all of a sudden,

I could "see" a full 360 degrees around myself. The shadows of the rocks around me, the views hundreds of meters away—the moment I turned my attention to it, I could figure out what it was. If I were still human, all this perception data probably would've fried my brain circuits. But now I was a slime. My cells could provide muscle just as easily as brain power.

So somehow or other, I withstood the torrent of information. Then—

Synchronizing extra skill Magic Sense with unique skill Great Sage... Successful. All information will now be managed by Great Sage.

Suddenly, my vision opened up. The brain-searing sensation from before was gone, and then I could see—so clearly that it was a wonder I wasn't able to do it before. Something told me that having the Sage at my side was almost cheating. It wouldn't be going too far to put it that way. If someone else had it, I'd probably bitch that it was against the rules. Since *I* had it, though... No problem.

Oh, I think I've got it. Thank you very much! I said, turning my attention to the creature in front of me.

Holy crap. He really was a dragon. He was covered in scales that shone a dark shade of black, tougher looking than steel itself but supple and flexible. A big, evil-looking...

Gahh! You're a dragon!!

He looked positively demonic, towering far higher than I anticipated. My internal scream welled up, pouring out of me, and I don't think I could really be blamed for it.

✳

What a surprise. I feel bad for ever thinking this guy was pet sized. This was...for real. Absolutely no doubt.

The body, startlingly similar to a Western-style dragon's, shone like obsidian. There were six fingers on each "hand," equipped with

claws that looked ready to tear through whatever they found. The two pairs of wings on his back—one larger than the other—came to a point at their respective ends, like swords honed to perfection and ready to dice.

Upon closer observation, the ominous scales covering his entire body actually radiated a dark purplish light—a mixture, perhaps, of their natural color and the unearthly force that made its way through the surface. There was something strangely beautiful about his vast shape, the picture of majestic dignity. I began regretting being so rude back when I couldn't take it all in, but that was all water under the bridge.

Turned out, by the way, that I was indeed oval shaped. Like a little bun. Kind of a...light turquoise, maybe? Lighter than the daylight sky, but not by a lot. A rather elegant color, I thought. Shame about the whole being-a-slime thing.

You do remember your promise, yes? And considering your previous complaints, you learned rather quickly, no?

Oh, of course! I was just joking a little, is all. I can see just fine, and plus I can hear now, too. I really appreciate this!

Hmph. You could have taken your time...

So he was fine after all. A little scary looking, but he was awfully kind to me, for no good reason. He really *was* lonely, I imagined. It was unfortunate that he looked the way he did. Kind of like that little story about the poor red demon who wanted to befriend the humans.

So what do you intend to do next?

Well, for starters, I figure I might as well look for some otherworlders from my home country. Not that I care too much if I don't, but...you know.

Finding some would be better, but it's not as if we're guaranteed to become fast friends. Plus, with my brand-new eyesight, scoping out the world could do wonders for me. Harvesting the light and sound around me had just expanded my world a thousandfold. Now, finally, I could say good-bye to my days of literally chewing the cud in my tiny cave or whatever.

That dragon, though.

The more I stared at him, the more sinister and terrifying he seemed. And yet he didn't move a single inch. He mentioned a three-hundred-year-old seal, right?

By the way, Veldora, you said something about being...sealed away?

Mm? Ah. Yes, I perhaps underestimated my opponent slightly. I eventually began fighting with, shall we say, more urgency, but...well, it was rather too late by then!

The dragon sounded almost proud of his losing performance. Magic was one thing, but I doubted there was a sword or lance in this or any other world that could scratch him. It wasn't as if I knew that much of this world yet—maybe it was crawling with horrifying monsters even more powerful than him, or something?

Was your opponent that tough?

She was...quite strong. She was what the humans call a "hero," one blessed with so-called divine protection.

A hero? My days in front of a game console had made me well familiar with that term. Simply doing hero stuff didn't make you dragon-slaying material, though. A lot of recent games had turned their so-called "heroes" into foils or parodies of themselves, besides. Maybe things were still a bit more traditional around here.

Now that I recall, Veldora continued, *the hero also said she was "summoned." Perhaps she hails from the same area as you.*

Oh? I dunno... Where I come from, nobody's that strong, you know?

Perhaps, but many otherworlders come here bearing special powers. Powers that are chiseled into their souls in the midst of their journey. The summoned will always bear one such skill—a unique skill, one exclusive to them and them alone. Unlike the otherworlders who come here by sheer accident, these people bear a soul strong enough to withstand the stress of the summoning process. The fact that said summoning process so rarely succeeds in this world otherwise proves as much.

When you say "summoning process," do you mean...magic, or whatever?

Precisely. A process requiring at least thirty magicians conducting a ceremony that takes place over three days. It is rarely successful, but it is seen as a powerful weapon to have in one's arsenal, should the need arise.

A weapon?

Mm. Those summoned in such a manner are bound by a magical curse upon their soul, unable to resist the orders of their masters.

Whoa, really? No human rights or anything?

Human rights? What rights would one possibly expect in this, of all worlds? Do not entertain such fantasies in this realm, little one. The only law that reigns here is survival of the fittest. Might, as they say, makes right.

Well, huh. If you got summoned to this world, no point hoping that your old values applied over here, I guessed. Bit hard to accept that.

So are you saying that otherworlders pretty much get treated like slaves here?

No. It depends. There is no Domination Stamp applied to them. If society accepts them, they are free to live their lives as they please. They can become adventurers or the like. Many otherworlder adventurers have sought my head… They learned the error of their ways soon enough! Hyaaa-ha-ha-ha-ha!!

So you're only forced into servitude if you were summoned here, huh…?

Not "servitude," exactly, but I suppose so, yes. I like to believe I know a great deal about the humans, but "a great deal" is not everything.

No… You're a dragon, besides.

In way, he knew almost *too* much as a dragon. At least conversing together put me on his good side—enough that he answered all my questions. So we kept talking—Veldora and I, dragon and slime, about all sorts of things.

How had the fight gone with this hero?

How strong was she?

Her skin was pale in color, the dragon told me; her lips were bright red and small. Her long hair was a dark shade of silver, kept back in a single ponytail. She was slim, not that tall, rather small for a human.

Her face was apparently covered by a mask, but there was no doubting her beauty. I asked him whether this beauty was enough to distract him, whether he was too enrapt to defend himself properly. *Enough of your nonsense!* he bellowed back at me.

Apparently she carried a long, curved sword. A "katana," it was called. She didn't bother with a shield. Taking advantage of two unique skills—Absolute Severance and Unlimited Imprisonment—and a wealth of other magic, she, as Veldora put it, "overwhelmed" him. There was more than a trace of nostalgic contentment in his voice, or so it seemed to me.

Something I picked up on as we spoke was that this dragon... I think he really *liked* humans. He kept calling them "wimps" and "garbage" and such, but from the way he put it, he never deliberately killed anyone who attacked him. Not unless they went out of their way to rile him. One time, three centuries ago—just *one time*, he emphasized—a certain chain of events made him reduce an entire city to embers. That was what made the people send a hero his way, and now—thanks to that hero's Unlimited Imprisonment—he was in his current predicament.

I had trouble enough figuring out my own feelings about a lot of things. Other people's, I could only guess at. But I was starting to get the impression that, well, maybe this wasn't such a bad dragon at all. I mean, I liked him. And he wasn't anywhere near as scary as before.

All right! Well, um... What do you think? Friends, then?

It was kind of...no, *really* embarrassing to put it like that. I'd have been blushing right then, if I could.

Wh-what? A mere slime, daring to seek the friendship of the mighty beast feared worldwide as Veldora the Storm Dragon?!

Oh, um, you don't have to if you don't want, but...

You fool! You foolish fool!! Who said anything about not wishing it?!

Oh, no? Okay, so, um...now what?

—Mmm, indeed... If you insist...I suppose I could consider it...

I could feel him sneaking furtive glances at me. It would have been one thing if it had been a cute girl sitting next to me at the movie theater, but it was quite another when it was a death-dealing mythical beast. Not fun. Pretty funny, though.

Yep. I insist. It's settled! And if you don't like it, then watch out, 'cause I'll never come back!

No! —Ah, so be it. I will become your...friend. I do hope you appreciate the gesture!

Heh. I wondered whether I could manipulate the other three

dragons he mentioned like this. I was made to exploit people, and he was made to be exploited. A perfect match.

Well, to future times, then!

Indeed! To future times! ...Ah, yes, allow me to give you a name. In exchange, you will give one to us both.

Huh? Why? Where'd that come from?

It shall chisel into our souls the fact that we are of the same rank. Something similar to the family names the humans use—except my name, for you, will also provide a kind of divine blessing. You are still nameless now, but through this, you will become a full-fledged named monster.

Mmmm.

So he wanted me to come up with a common name for us to share? And in exchange, I'd get my own name and all the benefits of named-monster status? Better think up something good. I'm terrible at this stuff...

Well, you said you were a storm dragon, so... I dunno, "Tempest" or something?

Ugh. Kind of on the nose, I know, but it sounded cool to me, so—

Perfect! So be it! A wonderful timbre to that title, yes.

He *liked* it?!

From this day forward, they will call me Veldora Tempest! And you... You will be called Rimuru. Proclaim to the world that your name is Rimuru Tempest!

Thus the name was carved into my soul. Not that it did too much to me. Or my abilities. But somewhere, deep inside my soul, something *did* change a bit. I suppose the same could be said of Veldora. And that's how we became friends.

Well, it was time to get going, I supposed. But before that:

Hey, so I had something I wanted to ask before I left, but...can't you do anything about that seal on you?

Not with my powers, no. Someone with a unique skill on the same level as the hero's would be necessary for there to be even a chance.

You don't have any, Veldora?

I do, but now that I am sealed off, I can access none of them. Telepathy is about all I can manage at the moment.

The hero's Unlimited Imprisonment could hold its target captive in an infinite number of imaginary spaces for all of time. It wasn't some weak barrier that would allow casual interference with the real world. Looking back, it should have struck me as strange that Telepathy was possible, even. It wasn't the sort of thing that would break down over time—but given that he could have any contact with the real world, and even exchange messages, perhaps it said more about Veldora. Neither of us noticed this at the time, though.

Well, here, lemme try something...

I rolled over to Veldora and tapped my body against him.

Invoking unique skill Predator to consume unique skill Unlimited Imprisonment... Failed.

I figured as much, but no, I certainly wasn't hero caliber. With a dazzling light, my unique skill tried to do its work but weakly bounced off without any further comment. I thought it might have made a small rip, but that was all. The barrier would repair itself shortly, no doubt. I was hoping that unique skill on unique skill would result in something, but it didn't.

Was there anything I could do, though? Something...

Received. Partial Analysis of unique skill Unlimited Imprisonment complete. Reporting a potential escape route.

Any escape involving a physical body is not possible. The chance of destroying the prison by physically damaging it is zero. Cannot analyze an escape route involving the annulment of imaginary space. One would need to be caught within the same Unlimited Imprisonment situation in order to analyze it from the inside. This is currently impossible.

The chance of escaping in spiritual form is one percent.

If a spiritual receptacle is prepared for the target on the outside to aid in the transition, the success rate is three percent.

This process is equivalent to transmigration. If the target is poorly compatible with the receptacle, he will lose all memories and abilities.

This concludes the report on potential escape routes.

—*Hmm. Kind of low numbers, it sounds like.* Unlimited Imprisonment looked like nothing more than a transparent membrane from my perspective...but physical damage did nothing against it? Maybe it had some kind of insurmountable defense attached to it, for all I knew.

Hey, did you lay any damage on this hero at all? Or vice versa?

Ah, I am glad you asked! Most of my attacks were evaded, but I did land several direct hits...which, I regret, had no effect on her. Death-Calling Wind, Dark Lightning, even Storm of Destruction had no effect, despite being completely unavoidable. A total loss... All I could do was laugh!

Veldora then accentuated the point with a loud, hearty guffaw.

It sounded as though you could also use this Unlimited Imprisonment skill to cover your own body, making a shield to protect from external attack. Pretty handy thing to have around. This hero was starting to sound downright omnipotent. Between that and Absolute Severance, she was all but invincible, wasn't she? I really wouldn't want to run into her...but then, I wouldn't have to. I would have liked to assume she had died in the ensuing three hundred years, at least. Either way, she was one tough character.

So if I was going to get him out of here, it would be through transferring his consciousness into a new body, huh?

I guess I need some kind of receptacle to get you out of here. Even if it's in spirit form only, it sounds like it oughta be possible...

No point telling him what kind of odds he had to go on. I'd just be hurting Veldora further if I dampened his spirits.

Mm? There is a way out of here?! Indeed... I feel my magical force will exhaust itself by no later than a hundred years from now. My magic continues to flow out of me, even now.

Yeah? So that's why there's such a concentration of it around here...

Indeed. Even high-class monsters would not dare approach. You saw how there were no weeds on the ground? The sort of plants that can thrive in this area are very rare indeed!

Right. I recalled all the hipokute herbs I'd churned through over my short life. It was that valuable, huh?

Yeah, so...you wanna try escaping, maybe? If I had the right receptacle, I think that'd help our chances a fair amount... Do you know what I'd need, though?

...Indeed, even if I escaped in spiritual form only, it would be quite difficult to regather magic and form my core once more. Your creating a small tear in the prison helped my chances immensely, no doubt. As for that receptacle—the new core, if you will—if you can bring one to me, all I'd have to do is traverse myself over to it. Transmigration, I suppose...

Yow! And here I thought he was a little slow. He knew exactly what I was getting at, didn't he? The exact same conclusion the Sage had made.

Pretty much, yeah. If it's something I can get on this side, I could look for it for you.

Hmm... To tell the truth, I do not need any core at all... You can keep a secret, I trust? As I said, I am both unique and the most perfect of my kind. A fully unique creation, one that takes purely spiritual form. I have no particular attachment to this body. It is merely the faith of those who live around me that forms the shape you see.

There he went again. Spouting off complete nonsense.

As far as I could piece together in the ensuing conversation, the basic idea went like this:

Using his consciousness alone, he could gather magicules toward him to form a physical body. Said body was currently being held in this prison, but that prison also prevented his will from collecting the magic he needed. Could he escape in consciousness form alone? No, because he needed some kind of receptacle.

If he simply burst out in spirit form, his essence would scatter to the winds like the magic itself, erasing his very existence. This would result in the birth of a new storm dragon, somehow, somewhere—I didn't care about the details by this point. But to sum up, *maybe* he could escape, but if he did, he'd wind up being something else. It wouldn't matter to him.

So much for that. But what if I used Predator to consume Veldora himself? I could either analyze him inside my stomach, or isolate him and annul the effect of Unlimited Imprisonment, and he'd be out. Would that work?

Received: It is possible to store the target Veldora in your stomach via the unique skill Predator.

Really...? In that case, if I could convince *him* of it, we could get going. If I couldn't, he'd have another century of isolation before he was reduced to nonexistence. So I spent a few moments explaining the Predator skill to Veldora, and what I wanted to do with it. It'd be impossible from the get-go without the Sage's help, but...

Mwah-hah-hah-hah-hah! Fascinating! Please, go ahead. I leave myself at your mercy!

You're that ready to believe me?

But of course! It'd be far more fun to break through this prison with you than sit around and await your return! With the two of us together, this Unlimited Imprisonment could fall quicker than we thought!

Now I got it. He was one, but now *we* were two. I liked his outlook.

So the plan was I'd use Great Sage and Predator to analyze this beast, and Veldora would try to destroy it from the inside. No worries about Veldora dissipating away in my stomach. I was starting to think this could actually work.

All right. So I'm gonna consume you, all right? Hurry up and get outta there.

Heh-heh-heh! Right away! You shall make me wait no longer! Let us finally join together!

Right! I summoned up my stores of resolve, touching him for a moment—then activated my Predation skill. In a moment, Veldora's massive form disappeared from sight.

It happened almost too fast. We were talking just a moment ago. Seeing him gone suddenly made me feel very small and *very* solitary. Using the skill on my first target created too much resistance to work at all, but with the help of a fully cooperative Veldora in all his hugeness, it couldn't have gone more smoothly. He and Unlimited Imprisonment itself were sucked in at once.

Kind of a surprise it all fit in me, though. Checking my stomach usage... Geez, 25 percent? How big *was* that thing, anyway?

Then:

Conduct Analysis of unique skill Unlimited Imprisonment?
    Yes
    No

This better work, I prayed as I thought *Yes* to myself.

●

A cataclysm shook the world on that day.

It was the only way to describe the reaction when the disappearance of the storm dragon Veldora was confirmed. It wasn't every day that a Special S-ranked monster simply vanished without a trace.

Monsters, as well as adventurers, were ranked on a system of six grades, from A to F. Pluses and minuses could be attached to these grades for extra precision. This system was first put into place by a man named Yuuki Kagurazaka, a rumored otherworlder and one of the few to assume the topmost rank of "grand master" in the Free Guild. It was quickly adopted, thanks to being much easier to understand than the previous, somewhat arbitrary four-tier system of "novice" → "beginner" → "intermediate" → "advanced."

The Special S rank combined the S rank, which comprised demon lord–class foes that deserved more than simply an A, with the "Special" tag reserved for those above even that class—monsters capable of single-handedly engineering calamities or natural disasters. A scale-breaking rank, existing wholly outside the six traditional ones. Normally, an A-ranked monster alone would be dreadful enough to threaten the existence of a nation—someone like Veldora was dangerous enough to plunge it into despair.

Three hundred years of penance had done nothing to affect the dragon's rank as a natural disaster–level threat. Just because he had disappeared didn't mean he couldn't be reborn somewhere, posing a new menace before long.

But twenty days after the initial report of his disappearance, the Western Holy Church issued a report that, as far as its investigations could tell, Veldora the Storm Dragon both no longer existed and showed no sign of existing anytime soon.

Word spread first in the area around the Forest of Jura, a broad plain dotted with a large number of minor countries. Once Veldora's fate had been broadly reported, each one of them sprang to their feet, the proverbial hornet's nest stimulated to action. Every king and every minister of every nation held day after day of emergency meetings, gathering information and debating what to do next.

It was a trying time for the Baron of Veryard, minister of the small kingdom of Blumund, but not half as trying as it was for the man Veryard had called into his private chamber that day. This was Fuze, a man just as renowned for his sharp, unrelenting eyes as he was for his small stature. He was the guild master for this kingdom, a position affording him a hefty amount of authority even in such a tiny nation.

"I believe you know why I summoned you here," the baron began the moment Fuze walked through the archway. "You have heard about the storm dragon by now, have you not?"

Fuze nodded. "Of course, my baron," he said in his low, hoarse voice.

"Hmph," Veryard spat out in response. "I suppose I should expect nothing less of you, my good guild master. Now, may I ask about how the guild intends to respond?"

"We have no particular plans at this time, sir."

"...I'm sorry, did I hear you correctly? You have no intention to take action?"

"Yes, sir," Fuze replied with a voice devoid of emotion, silently asking the baron what he was so perturbed about. "I do not feel any action is necessary."

The baron, not a great fan of this response, chose to keep those feelings hidden. "Rather a strange thing to say, is it not? Not necessary? The disappearance of Veldora the Storm Dragon may portend further monster activity in the space of days, even hours! And you are taking no measure at all against it?"

"It would strike me as rather strange to do so, sir, for taking such measures is the job of the state. I am responsible for the Free Guild, not for providing volunteer work when bidden."

This was the truth, as far as Fuze was concerned. The Free Guild was an independent, nongovernmental agency. Its members were afforded no special guarantees of security or comfort—unlike the assorted workers and craftsmen on the government ledger—but the basic rights that all citizens were entitled to. Their only official debt to the kingdom came in the form of taxes.

That was the system in Blumund, as it was in nearly all the nations that surrounded it. To put it another way, the Free Guild was a group that operated outside the framework of any nation—and one far more unified than a single government as well. It was a fact that some of their operations occurred without the knowledge or consent of these nations, whether the guild intended it to be seen that way or not.

"Is it not the responsibility of the state," the guild master meekly continued, "to protect the assets of its people? In the same way, it is the guild's responsibility to protect the lives of its members. We both have a lot on our plates, I suppose."

Fuze wasn't sure whether he had imagined the blue vein that had just popped up on Veryard's forehead or not.

He hadn't. The baron knew his position was being probed.

"Enough pretense, Guild Master! How many mercenaries can you provide us? How many adventurers with combat experience? What is the size of the defense force you can provide in service? I need numbers!"

The guild master gave a roll of his eyes and sighed. "I do hope we are on the same page when I say this, sir, but I will remind you, we are not an army of volunteers. If we are talking about a mobilization based on the terms of our agreement, I can provide you the equivalent of one-tenth of our members. If you wish access to anything beyond that, well, that would all depend on our compensation."

The population of Blumund was almost exactly one million. The membership log of the local Free Guild totaled around seven thousand, family members not included. Thus, if the kingdom decided to invoke its agreement with the guild and muster 10 percent of its members—seven hundred in all—these fighters would officially join the command of the national army.

Such an order, of course, would apply only to guild members who belonged to Blumund and no other nation. All Free Guild members fell under the same banner, but their home nations were also clearly stated in the logs for this reason. What's more, while a nation had the right to define its own mobilization period under this agreement, it was also obliged to give the guild a one-fifth discount on taxes collected during the entire period. This allowed governments to rapidly summon a powerful force, and the guild to make sure its men would not be obligated to the state for too much of their time. For a group like the guild, which was required to pay salaries to all deployed members in advance, it was the obvious approach to take.

Besides, even if a government asked for every man the local Free Guild had, there would be no way to handle them. After all, only about half of any guild's membership had any fighting skill.

The Blumund nobles were fully aware of this. Normally, they wouldn't have their top minister attempt to bully the guild master into better terms...but the times demanded otherwise. The monsters were stirring, for one—but even beyond that, they had more pressing motivations.

"Very well. Enough of this. Are you trying to wring the truth out of me, Fuze?"

Fuze's eyebrows raised a little at the mention of his name. Veryard rarely, if ever, called him by it. He turned his eyes toward the baron for the first time.

"The area near Veldora's prison was meant to be absolutely impenetrable," he said. "Now that route may potentially be open to direct navigation—and *that* means we must consider the possibility of the Eastern Empire taking action."

"Ah, certainly so!" the baron replied. "Whether they were letting Veldora be or were simply afraid of the seal being broken, we have been detecting sudden new movements in the Empire after a long period of silence. Do you understand what that means? If they can navigate that forest, this kingdom will be swallowed up instantly. And we can forget about the Western Holy Church providing us any meaningful support! The countries around the Forest of Jura have no meaningful alliance with each other. We will all become Empire vassals in the blink of an eye!"

"No support from the Church...? I fear not, no. They never were terribly interested in wars between mere mortals in the first place. Annihilating the monsters is what their doctrine calls for."

"Quite so. If we could have them deploy even one of their paladins, the Empire wouldn't be so quick to move... Not needing to prepare for monster attacks would buy us some time, at least."

"I doubt anything could stir the Church to action," Fuze said. "The destruction of a nation or two does nothing to affect their own finances. They cannot help everyone, nor even their own flock." He took a moment to gauge the baron's face. Veryard looked exhausted, as if he had aged rapidly in just the past few days. It was understandable.

The two of them were childhood friends. And even though Veryard was merely a baron, if the public knew of Fuze's close contact with a member of the nobility, it would create assorted difficulties for the both of them. They both had to pretend to use each other for their own personal gain, which was why they usually portrayed their relationship as surly and resentful.

It would take more than the power of a small kingdom to overcome this thorny obstacle they now faced. But perhaps, Fuze thought, his friend was being overly anxious. The Empire was on the move, it was true, but that didn't mean they should expect an attack before sunset.

"But how do we know the Empire will take action against us?" he offered. "I will gladly conduct my own personal inquiries into the matter. I'd advise you not to expect much, but I can at least gauge the situation in the Forest of Jura and around the Empire."

"…I would appreciate that."

Yes. There was no guarantee the Empire would act against them. If it was going to, it would undoubtedly be with a large force. It was never a nation to waste its time with small skirmishes. No, it would casually send over a force of a million or so and trample over every nation in the area, one by one. Assembling such an army would take time, at least three years or so. Which was not a generous amount, but it created some wiggle room to work with.

"I had best begin gathering information, then," Fuze said to close the conversation. "There is little time. I am off!"

"Thank you…"

The two of them nodded and went their separate ways. There was much to do.

●

Thirty days had passed since I swallowed Veldora. What had I been up to? Well, think about it. If you were being attacked by a monster, what would you do?

I mean, I was a slime now. It would be hard for me to zip away from a slavering attacker, much less defend myself. So I'd been spending my time thinking about how to fight back.

Along the way, I'd also been consuming any particularly odd-looking herbs or glowing rocks I stumbled across. There was a fair amount. I was still in the region Veldora described as teeming with local magic, and nearly everything I found there was hipokute herbs. Which was about what I figured. More healing potions for me, I suppose.

I also found that most of the glowing stones and such around here were what was called "magic ore," which could supposedly be refined into a metal harder than iron or steel and highly compatible with magic. I was kinda hoping for something a little less common, but I didn't even know whether orichalcum or crimson ore existed here, even if they were famous back on Earth. I shouldn't be too greedy.

So as I was chowing down on all these yummy herbs and rock, an idea came to mind!

If I could spit out water fast enough to give me powers of flight, maybe I could slice right through foes, too, like a high-pressure water jet cutter?

No, no, I know what you're thinking. You're thinking I was about to screw it up again, aren't you? You really shouldn't look down on people like that. I was good in a pinch, you know. They always wrote that in my report cards at school and stuff—"excellent work when he applies himself."

So yeah, I think it'd work.

Back I went to the underground lake from before. Just as I had imagined, the pool was pretty big. The air felt supremely tranquil to me. There were no creatures around—not even in the water, I assumed, what with all the magic soaked up inside it—which made it all the quieter. Pure, unadulterated nature! Truly a sight to see.

But back to business. I moved right into the "action" phase last time without testing a single thing, which was fairly ill-advised. That, and I ejected too much water at once, propelling myself far quicker than intended. No game plan whatsoever. *This* time, I'd keep it at water-pistol level, expelling just a bit at a time. Just taking a mouthful of water and—*thpbbt*—spitting it out.

Here I go.

Hmm. Not much water coming out. Too small of an exit hole? I expanded it a bit. Water shot out with a little more energy this time, dousing a nearby boulder I was targeting. A promising sign.

After a few more minutes spent adjusting my water levels, I

decided to boost the pressure just a tad more before opening wide. Launch. Then again. Then again, gradually upping the output as I kept my water-gun practice going.

It was starting to take form, yes. But, okay, while a shot of water might sting a bit, I didn't think it'd deliver a particularly decisive attack.

So now what? I thought to myself as I took a dip into the lake to gather my thoughts. Whenever I was tired, that was my cue to hit the bath for a bit. I wasn't just splashing around for kicks, all right? Besides, it also gave me a chance to use Magic Sense and observe myself floating and sinking in the water. I reminded myself of a jellyfish, kind of.

Maybe I could vibrate my body's surface to create currents or something? I gave it a shot, running magical force across my "skin" to control the particles around me. The vibration ran across my entire body, so I tried to point it in a single direction—and that was all it took to get me moving.

Nice! I spent a little while whizzing around the water like that, enjoying the experience. A nice change of pace, to be sure, but I totally wasn't just messing around, all right? Let's keep that straight.

Skill "Current Movement" acquired.

I thought it was the Sage for a moment, but it turned out to be the World Language instead. That bit of playing around just earned me a new skill. Oh, but it wasn't playing around, okay? I was just relaxing a bit.

Thanks to that, though, I could now flit around in or on the water at a pretty decent clip. If need be, I could use Water Pressure Propulsion to speed things up, too. Considering I didn't need to breathe, fighting in the water might actually give me an advantage, for all I knew. Good for fleeing into, at least.

That and other matters like it were on my mind as I left the lake. Break time was over, and it had certainly borne fruit for me. As I was relaxing, I had come up with a few new concepts.

If I was going to keep pursuing the water-gun approach, I'd have to apply constant pressure to my jet output for an extended period of time. Instead, I decided to picture the cylinder of a car engine, applying pressure to my *inside* while releasing a comparatively small amount of water per go. Adjusting the pressure and the diameter of my output hole allowed me to adjust the force of expulsion, just like before.

And thankfully, just as I'd hoped, it worked. A small jet, ejected sharply out of my body, slapped itself against the boulder—and it actually broke the rock slightly where it hit.

Success...I think. Better keep practicing before I forget the knack. Adjust output diameter, adjust pressure...and try putting a bit of spin on the water as you eject it, too. There was a lot to think about as I kept rehearsing it.

But that was it! That was the mental picture I had to keep in mind. Slicing through with water. I had to make the jets as thin and flat as possible, applying just the right spin to them.

So I gave it a whirl. And it worked! The cylindrical shot of water fought through the air resistance fast enough to leave afterimages, just like a blade...then slashed its way right through the rock. With enough force to astound even me.

It was the pinnacle of my efforts, the best results of my week of practice.

Skill "Water Blade" acquired.

Skills "Water Pressure Propulsion," "Current Movement," and "Water Blade" acquired. Combining and upgrading to extra skill "Control Water."

Whoa! It really *did* work. Extra skills were supposed to offer a completely different level of force than regular ones. Now I had a way of defending myself. It was just about time to head off.

Well. Finally.

One hundred and twenty days had passed since I got reincarnated at the banks of this cavern lake. Was I nervous? Yes. I still couldn't talk, exactly. I had no vocal cords, and I'd been poking around my body for something I could use as a substitute, but no dice yet. Staying here until I had more success was one option, but unlike with the water blades, I really had nothing to go on. For now, it'd have to be Telepathy or nothing—and if my would-be conversational partner couldn't use that, then so be it. Not the greatest of situations, but there you go.

Either way, I couldn't goof around in here forever. I wanted to see the outside world, and if I could, I'd love to run into some fellow Japanese otherworlder castaways. Learning some magic could be fun, too!

It was time to get started. No time like the present, and all that.

Veldora wasn't giving me any particular responses or signs inside me. It almost felt as though I'd lost him, but I knew that wasn't the case. We had a promise, besides. *Next time we meet, I better have some funny stories I can share with him.*

With an internal sigh, I traveled down the lone path upward from the broad underground cavern I had grown used to, my mind on the wide world to come. Who knew what would be awaiting me? I hardly knew what to expect, but I knew I *wanted* it.

Rimuru Tempest

Race Slime

Protection Crest of the Storm

Title None

Magic None

Intrinsic skills: Absorb Self-Regeneration Dissolve

Unique Skills Great Sage Predator

Extra Skills Magic Sense Control Water

Common Skills Telepathy

Tolerance Resist Pain

Resist Electricity Resist Temperature Resist Melee Attack

Resist Paralysis

A former human who transmigrated into the body of a slime on another world following his sudden death. Thanks to the Great Sage and Predator uniques he obtained just before dying, he has unusual strength and intelligence for his monster type. This is coupled with excellent slime-intrinsic skills, although he does not seem to be fully aware of them yet.

THE GIRL AND THE DEMON LORD

The main thing I remember is the fire raining down.

The grip of my mother's hand against mine felt so light, fleeting, and I was too terrified to see the way ahead.

An incendiary bomb went off nearby, turning our surroundings into a sea of flame. Where were we supposed to go? It was burning all around us...

I—Shizue Izawa—felt myself teetering on the brink of desperation.

Ahh... Is this where I'm going to die...?

Even at the age of eight, I understood that well enough. I had no relatives I could rely on; I lived alone with my mother. My father had been drafted into the war so long ago that I didn't even remember what he looked like. I was never quite sure whether I should be happy or sad about that, but either way, it had become my normal life, and I had to accept it for what it was. Me, and my life, and my fate to die in the flames.

And then—

"You want to live? If you want to live, heed my voice!"

—a voice echoed in my head.

Did I want to live? How should I know? I was too young to answer that question.

Still, though...

Looking at my mother, now just a pair of hands after she had shielded me with her body, I couldn't stop the tears from coming.

And I thought to myself—

I want to live!

Confirmed. Responding to summoner's request… Successful.

I can't take it anymore. It's too scary; it's too hot. Help me, Mom…

I lay there and cried, no longer fearful of the flame, as I wished life for myself.

Confirmed. Extra skills "Control Flame" and "Cancel Flame Attack"…successfully acquired.

Then my wish came true.

Just…not exactly the way I'd hoped for.

When I next awoke, I was inside the lair of a monster, a lone man in front of me. He had blue eyes, long blond hair, a well-defined face, and long, slitted eyes. His skin was so pale, I thought I could almost see through it. His sheer beauty would make nearly anyone mistake him for a woman.

His name was Leon Cromwell—one of the most powerful figures of this world, a so-called demon lord ascended from the human race. Also known as the "Platinum Devil." He sized me up.

"…Another failure," he whispered, seemingly disappointed at the sight of me, and he showed no further interest in me after that.

Perhaps that was why he never bothered killing me, not even with the serious burns I had all over my body. I was close to death, and I didn't even matter to him. Just a frail little girl clinging to life and no doubt dying soon enough if left alone.

I couldn't stand that thought. I was still alive. I didn't want to be abandoned. And I never forgot that experience. That moment of frustrated desperation as he sized me up and tossed me away. That memory wound up following me for the rest of my life's journey.

At the time, I had nobody to turn to, none of the strength I needed to survive. The only chance I had to keep going was Leon, my demon lord. He symbolized power to me, and being abandoned by him literally meant death.

I suppose I must have instinctually understood that, because without even thinking about it, I had extended a hand out toward Leon.

"Help... Help me..."

But the longing arm I stretched out to the demon failed to reach him. I gave up on myself, and with that came the anger.

Ahh... I really am going to die here...

The sheer selfishness of rescuing me and then leaving me to die was something I just couldn't let go of.

"You liar," I said, summoning what little strength I had left. "You asked me if I wanted to live."

I couldn't stop the tears as I glared straight up at the demon. I was no longer capable of forming a coherent sentence, but if I had to summarize my thoughts, I suppose they'd be along the lines of this:

You called for me, you gave up on me... I can't believe you ignored me! That's cruel!

In the end, it was another demonic whim that saved me. His eyes eerily lit up once more. "Heh. A liar, eh?" he whispered. "One moment..."

The ominous reply filled me with anxiety—but my near-fatal burns left me with nothing else to do. All I could do was prostrate myself before the will of this monster, this Leon.

"I had thought you were merely garbage," he said, "but maybe you're suited for flame after all." Then he activated the summoning spell for Ifrit, the fire titan. It was easy for him. No casting required at all. And when the giant appeared, he tossed him a casual order:

"I'm giving you a body. Use it well."

It was all the evidence anyone needed to show that Leon treated me as less than human. My frustration began evolving into hatred. The trauma was etched into my mind at such a tender age.

"You want to live? If you want to live, show me your will!"

It must have been my imagination. There was no way the demon lord could have ever said anything like that to me. No way he could have extended a hand out to me just before I succumbed to my burns.

But it was true: thanks to having my body possessed, I lived because of him.

The summoned Ifrit followed his orders, attempting to merge himself with my young frame. I immediately felt my limbs grow numb. It felt as if Ifrit was trying to snatch my body away from me. Just as Leon ordered, he was attempting to commandeer my body for his own use.

Confirming. Do you wish to be possessed by Ifrit in order to live?
    Yes
    No

As I cowered at the ghastly force flowing into me, I silently prayed to myself.

I don't want to die! Not yet! But...I can't... I can't let my old self disappear!

Confirmed. Possession by Ifrit...successful. Ifrit's possession is stabilizing Shizue Izawa's magicules... Successful. Furthermore, unique skill "Deviant"...successfully acquired.

Thus, thanks to a wild serious of coincidences, I managed to survive.

CHAPTER
2

BATTLE OF THE
GOBLIN VILLAGE

That Time I Got Reincarnated as a Slime

The path from the underground lake to the surface took the form of a single long cavern path, which I was currently bouncing and oozing my way along. I was moving quite a bit better than I'd originally pictured. Even in the dank darkness, harnessing Magic Sense made it look as bright as a sunny day to me.

Back when I was blind, I was too focused on my footing to notice, but slimes can actually truck along pretty quickly when they want to. I never got particularly fatigued, but there was no real reason to hurry either, so I tended to keep it at a regular walking rate by human standards. (This was definitely *not* because my last flirtation with exuberant locomotion landed me square in the water.)

As I plodded on, I found that the path was blocked by a large gate—the first man-made object I had seen in this cave. *Very* suspicious, but it didn't throw me off much. It was just like any of the dozens I had seen before in RPGs. Every boss room usually had a gate in front of it.

So how to get it open? Water Blade my way through the bars? It seemed like a decent idea, but as I thought it over, the door opened by itself with a creak. Flustered, I scurried over to one side of the path and watched.

"Whew! Finally got this thing open. The whole lockin' mechanism must've rusted out...," someone said.

"Yeah, I'll bet. Nobody's even tried going in for three hundred years or whatever, right?" replied a second voice.

"There is no record of anyone attempting an entry. Are you sure we're safe? We are not leaving ourselves open to sudden attack...?" commented a third.

"Gah-hah-hah-hah!" laughed the second one. "Come on. Maybe this guy was invincible a few centuries back, but it's just a big over-grown lizard, y'know? I told you guys 'bout how I bagged a basilisk solo once, didn't I? It'll be fine!"

"I was wondering about that, actually," the third replied. "Are you sure that's the truth, Kabal? A basilisk is a B-plus-ranked mon-ster. You truly handled that by yourself?"

"Quit playing dumb! I'm B ranked, y'know! Some huge reptile ain't gonna faze *me*!"

"All right, all right. Just keep your guard up, if you could. And remember, we can always use my Escape skill if things turn sour..."

"Can we save the friendly chitchat for later?" the first interjected. "I need some quiet. It's just about time for me to activate Concealing Arts!"

Three of them, it sounded like, none of them making much of an effort at stealth. And I understood everything they said, too. Odd.

Received. Your Magic Sense skill can be adapted to decipher sound waves that have willful meaning stored inside them.

Okay. So I couldn't speak to them, but I could get what they were saying. That was good. I was never too gifted at foreign languages. I was always one of those kids in the back of the class, bitching all like, "Why do I need this? I'm never gonna live outside of Japan, anyway! Save it for somebody who will!"

Now that I was actually in that position, something told me that excuse wouldn't work for much longer. Time to hit the books, I guess.

But that wasn't important. What should I do? That was a tougher question than opening the door, for sure. I didn't know what they wanted, but if I had to guess, they were adventurers. Treasure hunters, maybe? These were the first humans I'd encountered in this world—I had an urge to tail them to see what they were up to. But...ooh, if a slime who couldn't speak their language showed up, what would they do? Slice me up with impunity, I'd bet. Better save it for next time. Safety first. I could save the human stuff for when I could talk to them.

The slim man leading the trio did something, and the three of them suddenly began fading from sight. Not entirely, mind you. He *did* mention a "concealing" something or other—some kind of skill, presumably. *I wonder what he learned that for. Not for sneaking into people's bedrooms, hopefully. How scandalous. I'll have to make friends with him later.*

Once the trio went out of sight down the path, I sprang back into action. No need to rush this. It wasn't as if this would be my last chance to meet people. Slow and steady wins the race, as the ancients said, and I believe them.

Through the door I went, and before any of them could come back to check on things, I was gone.

✳

Proceeding a fair distance from the door, I arrived at an intersection with several paths branching out from it. Which one would bring me to the surface? Thinking about it wouldn't help much, so I chose a path and headed on down the cavern path.

Flick! Flick!

Our eyes met.

Slowly, I averted mine. There was a gigantic, ominous-looking serpent in front of me, a jet-black one with thorned scales, tough skin, and an appearance that made the snakes of Earth look positively cuddly. This creature in my path made me feel like a deer—or a slime—in the headlights.

My mind went blank. Maybe I'd be okay if it didn't notice me? Slowly, I tried to slide myself back. No luck. The black snake reared its head upward, matching my movements. It flicked its tongue at me as it silently menaced me with its eyes. *Damn it. It's not letting me off the hook!* We didn't need to exchange any words for that much to be clear.

Should I fight it? I had this killer finisher that I'd spent the last week training for, didn't I? It's just that...you know, fighting a monster like this would take a bit of an...extra oomph. In other words, I was crapping my pants.

But hang on. Get a hold of yourself. Thinking about it, I've been through scarier stuff before. Remember Veldora? Compared to that dragon, this guy... Hell, maybe it's not so scary after all. Maybe this is all gonna work out!

With a somewhat calmer mental state, I took a moment to size up the dark snake. It must have been thinking that it had stunned me into silence, that I was unable to move. Probably coming up with ways to land the final strike on me. Maybe it found the concept of swallowing me whole to be too bland or something.

Well, no point holding back. Without another moment's hesitation, I squared up toward the snake's neck and unleashed a Water Blade. With a lethal-sounding *fwissh*, the blade pierced through the air and struck the monster.

It all happened in an instant—so quick, I doubted my eyes. Without a single bit of resistance, the Water Blade lopped the black snake's head off. A snake so huge, so ominous looking, I was sure I'd be nothing but a midafternoon snack to it.

This skill...might have been a tad stronger than I thought. If I'd used it on that adventuring trio, things might've gone all slasher film pretty fast. Good thing I'd had the foresight to try it on a monster first.

Before I go on, let's do a quick recap of what was occupying my stomach at the moment. Veldora, 15 percent. Water, 10 percent. Medicinal herbs, recovery potions, and the like, 2 percent. Ore and other materials, 3 percent. Grand total, about 30 percent in use. Each Water Blade strike used not even a regular cup's worth of water, so...sheesh, I could probably spit out thousands of these before I even began worrying about running out.

Hell of a lot more efficient than some stupid magic spell. *I think I'll be relying on this against monsters for a while to come.*

So about this snake. Would it have any abilities I could steal by absorbing and analyzing it? No time to waste. Let's give it a shot.

The results were...not bad. In addition to the ability to disguise myself as a black snake, I gained the following two skills:

Sense Heat Source: Intrinsic skill. Identifies any heat reactions in the local area. Not affected by any concealing effects.

Poisonous Breath: Intrinsic skill. A powerful breath-type poison (corrosion) attack. Affects an area seven meters in front of the user in a 120-degree radius.

It looked as if this poison had a corrosive effect on its target, damaging whatever equipment or flesh it touched. A normal adventurer would probably have a lot of trouble against this guy, wouldn't they? Though who could say, really, given the kind of magic available in this world.

I spent a little while analyzing the skills of this snake I'd just vanquished. The more cards in my hand, the better, I figured.

The results:

1. Mimicking the black snake increased my bodily volume.
2. The skills I'd just earned could be invoked without having to mimic the snake's form, although their performance could suffer as a result.

To go into further detail:

1. I could break down and store the monsters I consumed with Predator in my stomach. I'd used Predator on my own body in order to repair damage, and this provided some spare cells to help with that, in other words.
2. "Intrinsic skills" appeared to be skills that were exclusive to a certain type of monster. My Absorb, Self-Regeneration, and Dissolve skills were intrinsic to me as a slime. However, to use intrinsics, I needed to take the form of the monster in question, or else I couldn't bust them out all the way. I could still use them in part, though, and some skills—like Sense Heat Source—seemed to work just fine either way.

Putting it all together: Predator freakin' *rocked*. I couldn't wait to track down some other useful skills with this thing.

✳

Three days had passed after my snake battle. I was still in the cave. I couldn't feel heat or cold or anything, but for all I knew, it was pretty chilly in here.

I had yet to see a single ray of sunshine, but my vision still worked just fine in the dark. However, a certain anxiety was starting to work its way into my head... I mean, I technically knew it wasn't possible, but I couldn't help but consider it.

"...I'm not lost, am I?"

No. I couldn't be. What kind of idiot gets himself lost in the *very first cave*? That first easy-peasy cave's supposed to be a springboard that helps you dive into the experience, isn't it? It looked as if that adventuring trio knew where the hell they were going, didn't it?

I'd be fine. It was probably just a really *long* path. Not knowing the exact way *did* make me a little nervous, though. Was there any way to get some help with that?

> Received. Display the paths you've currently taken in your brain?
>   Yes
>   No

Pfft. I laughed at myself. *Are you kidding me?!* I thought, unable to resist a little whining. *If I had something like that, why didn't you tell me sooner?!*

Of course I immediately picked "Yes." I used to think automapping was cheating once, too, but now I knew the error of my ways. With older games, you were expected to bring your own pencil and graph paper, filling in the squares with every step you took in the dungeon. That was what made them fun—making sure you were on the right track with every single step you took. As time passed, though, people became more reliant on strategy guides, and games started to be shipped with their own built-in mapping features. It sucked all the *real* fun out of the genre, you could say—but once you got used to the convenience, there was no turning back.

What I'm trying to say is...you know, if you've got such a powerful feature at your fingertips, you might as well use it, right? Besides, this wasn't a game. It was real life.

I scoped out the map that flashed into my mind.

Am I reading this right? It looks like I've been circling through the same area over and over again...

....

......

...

Following the map in my brain, I delved into a branch of the cave I'd never bothered trying before. There, I was greeted by a sight that had wholly eluded me for the past three days.

Heh-heh-heh. *Guess I'm lost after all. Flustering me like this... This must be one hell of a cave. I gotta hand it to the thing.*

(And my lack of direction was *not* the issue, all right?!)

I must have been getting close to the entrance—to the great outdoors. Moss and weeds were starting to appear on the walls and ground. And I didn't know where the sun was, but the light, dim as it was, was starting to make its way inside. Which meant it was daytime.

Along the way, I had a few more monster encounters. To be exact:

    A centipede monster ("evil centipede," rank B-plus)
    A big spider ("black spider," rank B)
    A vampire bat ("giant bat," rank C-plus)
    A big shelled lizard ("armorsaurus," rank B-minus)

No more of those black snakes, though. Maybe that was the only one.

They were all pretty strong. Not that I'm one to talk, given that Water Blade was still enough to end a battle all by itself. But the bat guy did dodge my blades long enough to get a few bites in, and my attacks just bounced off the lizard guy's body if I didn't hit it at the right angle.

They wouldn't all go down easy. The centipede concealed itself long enough to attack me from behind, but between Magic Sense and Sense Heat Source, I had enough of a bead on my surroundings that I was fully prepared. One Water Blade tossed behind me was all it took to end that encounter.

The spider, on the other hand. *Oof.*

I always had a hang-up when it came to bugs in the first place. It was as if I was physically repulsed by them. Just one look was enough for me, thanks. Transforming into a slime must've powered up my mental fortitude as well, though—enough that I fought that guy without running away screaming.

Sorry, dude, you're getting full blast! Five Water Blades at once, thrust deep into its thorax. I didn't want it in my sight for another moment.

Not that it stopped me from consuming it afterward, though, nor any of the other guys. Survival of the fittest and all. The spider and centipede gave me a *little* pause, yes, but I soldiered on.

If any cockroach monsters showed up, though, I was definitely making a sprint for it. It wasn't a matter of winning or losing. Just because I *could* didn't mean I always *should*.

Between this and that, I managed to absorb quite a few monsters in this cave. Let's go over the skills I acquired.

Black snake: Poisonous Breath, Sense Heat Source
Centipede: Paralyzing Breath
Big spider: Sticky Thread, Steel Thread
Vampire bat: Drain, Ultrasonic Wave
Shelled lizard: Body Armor

Whenever you get a new toy, you want to use it, right? Same here. So I harnessed the Great Sage to research all the skills I picked up.

Basically, I didn't use Poisonous Breath from the snake. I actually transformed so I could try it out against the lizard, and...like, *whoa.* All that armor didn't do jack for the armorsaurus. It literally melted into a puddle of goo before my eyes. Grossest thing I'd ever seen in my life, all those organs and bits of flesh all over the place. I had to spray another salvo of mist to break down the rest of the chewy bits. Last time I'd have to see *that*, hopefully.

Really, this breath was almost too much of a force to be reckoned with. I didn't want to use it much, if possible. Sense Heat Source, though, was awesome. Pretty much every living creature emits heat. Combining this with Magic Sense meant that I was all but impossible to ambush. There was no telling what kind of magic or special skills I'd run into once I started dealing with humans or intelligent high-level monsters, so I couldn't afford to let my guard down.

Next up, the centipede. I hardly wanted to mimic that guy, what with how it looked and all. Its breath had about the same range as the black snake's, and its form was about the same size as well. As I figured, trying to use it in slime form limited the range to only about a meter. It could come in handy for a surprise attack, I supposed, but if a foe was already within that radius, I'd be sunk unless I transformed or ran, so...

The lizard's armor, as I mentioned, put up zero resistance whatsoever to Poisonous Breath. I couldn't expect much from it. Besides, I already had Resist Melee Attack, so there wasn't much point. Using it in slime form just made my external surface a bit tougher, kind of like the metallic slimes that show up in that one RPG series and give you lots of EXP. It gave a nice metal sheen to my light-turquoise body; whatever it did to me must've changed the way the light reacted to my surface. I didn't want to test how I took damage with that on, though, so its effect remained a bit of a mystery. That little extra tint might help scare my foes into submission, though.

That about wrapped up those three. The real meat, so to speak, lay in the other two. They were pretty darn fascinating.

First, the spider. Who wouldn't want to imitate that famous superhero who does all the spidery stuff? Firing webs from his hands powerful enough to let him swing around skyscrapers, and all that?

Sticky Thread, it seemed, was originally meant to let the user encase their prey in webs, rendering them immobile. But could I use it to do some fancy web-rope slinging of my own? *Let's try it. Point it at that tree branch, and...*

Whoosh! ...Swiiiiiiing.........

So, uh, on to Steel Thread.

What? Sticky Thread? Never heard of it. Just some skill that leaves you hanging around motionless in the air. Pass. On to Steel Thread.

I guess this is meant to block your foe's attack. The spider uses it to help it create an effective (i.e., labyrinthine) web, the Sage told me. So I busted a thread out and whipped it against a tree.

Whoosh! Snap!

And lopped the trunk right off.

With Magic Sense, I could tell that this Steel Thread would be extremely difficult for the naked eye of a human to detect. If I worked with it a little, I bet it could be a decent weapon. I spent a little time doing just that in case it would come in handy later.

Finally, the bat. To be honest, out of this entire zoo, I had the greatest expectations for the bat.

But—I mean, geez, *Drain*. If it hits, you could use 70 percent of your target's skills for a limited period of time. Big whoop! Predator was far more effective. Talk about a precipitous drop in quality. And what's the point of sucking someone's blood when you can just analyze their data instead? *I'll just toss that one aside.*

Ultrasonic Wave, on the other hand, piqued my interest. This skill had the effect of confusing your foes or making them lose consciousness, but it was originally used for echolocation. Just like bats back on my home planet, you could use these sound waves to suss out exactly where you and other objects were positioned.

But the skill didn't matter to me. The *sonic waves* it emitted did. This slime was about to get his voice back. Talk about a stroke of luck. Instead of having to reinvent the wheel from the cells I had, I could just absorb a relevant monster and take the skill for myself.

Can I form it into a voice, though? That's the tricky part. So I continued my research. Restlessly, forgoing all sleep (not that I needed it), I walked around for three days and three nights, testing it out.

The end result:

"I COME FROM OUTER SPACE!"

Perfect!

It was still a bit distorted, like someone tapping at their throat while yelling through a box fan, but it was definitely a voice! Now all I had to do was fine-tune it!

Trying my best to calm my excitement, I began the long, arduous voice-adjustment process.

These supersonic waves were so useful. I thought I remembered reading something about a weapon that used sound waves. A sonic buster or sonic blaster or something like that? Could *I* do that?

Received. There is a chance that the skill "Super Vibration" may be derived from "Ultrasonic Wave." This cannot be acquired at this time.

So I need to derive it or change the skill somehow? Not much to go on, but nothing doing for now, I guess. Not like everything's gonna be handed to me on a silver platter. Maybe I'm getting too greedy, but the more cards in your hand, right?

No need to push things along too fast, though. Obtaining vocal cords is a huge coup by itself. I should be happy with it.

Looking back, I'd obtained a ton of skills in pretty short order as I wandered around, continuing with my research as I aimed for the exit.

And while it took some time, I eventually made it. The outside. The first time I got to bask in the sunlight of this world.

✳

Feels as if it's been a while, going outside like this. It has *been several months, come to think of it.* Hopefully the light wouldn't burn or melt me like a vampire…although as a monster, I would reportedly have an instinctual knowledge of what would be dangerous to my continued existence.

People do things they know are bad for them all the time, right? No joke. We could learn something from these monsters.

*   *   *

The cave, it turned out, was in a forest. The exit was just a hole at the foot of a mountain—more of a small hill, really, which stood out against the vast trees that surrounded it. In fact, thanks to the dense foliage, this hill was the only point you could see the sun from. Take a step into the forest, and all appeared to be dim darkness again.

Climbing to the top of the hill, I saw some kind of strange pattern carved into it. A magical pentacle or something? Sure seemed like it. Maybe those adventurers I bumped into were responsible? *Guess it doesn't matter much.* A wise man keeps away from danger, as they say.

I sidled off.

A fair amount of time had passed since I left the cave. The sun was starting to set, which indicated that I must have reached the cave exit right around midday. I had a surprisingly accurate internal clock, and it would've been nice if it could've aligned itself with a standardized sense of time.

And the moment I thought about it, it happened. Sheesh. *Is it this easy to do stuff like that? This Sage is one heck of a personal assistant to have around.*

Anyway, it was now past four in the afternoon. About time to prep for dinner, but sadly, I no longer had to eat. I *could*, but the meaninglessness of the gesture would probably just make me feel empty inside.

So I kept messing around with the new skills I'd obtained from the monsters I'd consumed in the cave. How to use them, neat ways to combine them, whatever else I could do with them, et cetera. Speech was a particular focus.

That was what occupied my time as I continued down the path I'd found. No particular destination. It would've been nice if there was a town or village with someone nice I could've talked to…but everything had been incredibly quiet over the past few days. After getting attacked so frequently in the cave, I hardly got any attention at all outdoors. Just once, while practicing my elocution, a pack of wolves started stalking me. I tried to threaten them—"Ah?" I said—and that was all it took.

"*Yipe!*" With pathetic yelps, they scampered away. We're talking multiple enormous canines, each easily two meters or so in length, and the sight of a slime freaked them out. Pathetic.

Not that I minded being left alone. *Getting a wolf's sense of smell would be neat, though.*

The reaction surprised me enough that I began paying closer attention to my surroundings. Turned out it wasn't just the wolves—not a single monster out there dared get within several meters of me. Were they really that scared? It sure seemed that way, but…like, why?

As I thought over that, my Magic Sense skill spotted a group of monsters approaching.

Nothing like a good crisis to come at you out of nowhere, huh?

They were small in size, their equipment plain and crude. Their faces were dirty and devoid of intelligence, but with their swords, their shields, their stone axes, and their bows, they weren't entirely bestial. It took a mere instant for my gray matter to figure out who they were—goblins, those infamous marauders of many a would-be adventuring party.

Talk about sticking to the script. No doubt they were here to attack the weakest of would-be heroes—which meant me, I guess. But, really, thirty of them against a single slime? Kind of a lot at once, wasn't it?

And yet, I didn't feel so much as a whiff of terror. My instincts told me I had absolutely nothing to fear. Their swords had rust on them, and their armor was thin and torn at the edges. Some of them were dressed in nothing but stained rags. Compared to the hard-scaled lizards and the spiders with massive serrated blades on their feet I had dealt with before, I couldn't imagine their gear inflicting any damage at all on me. Besides, if things got hairy, I could just go into black-snake mode and Poisonous Breath them all into puddles of goo…

As I sized them up, the goblins' apparent leader opened his mouth. "Grah! Strong one… Have you *business* here?"

Huh. Goblins talk. Or maybe Magic Sense is helping me decipher their grunting.

And—come on, "strong one"? First they're surrounding me with their weapons; then they're rolling out the red carpet for me... What do they want?

It got me curious. They didn't look ready to descend upon me immediately. It might be a good chance to test out my speaking abilities. No better time to start than now.

I gave the goblins a quick look-over.

To them, this must have been one of the most frantic moments in their lives. Their eyes, as well as their weapons, were trained on me, although at least a few of them were ready to flee at the least provocation. The leader, meanwhile, was every bit up to the post, his steely eyes practically drilling holes in my gelatinous form.

Hmm. They seem intelligent enough. Maybe this conversation thing could work out after all. But will they understand me?

I focused my thoughts on my still-newborn voice and gingerly tried a few words.

"Good to meet you, I guess? My name is Rimuru. I'm a slime."

The goblins murmured among themselves. *Does a talking slime surprise them, maybe?* I thought…only to find a few of them already prostrating themselves before me, weapons tossed away. Weird.

"G-garrh! Strong one! We, we see mighty power of you. Please! Quiet the voice of you!"

Mm? Did I put too much force into it? Maybe making myself understood wasn't such a big deal after all. Plainly, I was freaking them out.

I figured an apology was in order. "Sorry, I don't have this fine-tuned too well yet…"

"We, we need no apology from such great form of you!"

Guess that worked. This is turning into some decent practice. I was impressed that plain old Japanese worked on these guys. With all the politeness they gave me, I figured I should return the favor—but given how terrified some of them were, I might as well show off the confidence they thought I had.

"So what did you need from me? I don't have any business around here."

"I see. Village of us is ahead. We felt strong monster nearby, so we came to patrol."

"A strong monster? I didn't spot anything like that...?"

"G-gaah! Grah-gah-gah! Such joking! You cannot trick us, even with form of you!"

These guys totally have the wrong idea. Apparently they thought their powerful intruder had disguised himself as a slime. These *were* goblins, the world-famous lower caste of the monster totem pole. I shouldn't have expected much.

The goblins and I spoke for a while longer, and before long, I wound up receiving an invitation to their village. They were willing to put me up for a bit, even. Pretty nice guys, given how scraggly they all looked. So I accepted. I had no need to sleep, but a little rest never hurt a guy.

Along the way, I got to hear a bit of the local gossip. It turned out the god they worshiped had recently disappeared. Without it, the local monsters had started acting up a lot more than before. At the same time, more human adventurers—"powerful ones," as they put it—were starting to invade the forest. And so on.

And funnily enough, the more we spoke to each other, the more clearly I began to understand them. It must have been my Magic Sense skills getting more accustomed to however the goblin language was wending its way through the particles in the air. *Maybe getting in some practice with goblins before my big human debut was a good idea after all*, I thought as I followed along.

The village was shockingly dingy. Maybe I shouldn't have expected much from a goblin's den. They guided me to what I supposed was the most structurally sound of the buildings. It had a thatched, pitted roof that was rotting away in areas, the walls bearing nothing but a few pieces of flat wood nailed to them. No slum I'd ever seen in my world could out-filth this one.

"I am sorry to keep you waiting, honored guest," one of the goblins said as he entered. The leader of the expeditionary force I ran into earlier accompanied him.

"Oh, no need for that," I said, flashing my salesman's smile—or in this case, my slime smile. "Don't worry about me. I haven't been waiting for that long."

Something about smiling at your conversational partner always did wonders to keep negotiations moving your way. Once you were aware of it, it was scary how well it worked. Not that I knew what we were negotiating yet.

"I apologize we cannot provide you more hospitality," the goblin said as he brought out something resembling tea for me. "I am the elder of this village."

Even goblins must have this stuff, I thought as I took a sip (well, technically, slid my way over the teacup, but same difference). I couldn't detect any taste from it, which made sense, since I didn't have that sense. That might have been for the better, for all I knew. My Analysis skills didn't detect any poison, but reportedly it bore a bitter, acrid flavor.

It was good to see the goblins trying to play nice with me, though, so I made sure to politely drink it up.

Then I decided to get to the point. "So to what do I owe the favor?" I asked. "What made you decide to invite me over to your village?" This had to be more than monsters acting buddy-buddy with each other.

The village elder shivered a bit. Then, firming up his resolve, he turned to me.

"You have heard, I trust, that the monsters have been more active around here as of late?"

I had, on the way here.

"Our god has protected the peace in this land for generations, but about a month ago, he hid himself from us. That has allowed the nearby monsters to start meddling with our lands once more. We do not wish to let this continue, so we have fought back...but from a raw-power perspective, we face an uphill climb."

Hmmm. Was he talking about Veldora? It would match time-wise. But if the goblins wanted my help...

"I understand you well enough, but I'm just a slime, so I'm not exactly sure I can provide the help you need..."

"Grah-ha-ha! Trust me, no need for modesty! It is no mere slime who can emit the mystical force you do! I cannot imagine why you are taking that form...but you have a name bestowed upon you, yes?"

Mystical...what? What's that? I don't remember busting anything like *that* out. I focused my Magic Sense on myself instead of my environs. Then I realized it. There *was*, in fact, some kind of ominous-looking aura covering my whole body. You'd think I would've noticed that in the midst of all the monster transformation and Body Armor malarkey, but it was too late now.

Whew. Talk about embarrassing. Here I am, exuding all this mystical stuff, and I didn't even bother to say "excuse me." I felt as if I were walking down the middle of Main Street, baring everything I had to the world. With all the magicules in the air over in the cave, I'd been completely oblivious.

This is bad! Really bad! But at least it explained how the monsters in the forest reacted to me before now. Not too many of them would have wanted to take on *this* hombre. No one was stupid enough to be fooled by appearances.

Well, might as well run with it.

"Hee-hee-hee… Impressive, elder. You noticed?"

"Of course, my friend! Even in the shape that you are, there is certainly no hiding the strength inside you!"

"Ah. Well, if you spotted me, then I guess you guys have a lot of promise!"

Now *I'm diggin' this! Let's just pull the elder's strings for a bit and talk my way out of trouble.* At the same time, I tried to find a way to extinguish the mystical aura around me, futzing around with the surrounding magic to try to push it back in.

"Ohh… Were we being tested, perhaps? Then I certainly hope we are worthy. Many would be cowed to submission by such a force."

By this time, my mystical whatever was mostly hidden. I was back to being just a regular old slime. Funny to think, though—earlier, if I had looked like any old slime on the street, would the entire forest have tried to kill me? That would've been a bummer.

"You're right. Anyone willing to speak to me without being frightened by my mystic powers must be worthy indeed."

Worthy how? I wondered to myself silently.

"Ha-ha! Thank you very much. I will refrain from asking you why you hide your true form…but I do have a request of you. Would you be willing to listen to it?"

About what I figured. Nobody would go up to a fearsome, hideous monster for no reason at all.

"It depends on what it is," I said, trying to keep my swagger going. "But go ahead. State your business."

Here's the rundown.

It turned out some newcomer monsters from the lands to the east had been pushing into the area, hoping to seize it for themselves. The area was home to several goblin villages, including this one, and even the small clashes so far had resulted in a large number of goblin deaths—including some named goblins.

One of these named creatures was the sort-of guardian of this village, and with his death, the value of keeping this village intact had declined dramatically.

The other goblin communities had largely abandoned this land. Their reasoning was that they could coerce the newcomers to attack this village, buying them time to come up with countermeasures of their own. The village elder and the leader of the expedition who greeted me had tried to reason with them but were coldly brushed away. The frustration was clear in their voices as the two of them explained.

"I see," I replied. "So how many of you live in this village? And how many are battle ready?"

"We have approximately one hundred residents. Counting our womenfolk, about sixty of them are ready to fight."

Doesn't sound like much. Pretty smart goblins, though, if they're keeping track that closely.

"All right. And what types and numbers are we talking about with the enemy?"

"They are direwolves, we believe—certainly wolflike in appearance. Under normal circumstances, it would have to be ten of us against one of them for us to have a fighting chance...but they appear to number around a hundred themselves."

Huh? What kind of impossible game is this? I turned my eyes toward the village elder. He didn't seem to be joking; his eyes were as sincere and dedicated as a goblin's could get.

"So these goblin fighters took them on in such small numbers, even though they knew they couldn't win?"

"...No. This information I told you... Those fighters risked their lives to obtain it."

Oh. Might've been a rude question, there.

Upon further questioning, the named goblin they'd lost turned out to be both the elder's son and the older brother of the scouting party. I spent a moment weighing the options, the elder falling silent as he awaited my decision. It might have been my imagination, but I could have sworn there were tears in his eyes... I was probably just imagining it, though. Tears don't go too well with monsters.

Better pump up the swagger, I figured. That's how a feared monster should rightly act!

"Let's get something straight, elder. If I help this village, what do I get in return? Do you even have anything to give?"

Not that I minded helping them out on a whim. But it took ten goblins to *maybe* beat one big dog or whatever, and they'd be facing a pack of a hundred. It wouldn't be simple. *I think a little black-snake action could take care of them...but I can't just snap up this job without thinking a bit.*

"We shall give you our allegiance! Please, grant us your guardianship. If you do, I promise we will swear our loyalty to you!"

Honestly, as gifts go, that's not much. But after experiencing ninety days of silent solitude, even talking to goblins was kind of fun. The thought of saving this dive probably would've disgusted me back in my human days, but right now, I was a monster. No need to worry about falling in a puddle and picking up some infectious disease any longer.

Plus, those *eyes* on the elder. I could tell that he was truly relying on me to say the right thing.

I reflected on my past life. When someone asked me to do something, I always did it. Even if I bitched and moaned about it at first, even if the guys at the office yelled at me about it, I was never able to say no to my manager or clients.

"All right. Your request is granted!"

I nodded sagely. And that's how I became the guardian of a goblin village.

●

The direwolves ruled the roost over at the plains to the east, enough to give endless headaches to the merchants who plied their trade between the Eastern Empire and the kingdoms around the Forest of Jura. Each one of them was the equivalent of a C-ranked monster, hardy enough that an adventurer could find his leg bitten off if he wasn't paying attention.

The real threat, however, came when they roamed in packs. Only when a talented alpha was leading the horde did the direwolves show their real worth. The entire pack would act as a single mind, a single creature, every member acting in lockstep. Such a pack, in full motion, could easily be rated a B.

The eastern plains were located next to a wide grain-producing region, a vital lifeline for the Eastern Empire and one kept very well secured. No matter how cunning the direwolves were, no matter how advanced their skills, penetrating the Empire's defensive lines remained a difficult task. Even if they made it through, doing so would rouse the full fury of the Empire, putting the direwolf race's very future into question.

The pack's leader was fully aware of this. It was something he had learned through hard-fought experience, amid the many skirmishes he had witnessed against the Empire over several decades. Targeting the smaller-scale merchants who passed by wasn't enough to make the Empire take full action—but the moment wolves stepped into its grain fields, it would truly retaliate.

After so many failures, no more would the direwolves repeat the mistakes of their comrades. That was the alpha's way of thinking. But his monster's instincts also told him that, under the status quo, there would be no progress, nothing to push their pack forward.

As a rule, the direwolf race did not require food to survive. Attacking and consuming humans provided them with a nice little snack, but those didn't hold much in the way of magic.

To the pack, their real sustenance lay in the world's magicules. They would need to attack stronger monsters or slaughter humans in droves to evolve into calamity-level creatures. None of these options were particularly accessible to them. The Empire was just too powerful. But merely picking off passing merchants would never do anything for their dreams of evolution.

Then they heard tales of the southlands. A fertile territory, one with a forest that offered all its blessings—a vast store of magic. A paradise for monsters, so it was said. In order to reach it, though, they would have to traverse the vast Forest of Jura.

The monsters of this wood were, in and of themselves, no great foes. Their past experience hunting the stragglers wandering out of it proved as much. So why had they shied away from entering it themselves?

Simple: Veldora the Storm Dragon. He was the one and only reason. Even when he was within his prison, the waves of dreadful magical force shook their very hearts. The creatures in the forest, they believed, enjoyed the dragon's divine guardianship—which was why they could survive under those scorching waves. That was what they had to believe. Otherwise, the truth would drive them mad.

So despite how it pained them daily, the direwolves had given up on infiltrating the forest. Until now.

The alpha turned his bloodred eyes toward the forest. That evil, horrid dragon could no longer be felt. *Now is the time*, he thought, *to hunt the forest clean of monsters—and then we may become the lords of the forest*. The idea made him lick his lips and sound the howl commanding his pack to advance.

Okay. So now I'm a guardian. What should I do next? To me, it just felt like bodyguard duty, despite the grandiose terms the elder used to describe me.

To start out, I had all the goblins capable of fighting gathered around me. It wasn't a pretty sight. They were in awful shape. No way could I count on them on the battlefield. And from afar, the remainder of the village looked like…nothing but children and the elderly to me. Reinforcements, in other words, were out of the question.

The village elder must have been shaking at the knees. Even if they fled the village right now, they'd practically starve before the day was through.

Meanwhile, the goblins around me were all staring with an almost religious faith in their eyes. This was heavy, man. To someone like me, who lived a fairly easy-breezy life, those gazes added a lot of pressure.

"Right," I said, "do all of you know what kind of situation we're in?"

I wasn't trying to make a joke. I just couldn't think of anything inspirational I could say.

"Yes, sir!" the goblin leader instantly replied. "We are preparing for a battle to decide whether we live or die!"

The other goblins around him must have felt the same way. Some of them were visibly shaking, which I couldn't chide them for. A person's mind can think one thing and their body do something very different.

"All right," I replied, trying to act like the best general I could. "No need to get all worked up. Keep it chill, all right? Whether you're revved up or not, if we're gonna lose, we're gonna lose. Just focus on giving this everything you've got!"

That helped lighten *my* mood, at least. Maybe it worked better than I thought.

Might as well get started, then. If I screw up, that might be it for these goblins. But I gotta stick to my guns. I wanted to bring some swagger into this, and now I'm gonna!

With a moment to collect my thoughts, I gave my first order to the goblins—an order I would give many times to come.

Night. The direwolves' alpha had his eyes open. It was a full moon—the perfect night for a battle. Slowly, he rose, surveying the area, the rest of his pack looking on with bated breath.

Just the right amount of intensity, the alpha thought.

Tonight, they would level the goblin village, establishing a foothold for themselves within the Forest of Jura. Then, slowly but surely, they would hunt the monsters around the area, expanding their territory until they ruled the woods. Soon, when the time was right, they would turn their eyes toward the south, invading it for the power it held.

They had the strength to make it happen. Their claws could rend the flesh of any monster; their fangs could pierce any armor.

"Awooooooooooo!"

The alpha gave the signal.

It was time to let the carnage begin.

There was, however, one concern.

The alpha had sent a scout a few days ago who had come back with some perplexing news—news of a small monster that let off a strange, mystical force. Enough to surpass that of even their alpha.

He had shrugged off this report at first. It was too preposterous to entertain. He himself had detected nothing of the sort in the forest. Every monster they'd encountered was a comparative weakling. Up to this point, nothing even resembling resistance to their advance had appeared—and they were almost in the dead center of the wood. A dozen or so goblins had picked off one or two members of their pack, but nothing else.

The scout must have been too excited about the upcoming hunt to think straight. That was the alpha's conclusion as he kept his eyes forward.

Ahead lay a village. It was situated exactly where the scout said it was. He had followed the trail of a wounded goblin straight to it. Nothing about his report suggested it to be a threat.

This was not the alpha's first battle. He was cunning, and he never let his guard down. However, even he had to admit that the strange…*thing* around the village was a tad unusual.

It was…a fence, like one would see in a human village. The homes that once composed the settlement had been disassembled, formed into a defense that neatly covered all of the village grounds.

And there, in front of the single opening in the barrier, was a lone slime.

"All right, stop where you are, okay?" the slime said to them. "If you turn back now, I promise I won't do anything to you. Move away from here at once!"

Impertinent little bastard. Leaving just one entryway open to block a mass attack? Just the kind of shallow thinking one should expect from a garbage monster like this. Our claws and fangs would make mincemeat out of that rickety old thing.

It was time to show this slime their true power. The alpha gave the order. As if they were his own right hand, about a dozen direwolves immediately set off to attack the fence—the picture of coordination, the exact reason the pack essentially functioned as a single monster.

The Thought Communication skill enabled their collective behavior. It was far faster than giving verbal orders, letting the pack work in perfect tandem.

The first wave should have been all it took to destroy the fence. Instead the alpha, already picturing a screaming rabble of goblins struggling to flee after the miserable failure of their stratagem, let out a surprised yelp. The force he had sent toward the fence had been blown straight backward, some of them bleeding profusely as they writhed on the ground.

What could this be? The alpha kept his mind sharp as he surveyed the area. The slime by the entryway had not moved an inch. Did it do something?

One of his men sidled up to him to report. *It was him, boss! The thing with the mystical force that outclassed yours!*

Nonsense, the alpha thought as he looked at the slime. It was a small monster. They would occasionally be born here and there along the plains. Even calling them "monsters" at all seemed absurd—their whole existence was petty. *That thing, holding more force than me...?*

The alpha fumed.

Impossible!

Few, indeed, were the monsters more sly and crafty than the alpha. He had years of experience to draw upon, and he could summon it on the fly to calmly, nimbly formulate a new plan. And his years of experience told him that this monster could not possibly be stronger than he was.

Right there, for the first time, the alpha committed a fatal mistake—one that would ultimately decide his fate.

You wretched little worm of a monster—I shall crush you to pieces!

Yeesh. *That* was a shock.

I didn't think they'd go lunging at the joint straight out. I even gave them that heroic little speech about how I wouldn't do anything if they turned back, but they totally ignored it.

Instead, the direwolves all started moving at once, attacking the fence from pretty much every angle they had. I was hoping we could talk things over a little first, but they forced me to throw out my entire script. And after all that rehearsing I did while the fence was being built.

The first order I'd given the goblins was to show me where the wounded were. Adding a dozen or so survivors to the sixty fighters we had wouldn't make the work go much more efficiently, but given their devotion for me, I wanted to do what I could for them.

They were all lying down on the floor of a large, fairly unhygienic-seeming building. Looking over them, I started to think. *Apparently, they're using some herbs to treat them...but left to themselves, they'll die before long.* They were all in rougher shape than I'd thought—skin slashed by teeth and claws, and some were sporting nasty-looking gashes with God-knows-what growing out of them.

Better splurge a little bit, I figured as I took action. Consuming the wounded goblin closest to me, I sprayed some recovery potion on him, then hawked him back up. The elder prepared to say something to me, but he thought better of it as I worked my way down the row—swallowing, splattering, spitting out.

After I'd finished up with a few of them, I took a look behind me. There they were again, kowtowing to me.

What is with *these guys?*

They must've assumed I'd resurrected them with my powers or something. To avoid future misunderstanding, I opted to just spit the potions out directly from there on, healing the goblins' wounds out in the "real" world.

The healing process took a little time, but it worked. Once I was done with everyone, I gave the remaining goblins a new order—the fence.

A simple wooden affair would have been fine, I thought, but we didn't have much time or material to work with. We had to go with what we had, so that was what I did—without a moment's pause, I had them tear down their homes and use the wood and other components to fortify the whole community.

In the meantime, I ordered the goblins who were decent with a bow to go on scout duty. I warned them not to wander too far afield—wolves were bound to have good noses. I could tell by their eyes that they were willing to sacrifice themselves for the cause. They were ready to shout out "By my very life!" at any moment. A lot more bravado than I really needed right now, but I doubted there was any quick fix for it.

As night fell, around a day after I arrived at the village, the final planks were on the fence. The finishing touches were mine—spider silk to strengthen and solidify the paling and a few Steel Thread traps here and there. Anyone touching the fence without knowing the secret would be carved up before they knew what hit them. *I'll have to remember to go fetch a body or two later.*

I made sure the fence had a single entryway on one side. Once it was lined with Sticky Thread, my job here was done. All that remained was to wait for the scouts to come back.

By this time, the wounded goblins were starting to wake up, healed from their wounds. They furtively poked their bodies, staring curiously down at themselves. *Looks like that stuff packs a wallop.* I'd assumed I'd need to apply several doses to the graver-looking of the patients, but it worked a hell of a lot better than I'd thought. I had no complaints about that mistake.

After that, I had the goblins collect the extra material, pile it up in the center of the village grounds, and set it on fire. It reminded me of more than one camping trip, but now was no time for marshmallows. We would need to keep watch the whole night through. I offered to handle it alone but was sharply refused.

"Nothing doing, Sir Rimuru! We could never allow you to shoulder such a heavy burden!"

"She is right! We will handle watch duty for you. Please, Sir Rimuru, take the time to rest a little!"

The rabble around us echoed their approval. I appreciated the thought. They had to be far more exhausted than I was by now, but I agreed to handle the watch in shifts and rest when I wasn't on duty.

Just before midnight, the scouts returned—some wounded, but all safe. The direwolves had begun to move, they said. Funny how I thought they were these ugly, filth-ridden monsters two days ago. Now I was starting to feel actual affection for them. *If I had my way*, I thought as I applied the final Sticky Thread to the entryway, *I'd like to get them through this without losing a single one.*

So that was our prep process, more or less. Hostilities were under way, so there wasn't much else I could do. At this point, we had to stick to the plan.

I wasn't convinced the fence was strong enough to hold, but fortunately, the direwolves couldn't grab hold of it long enough to do much. The traps mostly sprang just as I'd planned. That was a relief.

Anticipating this, I had ordered small slits built into the fence at regular intervals. Those openings were for arrows so the goblins could attack from the inside and interfere with the enemy's movements. They opened fire, and even with their crappy aim, they made more than a few direwolves scream their last. A few of the enemy force tried to pry the spaces open and break in that way... only to have their heads caved in by the stone-ax-wielding goblins on either side of each hole.

Two hours wasn't nearly enough practice time, but this village was playing for keeps. They listened to everything I said, understood it, and took action. And we were reaping the rewards. The wolves were strong, yes, capable of taking on a gaggle of goblins at once, and maybe they were even stronger as a pack. But if they were powerful solo, we could just strike 'em all together. If they were powerful as a team, we'd make sure they couldn't team up. Use your head, and you can make it work. The strongest creature in the world, after all, is a human being with a little intelligence!

Your luck just ran out, I thought to myself as I stared into the cold eyes of the direwolf boss. *Some stupid animal beating me? How conceited can you get?*

The confused direwolf alpha was shocked at how far awry his plans had gone.

His pack was beginning to fall into disarray. That couldn't be allowed to continue. The direwolf tribe shone its brightest only when grouped together. Mistrust in the alpha would lead to fatal results. He understood that, too—and that was why he then made his greatest mistake of all. He was enraged at the weakness of his pack, unable to overcome a simple fence, but he was even more afraid that his team's frustration would soon be directed at him.

I need to display my strength to them, he thought. *I am the strongest of my pack. I am more than strong enough, even by myself!*

That was the moment when everything was decided.

My eyes were still firmly upon the direwolf boss. To the goblins, he had disappeared, I assumed, but to me, he was ambling along at a yawn-worthy pace.

Everything was going to plan. I had considered a few possible outcomes, and now one of them was playing out in front of me. These were animals, after all. Not ex-humans like me.

The Sticky Thread over the entryway immediately captured the boss. For all I knew, the silk wouldn't be enough to keep a direwolf leader stuck tight. There'd been no way to test it beforehand, but that didn't matter anymore. The Sticky Thread was there just so we could keep the boss in place for a single moment.

If I didn't hold him in place and he dodged the ensuing Water Blade attack, that would look *super* lame. Or worse, I could catch my team in friendly fire. In the midst of a battle, that was entirely possible.

That was why I devised the trap. But maybe I over-engineered it a little. These guys hadn't even gotten the fence down yet. I'd considered lining the entrance with Steel Thread instead but opted against it, worried that it wouldn't be enough of a final blow.

In situations like these, it was my job to play the ultimate strong-man, the ruler of the roost. That was what all this was for—and that's why, without another moment of self-doubt, I launched a Water Blade at the boss's head.

It hit home. The head launched upward, and then gravity took it. I had killed the boss—and more importantly, I made it look like a laugh.

"Listen, direwolves! Your leader is dead! I will grant you one final choice. Submit to me or die!"

So how will they deal with that? Will their boss's death drive them into such a frenzy that they'll bum-rush me? I'd like to avoid that, if I could.

The remaining direwolves showed no sign of moving. *Uh-oh. This isn't gonna be one of those "I'd sooner* die *than submit to the likes of* you*!" things, is it? 'Cause if it is, it's gonna be all-out war.* We were still losing numbers-wise, and we'd definitely take some casualties. We made it this far without any goblin blood—I doubted we'd lose at this point, but I'd prefer it ended without a struggle.

It was oddly quiet, compared to the pitched battle of a moment ago. I could feel the gazes of the direwolves upon me. Amid their stares, I gradually started glooping forward. I couldn't tell how they'd interpret this, but I wanted to hammer it home that their boss was dead.

In a moment, I was at the alpha's limp body. Nobody offered any objection. One of their pack, which had taken up position nearby, retreated a step.

Then I swallowed the corpse. As was my right as victor, yeah?

The Sage's voice rang in my mind.

Analysis complete. Mimic: Direwolf ability obtained. Direwolf intrinsic skills "Keen Smell," "Thought Communication," and "Coercion" acquired.

*　　*　　*

Sounds like a win to me. But despite seeing their own boss eaten in front of them, the rest of the direwolves still showed no sign of movement. Hmmm... At this point, they were either gonna freak out and run, or freak out and come for me.

...Oh, right! I told them "submit or die," didn't I? Ah, shit. That might've been throwing the baby out with the bathwater. *Better give 'em an escape route,* I thought as I transformed myself into one of them.

Activating Coercion, I spoke to them in a loud, guttural scream. "Arh-arh-arh! Listen to me!" I declared to them. "Once, and only once, I will let this go unpunished. If you refuse to obey me, I bid you to leave here at once!!"

I figured that'd be enough to make these dogs scamper off. I was wrong.

We pledge our allegiance to you!

Now *they* were kowtowing to me, although it looked more as if they were having a lie-down for a nap. But regardless, they had apparently chosen "submit" anyway. Maybe they'd been having a little Thought Communication conference about it while they were standing there like statues.

It beats having to fight them, anyway.

That, more or less, marked the official end of the battle at this goblin village.

✳

That's always the thing, though, isn't it? It's not the fight that's the hard part; it's all the goddamn cleanup afterward.

Who's the idiot that ordered them to destroy their own homes? What're we gonna do about those? And where're all these goblins gonna sleep tonight? And what am I supposed to do with all these dogs? I mean, sure, we killed off a fair number of them, but that's still, like, eighty more mouths to feed.

I, um... Ah, screw it. That's all for today, people! I'll think about it tomorrow, once everyone wakes up.

For the time being, I ordered the goblins to camp out next to the fire, told the dogs to go on standby around the village, and called it a night.

Morning came.

I had spent the previous night thinking, mostly. The conclusion I came up with: Let the goblins take care of the direwolves! Perfect!

We had a total of seventy-two goblins left in fighting shape. No casualties from yesterday. At most, a few scratches. Meanwhile, we had eighty-one surviving direwolves parked outside the town fence—some wounded, but none so badly that a little recovery potion didn't prop them right back up. They could've recovered themselves, I reckoned, with their intrinsic healing skills.

The morning began with me lining up the goblins who were awake. The children and elderly watched from the side. They couldn't help but stick out, given the lack of any homes to hang out in.

Next to me was the village elder. He wanted to help me out somehow, I guess, but there wasn't much an old goblin geezer could do for me. My personal aesthetic tastes remained unchanged from my human years.

That would never change, even though I was transmogrified into a slime. There would be no charming village princess I could ride off into the sunset with. I'd probably have to wait a while for that.

In front of this line of goblins, I summoned the direwolves. "Um, okay," I began, "from now on, I'm gonna have you all form pairs and live with each other, all right?"

Then I gauged the response. I didn't get much of one. They were waiting for me to continue, I guessed, not making a single sound as they stared at me. Nobody seemed to openly grimace at the idea of pairing up, at least, so I assumed I was on decent enough ground.

"Uh, do you understand what I mean? Like, groups of two, okay? Get to it!"

The moment I finished speaking, the goblins and the direwolves began exchanging glances with whoever was in front of them. Slowly and meekly, they followed my order. Yesterday's enemy is today's friend, and all that. They had to learn that the hard way, but at least everyone was on board.

Then I noticed something. *Hang on, do any of these guys have names at all? How are they supposed to call for each other and stuff? What a pain in the ass.*

"Elder," I said as I watched the pairing process unfold to my side, "it's too inconvenient for me to refer to you and your people. I'd like to give names to you all. Would that be all right?"

Everyone must have heard me somehow. Right at the word *names*, every single one of them was locked on to me—even the nonfighting goblins, clearly thrown by this turn of events.

"Are…are you sure…?" the elder timidly asked.

What's the big deal, huh?

"Y-yeah, um… If it's not a problem, I'd like to give out some names?"

It was as if I'd simultaneously blown the minds of every goblin on the premises. Each one erupted into enthusiastic cheering. *What the hell? It's as if they all just hit the lottery or something. If getting a name makes you* that *happy, why don't you just do it yourselves?* It all seemed so simple to me back then.

I started with the elder, asking him what his son's name was. He had been the sole named goblin in the village, now sadly passed. It was "Rigur," apparently.

So I added a *d* on the end and named the elder "Rigurd." No particular reason for it—it just sounded nice. "If your son was here," I joked, "you could have him state his name and just kinda add *d* to the end of it, y'see?"

No one laughed. They thought I was serious. "I… I cannot express my gratitude enough," he blubbered, "for being granted permission to take on my son's name!" *Yeah, great. I'm just shooting from the hip here, you know.* It was starting to make me feel a bit guilty…but ah, what the hell!

The goblin scout leader, meanwhile, I named Rigur. I could've added a "II" to the end of it, I suppose, but why make this more complicated than it had to be? "Rigur" was fine. Fine enough that it made him kneel before me in prayer, as if this was the most emotional moment in his life. Cripes. The apple doesn't fall far from the tree.

So on I went, down the whole line. I also did the rest of the onlookers while I was at it, having families figure out their names together and coming up with whatever for the orphans and singles in the village.

They aren't expecting to, like, keep recycling these names for generations to come, are they? If Rigurd has a grandson, maybe he could start calling himself "Rigurdd." Or if he has a great-grandson, he could be "Rigurddd" and "Rigurd" then gets passed on to the youngest generation. Something like that? Pretty random, maybe, but how else do family traditions ever get started?

"Sir Rimuru," the newly christened Rigurd plaintively asked, "we are so, so appreciative of this, but...are... Are you sure?"

"About what?"

"I mean, I am fully aware of the extent of your magical powers, Sir Rimuru, but...providing all of these names in one go... Will you be all right?"

What's he talking about? I'm just handing out names to folks.

"Mm?" I replied. "No, no problem, I don't think." Then I went back to it. Rigurd raised his eyebrows for a moment, but I paid him no further mind.

Once I was done with the goblins, it was time to move on to the direwolves. Their new leader would be the son of the old one—just as strong (and strong willed) as his father, and already looking every bit as stately.

Peering into his gold-colored eyes, I thought for a moment. Hmm. How about Ranga? That combines the Japanese characters for *storm* and *fang* into one peppy little word. Perfect! Cheap, maybe, but I rolled with it. I'm the Tempest; he's got fangs...

Whatever came to mind first was best, I figured. This wasn't my forte.

The moment I named him Ranga, I began to feel as if practically all the magicules flowing through my body were draining out of it. The sense of hollowness—of the violent emptying of my innards—was mind blowing. *What... What's going on?* It was a fatigue like none I'd felt before.

Reporting. Your body's remaining store of magic has gone below its acceptable threshold. Entering sleep mode. Expected to fully recover in three days.

I was still conscious. I didn't need to sleep...exactly, and I could hear the Sage's voice.

Slowly but surely, it began to dawn on me. I'd used too much of my...magic? Like hitting zero MP, sort of? What'd I do to manage that? Had I been wearing myself out this whole time without realizing it? It sure didn't feel that way.

I tried moving. No response. *"Sleep mode" must be something like hibernation.* I wasn't asleep, but I couldn't move at all. All I could do was sit around—which was fine, because the goblins had prepared a seat of honor for me by the fire, so I might as well bask in it. Nothing else to do, or that I could do.

I took the opportunity to reflect on what just happened. Why did I run out of magic after I started naming people? Did doing that consume magicules somehow? Come to think of it, it *really* started to flow out once I named the direwolves' leader, didn't it?

It was still just a theory, but it seemed clear to me that naming monsters actually required magic. That conclusion took around two days to reach.

It sure explained why Rigurd was so aghast at what I was doing, among other things.

This... Oh, crap, this isn't common knowledge among monsters, is it?

"Guyyyys," I wanted to shout, "you gotta *tell* me these things!!" But there was no point lashing out at others. Not that it'd stop me once I could move again, I imagined.

Initially, the goblins seemed kind of worried about how I fell stone silent, but...somewhere along the line, the question of who had the right to wipe my surface and take care of me almost erupted into violent conflict. *What are they doing? This is* one *harem I seriously wish I weren't involved in.* I was starting to feel like a magic lamp people could rub for three wishes.

Finally, the third day passed.

RECOVERED!

Despite depleting my magic earlier, I felt stronger and more magic-rich than I had before my little accident. Magic was the power to exert force upon the world, and the particles around me were the energy driving it. That seemed to be about the extent of it.

Is it one of those "that which does not kill me makes me stronger" types of things? I pondered experimenting with it further but decided against it. There didn't seem to be much need, and if I died in the process, I'd look like an idiot. Yet another case of me going overboard too soon.

Anyway.

The worker goblins, realizing I was awake, began congregating around me. They were joined by the direwolves, who were streaming in from their outside base. Which was fine, but...

"Um... Hey, guys? Have you all, like, gotten bigger?"

They had. Goblins averaged a little under five feet tall. Now they were all nearly a full foot taller. The guy next to me looked as if he was pushing six and a half, even.

These...are goblins, right? And check out the wolves. I remembered them being a lot browner. Now their fur was straight-on black, with a lustrous sheen. They had grown, too, with the bigger ones now pushing nine or ten feet in length. I didn't remember any of them being much longer than six feet before.

The one that really caught my eye was the wolf at their forefront, walking silently forward. I swear he had to be at least fifteen feet. I could feel the mystic force lashing out of every pore. This was nothing like the boss I beat a few days back—between his looks and his sheer force of presence, he had to be some higher-level monster. The star-shaped birthmark on his forehead and the magnificent-looking horn also raised a few red flags.

Kiiiinda scary.

"My master!" this beast of my worst nightmares bellowed in a fluent human tongue. "How it elates me to see you well once more!"

Holy... Is this Ranga? What happened over the past three days? I was left to wonder that for myself as the cheering, howling monsters surrounded me.

✳

All right...

So in the three days I was checked out, all the monsters around me grew. That was freaky. The only thing that could produce something like that was...evolution, I suppose. So does naming a monster evolve them?

And didn't Veldora go on about something like that for a while...? The difference between "nameless" and "named" monsters?

Oh, right! Something about how earning a name provides a sort of "divine blessing" that helps boost your ability as a monster. Hence the evolution.

Well, hell, no wonder everyone was so happy. And no wonder it tapped all my magic reserves at once.

Monster evolution happens fast. I'd say they didn't "grow" so much as become completely different creatures. The tepid, void-like eyes of the goblins now shone brightly with the pale light of intelligence. And the females... *Yow! They actually kind of look like women now!*

I was so shocked, I could barely even speak.

Huh? ...Huh?!

It made me literally do a double take. These guys were like little imps a moment ago, maybe closer to baboons than humans, and now—well, to use their official terminology—the males were "hobgoblins" and the females "goblinas," although the latter sounded pretty stupid to me. They had both evolved, and according to Rigurd, they had heard the so-called World Language when they did—something that all evolved creatures experienced. A very rare occurrence, and one that excited Rigurd to no end, judging by how he couldn't shut up about it.

This wasn't entirely a happy thing for me, though. The female goblins had covered their entire bodies in rags before. Now, thanks to their evolution, the skimpy clothing allowed one to see certain... things. There would be no brushing them off now. The males certainly seemed happy about it. Even though they were wearing nothing but loincloths themselves...

The village was in desperate need of food, clothing, and shelter. Better start with clothing first, I figured.

Another issue I had to deal with was Ranga. He was so delighted that I was back to full consciousness that he wouldn't stop following me around and bothering me. If you like those fuzzballs, I assume you'd be in paradise, but I was always more of a cat person. It wasn't the worst thing, but still.

"So, Ranga," I said, "I'm pretty sure I only named you out of the pack, so...how come all the other direwolves evolved, too?"

It was true. My magic stores conked out the moment I named this thing.

"My master! We, the direwolves, are both one and all. My brethren and I are connected together—my name is the name of our tribe!"

Huh. So the whole gang evolved together.

The "one and all" thing was something the previous boss never quite fully believed in, as Ranga explained. If he had, that battle might've gone in a different direction. Ranga, meanwhile, had already gained full control over his pack, it seemed, allowing them all to evolve from direwolf to "tempest wolf." "More power for everyone" is the way he put it.

"Nice work!" I said, since he seemed to be desperately fishing for praise. He whipped his tail back and forth, a display that was adorable on such an enormous beast. On the other hand, a happy five-yard wolf could produce nearly enough wind to launch me right out of the village.

"Hey, watch what you're doing with that thing!" I warned him. The downtrodden look he gave in response made me chuckle—and the way he then shrank his body down to around three meters long made me stop. His race could adjust their sizes, apparently. *How useful*, I thought as I instructed him to stick to the small side from now on.

The biggest issue of all, however, was where the heck we were gonna keep all these guys. The wolf-hobgob pairs seemed to be sharing households with each other by now—not that they had houses, so it was really more the hobs using the wolves as blankets. The lack of clothing was killing me, but housing also needed some attention.

So. What now?

∗

I saw a mountain of food piled up before me. That solved one of our problems, at least.

Once I used up all my magic, the rest of them began the evolutionary process. It took about a day to complete, and they wanted to celebrate with both that and the end of battle with a feast. The elder refused to allow it until I recovered, however, so instead they spent their time gathering the food first.

I had noticed them sparring with one another over who got to shine me up during my departure but not the evolution or food-gathering efforts. This "sleep mode" made me well-nigh defenseless, it looked like. I'd need to be careful with it.

The way they began taking action without waiting for orders, at least, was much appreciated. The evolution process must've done wonders for their intelligence. It might've impacted their mental strength even more than the physical.

And the food! Back in their regular goblin days, they'd eked out a living off fruits, nuts, edible plants, and whatever monsters and animals they could hunt down. Now, with the aid of their tempest wolves, they could cover a lot more terrain.

The pairs had, much to my surprise, gained the ability to use Thought Communication with each other—goblins who could guide their wolves more surely than the best of jockeys. I couldn't guess how much this improved their combat ability, but previously unbeatable foes were now simply a warm-up for them. This entire mountain of food was the results from the past two days alone.

But relying on hunting and gathering would leave them in danger if something happened to their environment. They'd have to start thinking about agriculture pretty soon. A steady food supply is the key to a life of plenty. I'd need to figure out what kind of produce grew well here, as well as what sort of grain crops (assuming there were different types at all on this planet). Always something new to explore, at least.

Today, though, I just wanted to shut off my brain and enjoy the feast. And I did.

Well into the night, we celebrated our evolution, the end of war, and—most important to me—my recovery.

The next day, I gathered the entire population around me. We had a heap of issues to tackle, but I had something even more important to tell them.

We needed to hammer out the rules of this village.

Rules, as everyone knew in Japan, were a must to maintain a communal society. "Because I said so!" was only gonna go so far around here, no matter how many times I used that phrase in my old life.

At the core, I had three rules in mind—three guiding principles I wanted to be sure to have them follow. Everything else, I imagined they could figure out.

"Everyone here? All right! I have some rules to give to you! Three, to be exact. The bare minimum I want all of you to follow."

And so I laid out my standards:

1. Do not attack human beings.
2. Do not fight among your friends.
3. Do not look down upon other species.

I could've gone with more if I kept thinking about it, but I couldn't expect them to follow too many from the start. Instead, I just stuck to the basics. But how would they take it?

"Could I ask a question?" Rigur shouted. "Why are we not allowed to attack humans?"

Rigurd gave his son the dirtiest look I've ever seen from a hob-goblin. Was he afraid I was offended? *I wish we could keep things a little more informal, but...*

"Simple: Because I like humans! That is all."

"Ah! Very good! I understand!"

You...do? Well, geez, that was easy. But I couldn't read a single hint of dissent on any of their faces. I was expecting a little more debate on the issue. Talk about a letdown.

"Human beings live in groups," I continued, giving my full expla-nation whether they needed it or not. "If you lay hands on them, they may retaliate in force—and if they throw everything they have at you, I doubt you would be able to defend yourselves. That's why I prohibit interfering with them. It'd help you all if you were friendly with them, besides..."

Really, though, it just came down to me liking humans, seeing as I used to be one.

Ranga nodded deeply at this. It seemed to make sense to him. He must have had his own reasons to think challenging mankind was a bad idea. The hobgobs, meanwhile, appeared even more convinced than before, so I didn't bother thinking about them much.

"Is there anything else?"

"What do you mean by 'Do not look down upon other species'?"

"Well, all you guys are freshly evolved, right? I'm just saying, don't let that get to your head and start lording it over all the weaker species! Just because you're all a little sturdier doesn't mean you're some high-and-mighty race now. Sooner or later, your rivals will get just as strong—or even stronger—and they'll want to get back at you. That'd suck, wouldn't it?"

I had the ears of everyone in the audience. *Looks like that worked well enough.* I was sure some of them wouldn't listen to reason, but it's best to try to nip these things in the bud, anyway.

"That's pretty much it. Stick to those rules as much as you can, all right?"

The first rules the village ever had were set in stone. Everyone nodded their approval, and with that, the curtain rose on a new life for them all.

With local laws out of the way, it was time to start divvying up roles. The village watch, the food-prep team, the group collecting materials for the village to make things with, the ones building homes and tools and such...

I decided to assign police duty to the extra Thought Communication–wielding tempest wolves. There were seven left after all the hobgobs were paired off, and with Ranga practically glued to my ass, that made six I could send on patrol.

Beyond that, I figured I'd leave the assignment details to Rigurd.

"Rigurd, I hereby appoint you 'goblin lord'! It will be your job to keep this village well run and well governed."

In other words, I tossed everything onto his lap. As hard as possible.

But think about it. I worked for a general contractor back on Earth. I'm no ruler. And if I got too wedded to this village, I'd never get a chance to visit a human town. Even if it meant being a tad pushy, I'd have to hand it off to him someday.

I was expecting some blowback, but—

"Y-yes, Sir Rimuru!! I promise you that I, Rigurd, will devote myself body and soul to this vital post!!"

He was sobbing tears of joy again.

Fair enough. Let the king reign, not govern. Or at least let him bark out orders now and then, and leave him alone otherwise.

You know, I seem to remember Rigurd being this doddering, wrinkled mess of a goblin when we first met. Now he's a hobgoblin in the prime of his life—fit, muscular, and bursting with energy. He might even be stronger than Rigur. How did that happen? The more I mess with this magic stuff, the crazier it all seems to me.

"Very well," I crowed. "It is in your hands now, Rigurd! Now, I was watching the construction work. It's terrible, isn't it?"

One could barely call the structures houses. These were stronger, smarter goblins now, but I suppose asking them to suddenly develop technical skills was asking a bit much.

"It pains me to admit so, Sir Rimuru. We never had a need for very large buildings in the past..."

"Yeah. You guys are bigger now, after all. As for clothing… You guys are all exposing *way* too much flesh. Could you maybe pass some clothes around?"

"Ah! Yes! There are some people I know that we've had dealings with several times. Perhaps they could supply clothing that could fit our needs. In fact, with their skills, they might know how to build homes as well!"

Hmm.

Having worked for a contractor, I had an eye for decent building quality. In terms of what I could actually construct, however, my skill was limited to your basic Sunday afternoon DIY projects. Not enough to serve as a building foreman. If these businessmen could help with that, perhaps it'd be worth paying them a visit.

"I see," I replied. "It wouldn't hurt to talk to them. What did you pay them with, though? Money?"

"No, Sir Rimuru. We do have some currency that we confiscated from adventurers, but that remains in storage. Instead, we have obtained the materials we need via either barter or short-term work."

"Oh. So who are these guys?"

"They are known as dwarves."

Dwarves! The infamous smithing race! I gotta check 'em out! And while the loincloth crisis had captured most of my attention, something had to be done about their defensive capabilities. Their armor provided no more protection than tatters—and they couldn't even use it, because it didn't fit anymore. It was certainly an issue, and tackling it right now would be killing two birds with one stone.

Just one problem. Almost nothing they had seized from passing adventurers was of much use any longer, and whatever money they had stored up couldn't be very much. What could we trade? Another problem to shelve for later, perhaps…

"I'll try visiting them. Can you make the arrangements for me, Rigurd?"

"Ah! Ah, of course, Sir Rimuru! I'll have everything for your journey by tomorrow afternoon!"

He sounded enthusiastic enough about it that I felt safe in his hands. He'd probably give me whatever money was left, too, not that I should expect much.

Currency, though, huh? It'd be funny if it was paper.

Thinking about it, though, I didn't have much money to *my* name, either. The fact that currency existed at all in this world was a nice surprise, at least. I'd figured it did, but I'd had no idea how it was circulated at all.

Once I reach a human town, I'll have to go around and check out prices. But that can wait until after the dwarves. After all the hard work getting this town in shape, a leisurely visit would do wonders for me. I'll be with my own humankind soon enough—checking out one of the other races could help me learn a little more about this wacky world.

Although technically a subrace of people, the dwarves apparently lived in large towns of their own. They had a king as well, although no goblin was ever permitted even a glance. Just being allowed into their towns was considered an all-time achievement for goblinkind.

I started to wonder about the state of goblin discrimination around here. I was a slime, after all. Would I be treated fairly? There were lots of anxieties to entertain, but I still couldn't wait to meet some of those little guys. The excitement remained fresh in my mind all throughout the rest of the night.

ROUGH SKETCHES

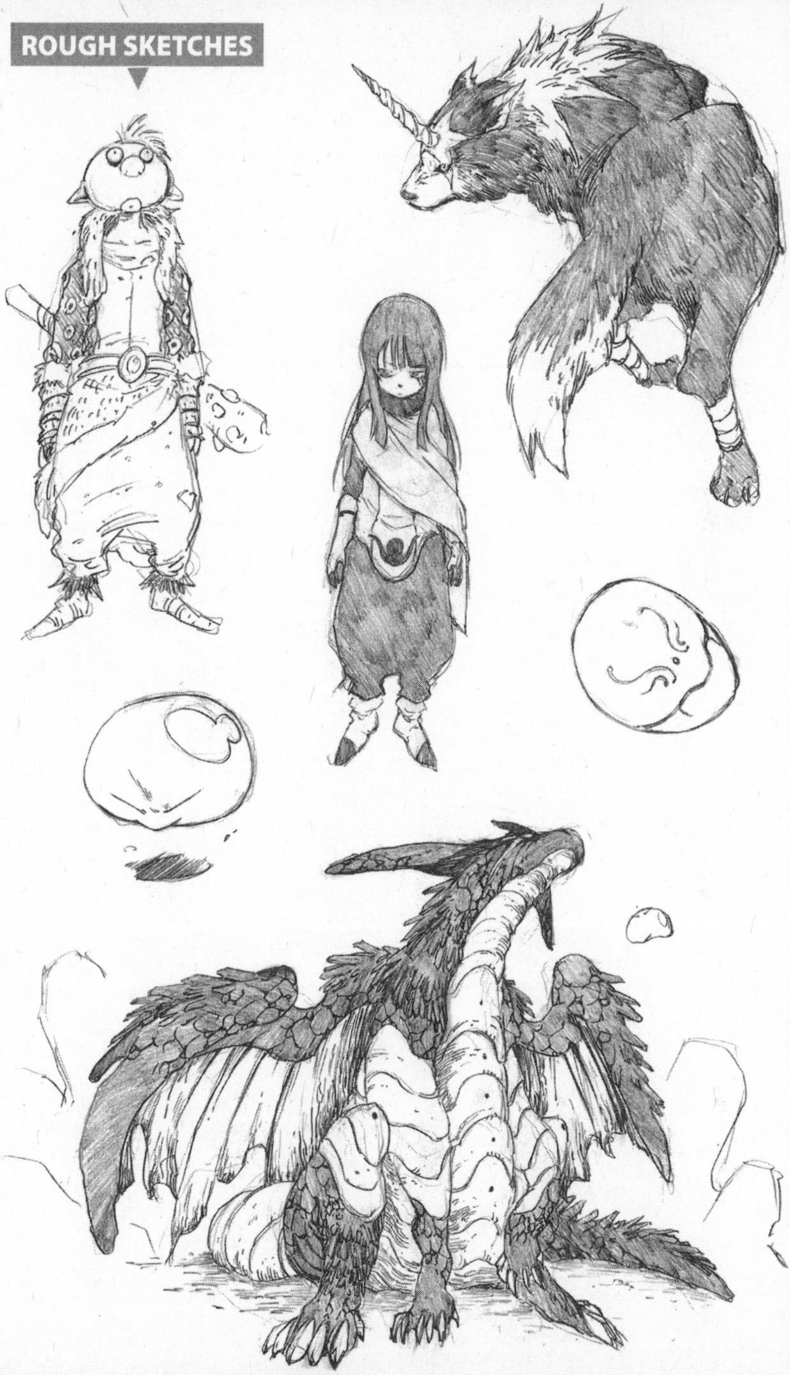

THE GIRL AND THE TITAN

Being possessed by Ifrit saved my life. That, I could never hope to deny. If I'd been left there alone, the burns from the air raid would've killed me. No matter what Leon the demon lord intended for me, I had to accept the fact that I owed my life to him.

As a high-ranked flame elemental, Ifrit had powers that were far beyond anything I could have imagined. He miraculously tamed the magic teeming inside me, ready to explode, as he took over my body. Thanks to my being stabilized beforehand—if you want to phrase it that way—I managed to gain an ability. The unique skill "Deviant."

Normally, being absorbed by Ifrit would have erased my consciousness from existence. It was Deviant that protected me. Ifrit may have held the right to rule my body, but I still managed to retain my sense of self despite the assimilation.

The demon lord always kept me near him.

Though Ifrit and I had become one, my body was still young and immature. The one who had summoned me towered over me, even seated in a chair. Ifrit held ownership over my body, so there was precious little to occupy my time. All I could do was stare at the things that came into view through my eyes. I never tired, but the long periods of boredom were a little painful to endure. I accepted it, though. It was all part of being assimilated.

Then, one day—

"Lord Leon! We have intruders!"

—one of the knights in the demon's service burst into his office.

I was standing next to him, as always. I had nothing else to do, and I couldn't do anything anyway.

A knight in black armor, standing at the demon's right side, took his sword in his hand.

Suddenly, a mysterious figure—a sort of mix between bird and man—shot into the room, cackling in his rasping voice.

"Kehhhh-keh-keh-keh! Greetings from König the Magic-Born! When I defeat you, Leon, I will be a demon lord for all time. An ex-human like you, declaring himself to be a demon lord? Know your place, fiend! I'll be happy to take *yours* once your body is firmly buried in the ground!"

Nothing the man blurted out did anything to change Leon's facial expression. "Hmph," the knight in black calmly said to him, "I see leaving me, at least, to guard you was a wise choice. It looks like one of the rank and filers sniffed this place out."

"Bah," the demon replied just as the knight was about to unsheathe his sword. "Another would-be meddler from the gallery. Very well." He looked at me. "It is time, Ifrit."

What did he mean? I was confused.

"Hmm? What is it, Ifrit?" he asked, an inscrutable look on his face. My bewilderment must have shown in my body's eyes.

"Ignore *me*, will you," the one known as König—a high-level magic-born, as it turned out—said as he spread his winglike arms out and crossed them in front of his face. For a moment, I could see his hands glow.

Confirmed. Extra skill "Magic Sense"…successfully acquired.

*　　*　　*

Ignoring the unfamiliar voice booming in my head, I unconsciously began to walk. One step. Two steps. Then, before I knew it, I was standing in front of the demon lord Leon—face-to-face with König.

"Are you in such a hurry to die, brat?" he rasped out. Something about that voice rankled me to the core. "You will perish by my hand sooner or later. But once I kill that demon lord pretender—"

I could see that the wings extended in front of him held a decent amount of magical force.

"Die, bastard!!"

Before he finished speaking, he fired a volley of feathers. I could tell he had aimed them straight at me. Each one had an ample amount of force behind it—touching one would make it explode, which looked a tad painful.

The moment that occurred to me, I was suddenly taken by a violent rage, my head heating up until I thought it was going to boil. I think it was the wrath of Ifrit inside me.

What happened next took place in the blink of an eye. In a single moment, all the feathers turned to ash, and flames were dancing around König's body. Looking closely, I could see a plume of fire, like a whip, extending from the palm of my outstretched right hand.

"Ah, ahhhh! S-stop! Burning, stop, stop it—"

Whatever König was attempting to shout, he never quite managed to piece together a full sentence. My flames consumed him.

My heart filled with fear. I knew that right here, by my own hand, I had killed a magic-born person. Yet I could feel my whole body lightening with a sense of strangely deep satisfaction. It was hard to explain—as if I had just completed something I was meant to do. It felt as though my mind belonged to someone else. The terror was unbearable.

But... In another moment, it all fixed itself. Ifrit's consciousness filled my soul anew, bottling up my anxieties and my fear.

It did, in the end, keep me from going mad inside. It helped shelter me from the guilt I should have felt at killing. Not that I was incapable of that emotion—Ifrit just exercised his complete control over me to ensure I never felt it. To ensure that I, his host, never lost my mind and died on him.

So began my strange symbiotic relationship with Ifrit, something I neither wanted nor hoped for. The same thing happened again, numerous times—and again, I killed the intruders for Leon, never feeling a thing.

I had no regrets. I was young; I still didn't know right from wrong, and I left everything to Ifrit. I simply acted, unfeelingly, dragged along by the creature's will to dispatch those in his way.

One day, the demon lord spoke to me. "Heh-heh. Ha-ha-ha-ha! I love it," he said. "You've shown your will to me, haven't you? You've shown you can survive. I'm impressed."

For some reason, this observation didn't discomfort me at all. In fact, I almost felt proud.

"What's your name?"

"Shizu...e."

"Shizu-eh? All right. Your name is Shizu. You will call yourself Shizu from now on!"

I meekly accepted it. *I am Shizu. Not Shizue Izawa. The name I live with is Shizu.*

That was how I came to stay at the demon lord's castle, serving as his flame titan—an upper-level magic-born. His close assistant.

Several years passed after I gained the name Shizu. After a while, I was able to move around somewhat under my own volition. I was perfectly at ease with my symbiosis with Ifrit.

The demon lord Leon's castle included a training facility.

There, the black knight served as an instructor, providing guidance for the titan and nonhuman children there—although there were some adults as well. It was a grueling process, and those who failed to keep up would often find themselves with nothing to eat. We all struggled to keep up, with everything we had.

It was there that I learned how to fight with a sword, without borrowing Ifrit's power. I didn't want to lose out to any of my fellow students, and I hated being treated like someone special. That was what drove me to improve.

One day, I befriended a young girl named Pirino, a gentle, quiet girl just a tad older than I was. We were in the forest, on a hunt as part of our practical battle training, and we struck up a conversation. Pirino would always go off on her own, which struck me as odd, so I decided to follow her.

"Fwee!"

There, I spotted her playing with a baby wind fox. She had been giving it food, taking care of it on the sly. It was a monster, a magical beast, but also cute and still too small to go hunting by itself. It was alone, separated from its parents, but it was alive and thriving.

"Ah...!" Pirino hid the wind fox behind her as she whirled around, shocked by my presence. "I—I was caring for this," she stammered, realizing I had seen it. "It'd just be mean to leave it to die... Don't tell anyone, okay?!"

Her eyes wavered with anxiety. I could tell her aims were noble. This was a small life in her hands; she wanted to protect it. Maybe I was jealous of that wind fox. It wasn't alone anymore, I felt, but I was.

"All right," I bashfully said, "but...can I take care of it with you?"

Pirino stared blankly for a moment, then flashed a serene smile. "Of course! In fact, I hope you can. My name is Pirino!"

I gave her my name, and we exchanged a few pleasantries. She was the first friend I ever had in my life.

"What did you name it?" I asked her.

Pirino gave me another look. "Name it? Monsters don't have names. They can communicate with each other through their minds."

"But I'd feel bad if this guy didn't have a name, though. Hey, is it okay if I come up with one?"

"Really? But they said we aren't allowed to name monsters..."

"Please? Come on, just once?"

I didn't quite understand what Pirino meant. No matter what it took, I believed the wind fox deserved a name. After a few more moments, she grudgingly nodded at me—and in another moment, we were both having fun coming up with names.

Ultimately, we settled on "Pizu," a mixture of Pirino and Shizu. It seemed to symbolize our newfound friendship, in a way. I was happy with it.

"Fweee!!"

It would always cry with glee like that whenever Pirino or I used its name. It must have liked what we chose, and I enjoyed the reaction. Pirino would smile, too.

This is so much fun!

I had been so alone, but Pirino and Pizu were there to soothe my heart.

*　　*　　*

We came to visit Pizu on regular occasions.

A few days after we named it, the wind fox grew from something we could keep on our palms to a creature about the size of our heads. It surprised us, but considering how attached it was to us, we didn't mind. If anything, we were glad it was large enough to hunt for itself. Sometimes, it'd even have a bird or wild hare for us when we visited.

"Do you think we could take it to the castle, Shizu? It's really smart, and maybe it could help out around the place…"

"Huh?"

Frankly, I wanted it to remain our little secret. But faced with Pirino's pleading eyes, I couldn't bear to say it. I didn't want my selfishness to sadden her.

There were other assorted magical creatures being kept in the castle. A wind fox this intelligent and this friendly to people—Pirino insisted—could easily be recognized as a servant beast.

That was the start of the tragedy.

"Fweeeeee!!"

I suppose you could say it was just bad luck that we passed by the demon lord Leon in a castle hallway. But it wasn't. It was our fault for assuming we had the strength to watch over anything in life.

"Run… Run, Pizu…!!"

Coming across Leon spooked Pizu beyond all consoling. It leaped right out of Pirino's clasped hands, hackles raised at Leon in a show of intimidation.

The act made my titan awaken. The moment it did, I lost all autonomy. Pirino was so close, but she sounded so far away. Ifrit didn't care how I felt and lashed out at the snarling Pizu. There was no stopping my body, no matter how hard I struggled, as it grabbed Pizu and incinerated it. With my very own hand.

That wasn't the end of it. The flames from my hand formed a white, swirling vortex, attacking the girl that had brought Pizu to Leon. Without so much as a sound, it rendered her into a pile of ash that disappeared in moments. As if there were never anyone there at all.

The flame elemental, finally satisfied at a job well done, gave a loving salute to his demon master before quieting down.

…What was that? I stood there blankly, unable to parse my new reality. *My hand… My…my body… It moved by…itself? Why did…did the flame… Did I…?*

It took several more hours to realize that Ifrit had determined not only Pizu but also its keeper Pirino to be enemies of the state. By my own hand, I had slain my friend.

It made me sick. For hours on end, until nothing came out any longer. He should have just killed me, too, while he was at it. My entire body surged with maddening regret and sadness—and then, like nothing had happened, I was serene. No tears spilled from my eyes, even though I wanted to cry. No madness overtook me, even though I wanted to lose myself in it. No voice escaped my throat, even though I wanted to scream.

Did the magic-born titan take over my mind, too? My heart was buried in a swell of terror, and then instantly, the calmness came back. I was no longer even a person. No matter how much I wanted it, I would never attain the kind of happiness others were entitled to.

From that day forward, I stopped crying. I had already cried all my tears out anyway. There was nothing left to shed. I had lost something far too important to myself on that day.

And Leon, my demon lord, simply looked on coldly. Quietly. Never punishing me.

CHAPTER
3

THROUGH
THE DWARVEN
KINGDOM

That Time I Got Reincarnated as a Slime

As he'd so boldly proclaimed a day earlier, Rigurd had everything I needed that afternoon. He had even chosen the team members for my expedition into the Dwarven Kingdom already.

By the way, did Rigur really have to be our expedition leader, too? I was a little concerned about that, but he seemed to be all for it.

Well, his father did recover his youthful looks and the enthusiasm to go with it. Maybe I was worrying too much.

Once I picked up my luggage, Ranga eagerly allowed me onto his back. I boinged myself up and nestled into his fur. There was a lot more fuzz than I'd thought, and it sure did wonders for comfort.

I braced my body with Sticky Thread to keep from falling. Not having any arms or legs was a real pain at times like these, but at least I had the skills to do something about it. Gotta use the tools you have on hand.

I had actually been practicing a bit with my silk during the off-hours. What red-blooded hero hasn't wanted to slap his enemies down with a lightning-quick whip strike? I didn't know if I could yet, exactly, but I had time. Practice makes perfect.

My luggage primarily consisted of money and food, three days' worth. If we took longer than that, we'd have to forage a bit. We could've brought along some hardier rations that'd keep over longer periods of time, but I wanted to travel light, if I could.

Not that I couldn't just swallow whatever up and bring it along... but I didn't want to get soft. I didn't need food anyway.

On the monetary side, we had seven silver pieces and twenty-four bronze pieces. Even I could tell that wasn't much. My expectations weren't high, though, so that was fine. We'd just figure out what to do once we showed up.

*

For a goblin on foot, it would apparently take around two months to walk to the Dwarven Kingdom. We would be largely following the Great Ameld River, which flowed through the forest, up to its source in a mountain range that held the settlement we sought.

These were the Canaat Mountains, which neatly separated the Empire to the east and the small litter of nations here and there around the Forest of Jura. There were, by and large, three trade routes that ran between the two pockets of civilization. One put you right through the forest; another was a more treacherous route through the mountains; the third was by sea. The Jura route would normally be the shortest and safest, but for some reason, it was only rarely taken advantage of—most travelers challenged the mountains instead, what with the travel costs and potential sea-monster interference a ship route presented.

In addition to these three routes, there were a handful of other ways to reach the Dwarven Kingdom, but they all charged tolls. This was mandatory, supposedly to keep people from transporting dangerous goods along the paths. It was a decent enough option for small bands, but the larger caravans avoided them for the costs and time involved. They were safe, no doubt, and we'd have to consider one of them later, depending on how our finances held out.

We had no business with the Empire, so there was no point traveling east to leave the woods. It was straight north to the Canaats. We wouldn't have to go up to any peaks, at least—the kingdom was situated at the base of the mountains, in the upper reaches of the Great Ameld. A beautiful hub of civilization, by the sound of it, built into a gigantic natural cavern.

That was the Dwarven Kingdom.

So we followed the plan, tracing the Great Ameld River's route northward. It certainly kept us from getting lost. I had a map in my brain anyway, just in case. We had a guide with us—Gobta, who apparently ran a trip of his own to the kingdom once—so we followed his lead, and I took up the rear.

These black wolves are fast! And they never seemed to tire at all. We had been going for about three hours without a single break, and we had to be averaging nearly fifty miles per hour the whole way. We had a few rocky outcroppings to navigate now and then, but they sure didn't care. And this was all while making sure we stayed balanced on their backs! It made the trip a breeze for us.

At this pace, we might not even need a week for the whole trip. Not that I was in a hurry. I wanted to work out the housing and clothing situation back at the village, but that wasn't a problem we could solve in a night and a day regardless.

"Hey!" I shouted. "Don't wear yourself out, now!"

Ranga, for some reason, upped his speed a little.

I had spent the past three or so hours enjoying the wind and the motorcycle-like sense of speed, but I was starting to get a little bored. Trying to converse in these conditions would normally be impossible, but not with the Thought Communication skill I stole from the direwolf boss. Maybe it'd be fun to chat up the gang while I took in the journey.

In my mind, I formed the required network of thought. *Right, what to talk about...*

"Hey, um, Rigur? By the way...who was it that named your brother, anyway?"

"Ah, thank you for recalling my name, Sir Rimuru! My brother was named by a passing member of the magic-born races."

"Oh? One of them visited a random goblin village?"

"Indeed, Sir Rimuru, about a decade ago. I was still a child. He spent several days in my village...and he claimed to 'see something' in my brother, in his words."

"Huh. Must've been a nice brother."

"Oh, absolutely! He was my pride and joy. Sir Gelmud, the one who bestowed the name, said it himself. 'I would love to have you among my men,' he said!"

"But he didn't take him along on his journey?"

"No, Sir Rimuru. He was still young at the time. Sir Gelmud said he would return in several years, once he was stronger, and then he set off."

"Ohh. Bet he'll be pretty surprised at how much everything's changed when he gets back!"

"I imagine so, yes. Now, though, we serve you, Sir Rimuru. We may not be able to follow Sir Gelmud to his honorable demon horde, but..."

"Demon horde? Wow, he's got one of those, huh? You sure he would've been willing to invite the rest of you guys, too?"

"I am rather positive, actually. My brother evolved himself as a named monster, but the changes that wrought were nothing compared to what you provided us. Clearly, this evolution was on a different caliber. Heavens, I thought I would never hear the World Language once in my life. Such an honor!"

The hobgobs listening in on us all nodded their earnest agreement. *That kind of thing, huh? Naming someone evolves them, but how it turns out depends on the namer...? I'd love to recruit someone to help me experiment on that a bit. We could have a name-off.*

But...dang. A real-life demon horde. I knew there had to be one of those around here! Is the king of all demons going to attack us sooner or later? Actually, which side should we be on if that happens? Maybe I should save that question for when it actually comes up, if it ever does.

I already know there's at least one "hero" out there, besides, so I'm sure that king or whatever's gonna be mostly focused on whoever that is. Not too sure the one Veldora told me about is alive after three centuries of retirement, but given how easy it apparently is to transmigrate and revive and so on around here, something tells me she's still up in some mountain shack right now, training away.

Better make a mental note of that Gelmud guy, at least. Now, next question.

"Ranga!" I called out to the black wolf that was suddenly my biggest fan in the universe. "I'm kind of the guy who killed your father, aren't I? You don't have any lingering, you know, resentment about that?"

"I do have thoughts about it, my master. But to a monster, victory or defeat in battle is the only absolute in life. No matter how it turns out, we are aware of the fact that might makes right. Win, and the day is yours! Lose, and nothing shall remain! But...not only did my master forgive; he even gave me my once and future name for all time! I am filled with thankfulness, not resentment!"

"Hmm... Well, if you want a rematch, I'm open any time."

"Heh-heh-heh... But, indeed, my evolution has made it all the clearer in my mind! If you had unleashed your full force in our previous battle, the whole of the pack would have been wiped out. We would have been lost to the winds of time, never able to realize our dreams of evolution! Our loyalty, our devotion, belongs to our one true master alone!"

All...right?

Certainly, in black snake form, I might've been able to do 'em all in with one breath. But I didn't want to have to try anything so risky. *He's really thinking way too highly of me.*

Not that I mind him having the wrong idea, but...

"You realized that, eh? Guess you really *have* grown a little!"

"Ah-hah-hah! It pleases me to hear such words!"

I nodded to myself. *I mean, I killed his dad. There's no way he's not at least a little miffed about that.* If Ranga wanted to exact his revenge someday, I'd gladly hold up my end of the bargain. He could definitely give a black snake a run for his money, at least.

We chatted a bit more as the road wore on. All of us were moving far, far ahead of schedule.

"Hey, you guys aren't going too fast for your own good, are you?" I asked.

"Not a problem, Sir Rimuru!" Rigur shot back. "Thanks to our evolution, perhaps! We are not terribly fatigued at all!"

"Do not worry, my master!" added Ranga. "We are not wholly freed from the bonds of sleep as you are, but we do not require an extended period of rest! Nor do we need frequent stops for food. It will be no obstacle, even if we fast for several days!"

I scoped out the rest of the crew. They all looked just as gung ho as when we set off. *Sheesh, I'm probably the least enthused out of them all. And why shouldn't I be? I've got nothing to do up here.*

We wound up running, running, and running some more for around half the day. Talk about tough.

As the group took their evening meal at the end of the second day, I decided to ask Gobta about the Dwarven Kingdom we were headed toward.

"Y-yes, sir! Umm, it is officially known as the Armed Nation of Dwargon! Their leader is known as the Heroic King, and—"

Something about his shouty reply indicated that my speaking to him made him terribly nervous. I was afraid he'd bite his tongue in his panic.

According to Gobta's account, the current king was Gazel Dwargo, third in his line from the original. A great hero, one whose might and presence made the elder dwarves recall his grandfather in his younger years, but also an intelligent one who ruled his realm with a steady, even hand. A living hero, in a way.

It had been a thousand years since Guran Dwargo, the first Heroic King of the dwarves, established this kingdom. Since then, his descendants had carried on his will, preserving and developing his people's history, culture, and technical skill.

In a nutshell, that was Dwargon. Given how long its kings apparently lived, it must have been a hell of a place. Hearing about it got me excited.

"In that case," I asked, "how much longer will it take, Gobta?"

"If I had to guess, we should arrive by the morrow, sir! The mountains are starting to loom high!"

He was right. The peaks weren't even visible until yesterday. We were advancing at an astounding clip.

"I've just thought of something, Gobta—what errand brought

you there in the first place? I thought you had merchants visiting the village regularly."

As far as I had heard from Rigurd, there were bands of kobolds who stopped by on regular occasions. Why would a goblin want to take the two-month journey over here, then?

"Y-yes, sir! The dwarves pay high prices for magical weapons and armor, you see. They paid us with tools and such, but the merchants helped me carry them back, thankfully! None of the monsters around the village could use that magical gear anyway…"

Aha. So they sold the weapons and stuff they found off passing adventurers? No wonder there was nothing decent left at the village. He must've carted it all to the Dwarven Kingdom because the kobolds didn't have any way of appraising it on-site. Of course, any adventurers who'd lose to a bunch of goblins almost certainly must've been utter beginners, so inexperienced that they couldn't even use a compass to keep from stumbling into monster villages. I doubted any of their gear could've been worth much.

"Plus," Rigur added to Gobta's roundabout reply, "all the goods the dwarves make—the weapons, mainly—it's top-notch. Even the humans recognize it as the best make in the land, and they gather at the kingdom to seek out the latest works, along with the subraces and intelligent monsters. It's been tradition for years now, and all conflict between races is prohibited there, in the name of the king."

So we were traveling there less to sell some junk and more to buy the tools they needed. The fact that they could do so on neutral turf, without getting laughed at by the other monsters, must've been another attraction.

"Such an arrangement," Rigur continued, "is made possible by the Armed Nation's astonishing military might. As far as the kobold merchants told me, the dwarven armies have not tasted defeat in a full millennium…"

The kingdom enjoyed the defenses of a massive, powerful, magic-driven army corps and a wall of heavily armed infantry. Any would-be attackers would find themselves first blocked by the infantry, then turned into dust by a rain of offensive magic.

The equipment that backed up such an offensive juggernaut must have been very high-tech indeed, for this world. As Rigur put it, it was overwhelmingly superior to any human-made weapons or armor. I doubted anyone had the guts to mess with them at this point. It'd be the intelligent thing for a nearby nation to try to stay on their friendly side. No wonder none of their visitors were stupid enough to squabble with any other monsters within their territory.

Still, dealing with any species, regardless of what they look like? *The dwarves must be pretty chill dudes. Maybe I could make a few connections myself. In fact, I'd better.*

This was a realm where people intermingled freely with monsters. A land that began with the surface city and extended down, down, down. A kingdom armed to the hilt that walked the path of peace. No place in the world boasted as many weaponsmiths and merchants, and yet it sounded like the farthest point in the universe from any kind of conflict. A bit ironic, maybe.

The way the Dwarven Kingdom was starting to sound from these conversations, I couldn't wait to arrive.

Exactly three days after we began our journey, we reached the grasslands at the foot of the Canaats. The city truly was beautiful—chiseled into the vast mountain cavern, a natural fortress created by nature.

It was the Armed Nation of Dwargon in all its mighty glory.

*

And, of course, there was a line to get in.

The front gate was enormous, built to block free entry into the vast cave opening.

This gate opened only whenever the army went inside or out, and that, I heard, happened just once a month. Today it was firmly closed, but at the bottom of the great doors were two small entryways meant for regular traffic. The right-hand one had nobody in front of it—probably meant for the nobility or any other lofty figures who showed up. The door we were waiting for was on the left, and while some people bore passes that allowed them free entry, others had to undergo luggage checks in a separate chamber. All of this, of course, was guarded by a security detail whose equipment certainly reminded you that this was the Armed Nation. They weren't clowning around.

Once you were through security, you were pretty free to do what you wanted around the city, it seemed...but *man*, what a line. We were bound to spend more time waiting than traveling at this rate.

"Guess we're really here, huh?" a nearby traveler ventured as I scanned the line of people down the corridor. "That's a fancy gate."

"Look at the armor on that soldier!" his companion exclaimed. "We probably couldn't afford gear like that after ten years on my salary."

"Yeah, I'll bet! Even the Eastern Empire tries to keep things peaceful with these guys—in public, at least. With that kind of equipment, I see why."

"You said it. They sure ain't gonna give you a second chance if you try anything. The blowback would be one hell of a headache for any nation that tried it!"

Maybe the dwarves of this world weren't the kind, gentle, almost lovable beings I was picturing. They could be a lot more violent than that, for all I knew. Still, as a free city and a hub of trade across races and species, it maintained at least a public face of neutrality. The fact that the Heroic King never allowed combat inside the city was fairly common knowledge among adventurers. I supposed that even in this world, you could afford to be neutral only if you had the muscle to back it up.

As I mused over this, I began hearing some more sinister voices.

"Hey! Hey, check it out, there're monsters out here! We can kill 'em, right? We aren't inside yet."

"Yeah, what the hell're you guys standing in line for? You think we're gonna letcha do that, you little runts? Gimme your spot before we kill you! And leave your crap there, too, all right? Then we'll letcha go!"

I figured they had to be out of their minds, but then again, it was just me and Gobta.

A bunch of loinclothed goblins riding gigantic wolves would have been bound to stir up at least a little attention, and not the good kind, so I'd decided to go in solo with my guide. Rigur had wanted to join me, but I'd turned him down.

They were all camped out at the forest entrance now, waiting for our return. Which left the two of us. I'm sure we looked as if we had giant targets painted on our asses. Now this pair of adventurers was accosting us, whining about not liking our faces or whatever.

"Hey, did you hear something, Gobta?"

"Yes, I did..."

"Did you run into any trouble last time you were here?"

"Of course I did, sir! Ooh, they beat me silly! The kobold merchants had to pick me up off the ground! Might've died if they didn't, eh?"

"...They did, huh? So we can't avoid this?"

"It is, uhh, the fate of the weak...?"

He'd all but expected it. Sheesh, could've told me beforehand. Gobta hung his head, realizing what was in store for him. He was finally getting comfortable talking to me. I was a bit worried this threat would make him flee back into his shell again.

"Yo! You think you runts got a right to ignore us?!"

"Hey, isn't a talking slime pretty rare? Maybe we could get some money outta selling it."

The adventurers kept yapping at us. People (maybe could have) said I had the patience of a saint back home, but this was starting to irk me.

"Gobta... You remember the rules I gave you all before?"

"Y-yes, sir! Absolutely!"

"Good. In that case, could you close your eyes and cover your ears for me? No peeking!"

"Um...? All right, but...!"

Right. Laying out some simple rules for my people, then promptly violating every single one of them three days later wouldn't exactly make me a role model. But with Gobta out of my hair, I was free once more to take out the garbage.

Just then, the hostile adventurer on the right shifted his gaze, and I followed it. It led to another group, a trio, grinning as they watched the spectacle unfold.

One of my adversaries carried a sword; the other was clad in light armor. Bandits, I figured. The other three consisted of two robed figures—wizards or monks or something—and a big, brawny fighter. If I had to guess, they were all in the same party, and these two were sent over to chase us out and nab our position in line while the other three finished us off and joined the others as if nothing had happened. That kind of thing.

A neat and easy way to pick off the weaker monsters and take their possessions. Nicely planned. Too bad they picked the wrong target!

"Whoa, whoa, back of the line!" I said to rile them up. "I'm feeling generous today, so I'll let all that slide if you line up out back!"

The duo looked stupefied for a moment. Then their faces turned bright red.

Didn't take much to tick *them* off.

"What the hell're you talking about, you little pissant?" one of them bellowed in his best evil-underling voice. "You wanna start something with us?!"

"You're dead! I promised you'd live if you just left all your stuff there, but you know what? Now that you've pissed me off, that's off the table."

Heh. Back in my contractor gig, I pushed people around that looked a hell of a lot scarier than these guys. I had to if I wanted to get any work done. Some of the old rascals even had tattoos all over them. Compared to that, this barely made me break a sweat.

"Little pissant, huh? You mean me?"

"Who the hell else am I talkin' to? A slime's the pissiest out of 'em all, man!"

"Get over here! If you're so eloquent, we'll make you into our slave instead!"

A monster slave? Do those even exist? Let's look into that later. The merchants and apparent adventurers around us had started to notice the shouting. *Better keep their eyes on me, for starters. I don't know if* the concept of justified self-defense exists in this world…but it wouldn't hurt to have as much eyewitness testimony as possible.

Too bad it didn't look as if any of the humans were interested in lending me a hand. *Really? If I were a little girl, I bet it'd be a different story.*

"Think you can call me a pissant and get away with it, huh? And you just called me a slime, too…?"

"Well, duh! What *else* are you?"

"Piece of shit… You think I'm gonna let you treat me like an idiot? You're dead! Too late to beg for your life now, man!"

The two of them drew their weapons. *Oop! Off they go.*

Man. Talk about a stroke of bad luck, having these guys be the first humans to ever talk to me. Can't believe how much friendlier the monsters were.

The people around us began edging away to safety. I supposed they wanted to keep from getting involved. The gate guards must have noticed as well, because they were starting to hurry over.

Keeping my eye on them, I casually rolled myself forward.

"Heh-heh-heh… A piece of shit, huh? A slime? Where'd you get the idea that I was a slime, huh?"

I let them fill in the rest themselves.

Of course I was a slime. Anyone would've said so.

"What? Cut the crap, man!"

"Yeah! If you ain't a slime, show me what you really are! It's gonna be tough to make excuses once you're dead!"

They were practically waiting for me to transform. Just like I'd hoped! I was sure I could win as a slime, but it was kind of hard to hold back my skills. I'd be liable to slice each of them into two neat pieces with my Water Blades. Toning it down and just knocking them out was harder.

"All right!" I shouted, keeping up the performance. "Allow me to show you my true form!" Then I released the mystical aura I had been covering up. Just a little, of course.

I looked around, seeing whether the audience had picked up on it. A few among the handful of people around us had. The two idiots in front of me, meanwhile, seemed oblivious.

All bark and no bite, I suppose. Enough sizing them up. Now, what to transform into...?

A black mist sprayed out from my body, shrouding it completely. When it cleared, a different monster stood there instead. A black wolf.

Um, hang on, wasn't I a direwolf when I absorbed the boss and transformed right after? Now I was just as dark as Ranga and his pack. If anything, I was actually larger than Ranga.

That, and I had two horns on my head.

Form: Tempest Starwolf.

...Well. I guessed if a monster type I consumed evolved, my mimic form evolved with it. I was one level ahead of the evolved Ranga, even. After all, he had only one horn.

Less trivially, I felt a terrific amount of power well within me. I was sure the sight would make these fools drop their swords and instantly run away.

But they didn't.

"Hah! I don't care how badass you look! You're still a runty goddamn piss-slime to me!"

"You think that was enough to freak us out? Come on, man!"

They aren't picking up on this at all! You're really supposed to by now, guys... I mean, don't I look threatening enough? And even if you think it's just an illusion, shouldn't a shape-shifting slime give you at least a little pause?

And yet it didn't faze them at all. Maybe they figured they still had their three friends for backup.

I had a few more skills on hand, too. Five, according to the Sage. Keen Smell, Thought Communication, Coercion, Shadow Motion, and Dark Lightning.

Shadow Motion was something Ranga and his pack were actually practicing at the moment. They could hide inside the shadow of their partner, then reappear on the spot whenever they were called. They were still getting the hang of the "get inside a shadow" bit, so it'd likely be a while to come.

Dark Lightning, meanwhile… That, I didn't even have to test. If I tried it out now, my adversaries would be charbroiled, I was sure. I had underestimated the stupidity of them both, so things could get ugly around here. Either way, Dark Lightning was out of the question.

Sure would have been nice if Coercion actually worked on them! Talk about being too stupid to find your ass on the bottom of you. The audience, meanwhile, were clearly quaking in their boots. Some had already lost their footing.

"Sheesh… Well, whatever. I've had enough of this. Take me on!"

I gave them a free swipe to start.

Speaking of, what would happen to the form I was mimicking if I was damaged? I did actually test that once—I deliberately kept getting myself attacked in armorsaurus lizard form. What I found was that once I took enough damage, I automatically reverted back to slime form—although the damage would be applied only to the mimic, not to my slime body. I supposed the magicules forming the mimicry also protected my body from the blows.

The restrictions I had to work with were the three-ish minutes I had to wait before switching to another form, and the magic I had to consume for each mimic type. But the magic wasn't a problem, really, considering the amount I could work with.

In other words, I could let these guys flail at me all they wanted. Even if they were a hell of a lot stronger than they appeared, I'd just revert to slime form and scoot off. Simple.

"Hah! Prepare to die!"

Answering my call, the swordsman lunged at me with a shout.

"Hrahh! Windbreaker Slash!"

Is that a swordsman skill? The blade of his sword started glowing green. But it didn't hurt me, sad to say… My hide snapped his mighty blade cleanly in half.

As he attacked, his partner threw a set of three daggers at me. I appreciated the gesture—three at once had to be tricky to pull off—but none of them had enough force to even split a tempest starwolf's hair.

"What was that?" I sneered at them, trying my best to play the villain figure. Really, though, what was that? I was completely undamaged. Was that skill name just for show?

"N-no! That pelt of yours... It's too tough!"

"It can't be... I...I... It *can't* be! My sword is crafted from silver! It's supposed to hurt monsters more!"

...Silver's a relatively weak metal, isn't it? Brother.

"H-hey! Help me, you guys!"

Apparently the swordsman didn't care about saving face any longer. I guessed that other trio was with him after all.

"Hah! It's over for you now!"

"Oh, man... I *really* didn't think we'd have to wade into this, man."

"A transforming slime, huh? Interesting. Think I'll dissect it once it's dead."

"You haven't moved this whole battle, have you? Bet that magic fades away the moment you do, huh? Am I right, or what?"

The three of them prattled on as they joined their friends, making for a total of five surrounding me, and went on the attack. The swordsman summoned magic blades of wind, his companion producing a shortsword to swipe at me with. Their heavy fighter shouted "Grandbreaker Slash!" as he hefted up a great ax and slammed it down. The wizard tossed a few fireballs my way, and his monk friend built a magical defense for himself, expecting me to target him first.

As parties went, it was rather well balanced. The only problem they had was that none of their attacks did a thing against me.

Once the dust settled, the group lifted their eyes, daring to take a look at me. They were too shocked to speak. Maybe Coercion would work now.

With an earth-shaking roar, I invoked it...but, alas, I screwed it up. I didn't mean for the *audience* to faint to the ground, too, with assorted substances welling up around their pants.

What a disaster. Now what? This'll be such a pain to deal with. Hmm? The party? Well, they had just taken a Coercion blow at point-blank range. I doubt I need to go into detail on what happened to them.

My Magic Sense skill started picking up on the dwarven security force running our way.

"It's over," I whispered. Over, indeed. I looked down at them, wondering how they were ever going to clean up their undergarments after this—trying to keep my new reality at bay for just a few more moments.

∗

"I'm really sorry about this!!"

I bowed deeply—or intended to, anyway—inside the guardroom.

After the ruckus we had caused, there was no way security was going to let the lot of us off with a slap on the wrist. After only a few moments, a squadron of guards was surrounding us. Well, me, really, given how unconscious the other five were.

I know! I thought. *I'll just turn into a slime and slink off!* And I tried to. But before I could move, they grabbed me en masse and—*squish*—lifted me up. So much for that.

The soldiers flashed me their best "no struggling, now" smiles. The sweat running down their foreheads, however, indicated the effort they had to expend to make this arrest.

"W-wait!" I shouted, doing my best frenzied-Gobta impression. "We didn't do anything! We're the victims here!"

"All right, all right," came the smiling reply. "We'll hear you out in the guardroom. Can't expect to run off after *that*, now can you?"

Not much else I can do, I guess. What's Gobta doing? I glanced back, only to find he still had his eyes closed and his hands over his ears. *Oh, for... What is he thinking? He's not, clearly. He's too stupid to. At least he takes orders well.*

Luckily, I managed to shout loudly enough to attract his attention. Before long, we were all on our merry way to the security guards' office.

So here's what happened!
1. I got accosted!
2. I turned into a wolf!
3. I kind of howled a little.

Whatcha think? Not my fault, right? I thought as I glanced at the soldier standing above me.

He was still smiling at me—the expression suited this gruff, friendly-looking dwarf and his long, bushy beard. Except for those unfortunate veins popping out of his forehead.

"Umm, why did you take me along with you, officer?"

"You damned fool! What do you think you're saying? Our chiefs are yelling at us *because* you were accosted."

"What?! Really? I'm sorry... I've messed up again, haven't I...?"

"Well, there's nothing to be done about it this time, but try to be a bit more careful, all right?"

Whew. Guess they finally saw the light. Good thing my "Blame Everyone Else" skill from my human years was still going strong. It was an advanced ability, earned only after years of life experience. The key was to never give your foe a single moment to doubt you. It was hard!

And maybe I phrased it a bit jokily, but my account pretty well summarized the whole thing. It sounded as though the witnesses they talked to said the same thing.

"So what was that wolf, then?" the soldier watching over me asked. *What's he mean, "What is it?"*

"Um, the species, you mean? It's a—"

"No, not the name. What I mean is, why did that kind of monster show up around here? Where'd it come from, where'd it go... I wanna hear everything you know!"

Mmm? I'd told him that was just mimicry. He didn't believe me? I thought I was pretty open with him. I knew it was standard procedure for a hero to hide his secret identity, but I wasn't exactly a hero anyway.

"Well, I told you... That was just me transformed!"

"Huh? Look, it's already rare for a slime to talk, and you want me to add shape-shifting to the package, too?"

"No, I mean... Look, would you like me to show you?"

"Hmph. Nah, it's fine. But if you can shape-shift, how is that possible? You're a slime, aren't you?"

That... Wait. How should I answer that? I don't think he'd buy it if I just said "It's an intrinsic!" or whatever. That'd just put me on the same level as Gobta. Think, man. You gotta come up with a decent excuse, now!

"Well... I was actually cursed. My talents must have sparked some jealously, I guess... I'm capable of wielding illusory magic."

"Oh, really? A curse, is it? Then what?"

"Then, um... Well, I know a few illusory spells, but I was still just a student at the time, so this evil mage turned me into a slime... I'm on a journey to find a way to undo the curse, and, um, that's pretty much it!"

"Why'd you run into an evil wizard, then? Why'd he curse you instead of just killing you?"

Nnngh... This would go a lot easier if you'd just believe me, man. You don't have to be so obstinate about it. Though I guess I'd be, too. If he actually bought my story, that'd make him more gullible than a goblin.

This little back-and-forth between me and the soldier went on for another two hours or so.

....

......

...

By the end of our intensive debate, I had just about an entire novel's worth of backstory. A story about a forlorn young (and beautiful) girl, brutally transformed into a slime by an evil mage.

In the midst of our tit for tat, if you want to call it that, the soldier's questions helped me weave a grand story of heroic tragedy in my mind. I was a young prodigy, a girl inherently gifted in the arts of transformation and illusory magic. A cruel witch had cast a terrible spell on me, and I was traveling to rid myself of the curse.

Why did this have to happen? And why did I turn myself into a magical girl along the way?! And the worst part of it was, whenever I said something that wandered off-script, the soldier's next question would help me fix the mistake. *Oh, right!* I'd say to myself as the tale meandered its merry way down the path.

By the end of it, both myself and the soldier were enthralled, hoping against hope that the girl would somehow succeed on her quest. Our eyes burned with passion—at least, his did. Truly, we had a connection that went beyond mere words.

"All right! That's it for the report. Thank you for your cooperation! But we're going to need to—"

Slam!

Before the soldier could finish, the large door behind him opened. Another soldier rushed in.

"S-sir! An armorsaurus just showed up in the mines! It's already injured several miners at their posts!"

"What?! Well, did you defeat it?"

"We're good there! A suppression force is on its way. But some of the miners are fairly roughed up. I don't know if there's a war under way or something, but the city shops are out of medicine, and the castle won't let us access their stockpile…"

"What about our healers?"

"That's the thing, sir… The injured were deep inside, mining magic ore. The healers at the guardhouse are all out handling other calls, so all we have left is a single novice!"

"Ah, damn it all!"

Sounds rough. Not that I care. Just take some from the castle, if it's that important! I thought, but…

I do have a few potions on me, though. What should I do?

It wasn't as if I expected the gesture to testify to my character and get me off the hook. We just need to make the world a better place is all. I know it sounds fishy coming from me, but… Compassion is its own best reward, and all that. I'll get karma back for it someday.

"Um, sir! Sir!"

"What? I'm busy. I'm done with you for now, but I can't let you go yet. Stay in this room until things calm down a little!"

"No, not that, um… I've got this."

I took a recovery potion out. Or spat it out, is the way he probably saw it.

"…Um, what's that?"

"A recovery potion. Drink it, rub it in—it's high quality!"

"Eh? What's a slime like you doing with that?"

Oh, come on. What happened to my story? Why's he treating me

like a slime again? He was egging me on during that entire inter-
rogation, wasn't he? Not that I wasn't an eager participant, but…

"That kind of doesn't matter right now, does it? Go ahead, try it.
How many do you need?"

"We've got six men down…but are you sure?"

The soldier who'd just stormed in gave me a quizzical stare. If I
were him, I probably wouldn't take a potion from a monster, either.

"Tch… Stay here, all right? Let's go!"

"Um? But, Captain, that's a monster…?"

"Enough from you! Just take me over to them!"

The bushy-bearded captain snatched up the six recovery potions I
provided and ran off. What with the grand fantasy tale we'd just woven,
I supposed I had gained his trust somewhat. Maybe he was a nice guy
after all. Didn't expect him to be a full-fledged captain, though.

"Is it over?" Gobta asked after silently nodding at everything I'd
said before now.

"No, but I guess we'll sit here and see what happens."

"Got it, sir!"

Then we stared into space. The soldiers who peeked in on occasion would give us confused looks, but otherwise, not much happened for an hour. I was practicing my Sticky Thread moves a bit
when I heard the captain's heavy footsteps. The silken whip zipped
back into my body as I waited for him to come in. Gobta was asleep,
proving that maybe he was smarter than I was all along.

"Thank you, sir!" the bearded captain thundered as he stormed
into the room, head bowed. The miners filed in behind him.

"You're the one with the potions? Thanks a ton!"

"My arm was pretty torn up. I didn't think I'd ever work again,
even if I survived… Thank you!"

"……"

The last guy didn't say anything before they all left, but I was
fairly sure he was thankful, too. *Glad to see the potions worked.*

By this time, it was past sunset. It was almost fully dark outside
when the captain started talking with me again—seriously, this time.

It turned out the quintet who'd tried taking me on were members
of this nation's Free Guild. They had talent, but they also had a

prior reputation as rabble-rousers. "That oughta teach 'em a lesson!" the captain said with a roaring laugh.

The guard was already certain that we were guilty of nothing, but I was still being detained out of respect for the other "victims" I had inadvertently inconvenienced with my actions. Nobody was pressing charges, though—I suppose they figured asking restitution for crapping their pants wasn't the shrewdest of social moves.

So I told him the truth. I was helping rebuild a goblin village, and we needed arms and clothing, as well as someone who could provide a little on-site guidance. The captain listened intently, some of his men chiming in on occasion. They even asked Gobta a few questions, despite his darting eyes and bewildered expression.

The next day...

We were still in the guardroom. Gobta had borrowed another cell to sleep in, which I assumed he was still using. Having nothing better to do, I was watching some dwarven personnel run through morning training in the field behind the guardhouse. Swinging heavy wooden swords around to work on their speed, sparring a bit in simulated combat, running a few laps, the usual.

I sat there, taking it all in and imagining how they'd fare against the assorted creatures I had Predated by this point. It was a bit like a game to me...but would the Sage mind if I used it like this? *Seems like kind of a waste of talent—but what the hell? It'll be fun.*

Turned out, the guards barely stood a chance. Even if I gave myself a handicap, there were only *just* a few of them who could beat the bat and the lizard.

In a one-on-one matchup, the scales tipped pretty heavily toward the monsters, but since the dwarves always seemed to operate in teams of four to six, a few of the combined parties could take on the spider fairly well. Even all twenty of them out in the field couldn't take on the centipede, though. I wasn't expecting these guys to be Special Forces types, of course, so the results made sense to me.

They were just about wrapped up by the time Gobta awoke. The captain checked in at around the same time.

"All right," he said, "you're free to go. Sorry I kept you in here for so long—I was beholden to keep you overnight, at least. Apologies!"

"Oh, no, no. It saved me one night's hotel cost, at least."

"Glad you see it that way. Here, let me make it up to you. I can introduce you to a talented blacksmith I know!"

"That would be perfect. Thank you!"

Things were looking up, finally. We just got priority entry, one—inspection, *schminspection*—and we had some extra money to spend. I thought finding a weaponsmith who wouldn't rip me off at first sight would be a chore, too, but a military referral was about the best I could ask for! *Maybe I can afford to be a bit optimistic after all!*

"In exchange for that…"

Mmm? A catch? The only "catches" I ever liked were the ones on porn sites.

"If you have any of those recovery potions left, would you be interested in letting go of them?"

Aha. They must really be short on them, huh? That soldier mentioned that yesterday. Well, I've got a ton I could sell you guys…but I don't really know the going rate.

Now what?

…*Ah, why not?* I had a manufacturing cost of exactly zero on those things anyway. If he wanted some, he could have some.

"All right," I replied. "It'll depend on how many, though. I need to keep a few for myself, too."

"Any extras you're willing to part with are fine by me. Even if it's just one."

Mm? Rather odd way of putting it, isn't it? I thought he was trying to rebuild the guard's stockpile. One's not going to be enough in a pinch, is it? …Well, whatever. Maybe times were just that tough.

"Okay, um, well, how about five, then?"

"Five! Ah, that'd be wonderful!"

"Sure. Oh, also, I'm pretty sure they'll still work even if you dilute them a little bit, all right? If it's just a regular slash wound, ten parts water to one part potion oughta do the trick."

The captain nodded eagerly, fully convinced. I spat out my five potions, and he responded by giving me a small pouch. Inside I could see a selection of gold coins. "I know it's not much," he explained, "but I hope you'll accept this. I'll give you five gold pieces for each one of these!"

Twenty-five gold, then? Fine by me. I don't know if I'm undercutting myself or not, but I'm not in a position to haggle. Better figure out how much that is, though, exactly.

"Uhmm, if I could…"

"Not enough? I'm doing my best here, sir…"

"No, no, the price is perfectly fine, but I needed to ask you…"

"Huh? It is? So… So what did you need?"

Ooh. Mmmm, that's not a good reaction. So I'm being ripped off after all? I knew I should've started higher. Oh well. The captain seems like a nice enough guy. I doubt he's fleecing me that badly.

"I'm sorry to admit it, but I'm not exactly sure what this money is worth, or what prices are even like around here… If you could give me some guidance, that would really help! I'm just a slime, besides!"

Way to contradict yesterday's magical-girl saga, man. Good thing he apparently never bought it in the first place.

We wound up having a long conversation before Gobta and I set off. Soon, I was out in the fresh air of freedom again…but not before lunch. The captain insisted. I couldn't taste anything, but the appreciation was sweet, I guess.

For the first time in a while, I enjoyed a meal.

Ugh… Why do I have to be so busy…? Kaijin the dwarf grumbled to himself. *What do they mean, the Eastern Empire might be on the move? That's the most ridiculous thing I've ever heard!*

He had reason to doubt it. Peace had reigned over the kingdom for three hundred years. The Empire had all the riches it could ever want—what motivation could it possibly have to stage an invasion? That was what he didn't understand.

Of course, Kaijin added to himself, *I doubt the weaponsmiths of this city would mind a good war to fill their coffers. But...arrgh, why is my work so busy all of a sudden?!*

And that wasn't his only problem.

He scowled. *Curse that damned minister!* He rubbed his forehead as he imagined himself taking a hammer to the man and sighed. A lot of sighing lately.

There wasn't much time left. A refusal would damage his reputation. "I can't do it" wouldn't be an excuse. He was waiting for some of his friends to get back to him, and depending on their reports, all could be lost.

He had built a decent name for himself as a weaponsmith, but he wasn't omnipotent. What kind of smith could craft weapons without any raw materials to work with?

Finally, he heard the news he had been waiting for.

"Sorry," one said as he came through the door. "We wanted to contact you yesterday, but we ran into one heck of a distraction..."

They were three men—dwarves, all brothers, the trio Kaijin had assigned mining duties to. The eldest was Garm, an armor crafter with long, muscular arms. The middle child was Dold, who was known around the kingdom for his intricate handiwork. The youngest, Mildo, rarely spoke but was skillful at almost anything he did—architecture, art, you name it. A sort of savant.

Any one of them could've been talented enough to run a successful business by himself—but they all had a critical disadvantage. Outside of their individual God-given talents, they were utterly hopeless, barely capable of dressing themselves without an instruction manual. None of them had a head for business or laying the groundwork for a successful career. They seemed to prefer letting other people use them instead.

That was how they wound up entrusting their shop to someone who stole it from them, falling into the trap of an apprentice jealous of their natural talent, getting bullied by the government after they botched a ministerial request... In the end, with nowhere else to go, they turned to Kaijin, an old friend and practically a fourth brother to them in their youth. He wished they had called on him sooner, but that was neither here nor there—they needed someplace to lie low, and he could use some help around the shop.

The only problem was that Kaijin had no work for them. He was a merchant dealing in battle gear, and he already had steady connections for all his merchandise except the weapons. Those he made himself, and he figured he could keep the trio busy making the rest of his lineup…but he couldn't have them start immediately. Telling his armor and accessory contacts out of the blue that their services were no longer needed would lead to easily avoidable trouble. Until things settled down a little, he would have to continue with business as usual.

Instead, with few other options available, Kaijin was having them direct a team of laborers as they mined for ore and other materials.

The brothers had arrived in Kaijin's shop with a wild story about a monster. It was the last thing he wanted to hear. He rubbed his forehead.

"Well, at least you're all fine," he told them. "Glad you got away before you were hurt at all!"

And he was. If they weren't injured, they could go right back to ore collecting. His friends' safety was naturally important, but…still.

The three bothers gave each other awkward looks.

"Well…we didn't get away, exactly."

"No. In fact, we can still hardly believe what happened to us yesterday!"

"………"

They moved on with the story—a tale of a mysterious slime who provided them life-saving medicine. It seemed like a bunch of ridiculous ravings, but these people weren't ones to make up stories. They didn't have the talent for it.

So did the whole affair really happen? Perhaps it didn't matter. It was true enough, he knew, that people had been attacked in the mines. And that meant no mining for a while. The workmen he had hired all quit yesterday and headed for the hills the moment the monster news broke. And why wouldn't they? Their brethren were injured, no doubt.

Now would be the perfect time to call on the services of the Free Guild, but that was probably equally impossible. He had filed a mining request long ago, to deafening silence. He knew he wasn't the only one, either. A shortage was starting to rear its ugly head.

Hiring guild members as mine guards wouldn't accomplish much, either. They weren't cheap, and even then, they didn't lift a finger beyond what the guild paid them for. Guild guards did just that—guard—and nothing else. And if this was the kind of monster that could take out a B-minus-graded adventurer...

It was hopeless! There was no way to turn a profit. In fact, this would bankrupt him. Bah! Why did such a powerful monster have to show up in such a damned shallow part of the mine?!

Kaijin let out a deep sigh. Now what? There wasn't much time left. Maybe he'd have to just go down there and grab the ore himself. No better ideas were springing to mind. All that filled it right now was the passing ticktock of his destiny.

The four of them exchanged glances, all at a complete loss. That was right about when a set of rather odd-looking customers showed up.

"Yo! You in there?!" shouted the captain—Kaido, as it happened.

As we had conversed, we'd grown friendlier and friendlier with each other. We were on a first-name basis now, and it turned out his older brother was in charge of the shop we were visiting.

It was a cozy place, the kind where you'd expect the owner to be a gruff old man behind the counter.

"Hello!"

"Excuse us," I said as I followed Kaido in. The moment we entered, we felt several dubious gazes upon us.

"""Ah!!"""

The three miners who had thanked me for saving them yesterday lifted their eyebrows high. They looked right as rain, but their expressions weren't exactly jubilant.

Just as expected, the man behind them was a perfect image of the grizzled, grouchy old civil-works guys I once had to deal with. He was the proprietor, no doubt. Didn't look much like Kaido.

"Whadda you want? You know these guys?"

"Kaijin, this is it! The slime! The one who saved us…"

"Yeah! It sure is! And you're our boss's brother, aren't you, Captain?"

"………"

"Oh-ho! The slime, you say? We were just talking about you! Thanks for getting these guys out of a bad way yesterday."

"Oh, no, it was nothing… Okay, it was *something*, but, ah, you know. Ha-ha-ha-ha!"

It should be against the law to compliment me. I always let it go to my head, until I finally float up into outer space. I probably wouldn't be coming back down for a while.

"So," the old guy said, rearing back a bit, "what brings you here today?"

I decided to go into full detail. We all piled into seats situated deeper inside, and Kaido was kind enough to provide a quick recap for me. I added a few choice details, and things moved along at a good pace.

That younger one, though… Mildo, was it? I wish he'd say something. Like, how's he managed to stay in conversations by saying nothing at all? It floored me.

"All right," the old guy answered. "I understand. But what do you want? I can't do anything for you. I've got a job from a certain country I gotta deal with, too. None of this leaves the room, but…"

Then it was his turn to talk, deliberately leaving out some of the finer details, as it was all classified. Basically, a number of countries were sending out orders for weapons and armor, spooked that a certain "idiot nation" might be trying to hatch a war on them all. It connected to why the guard was out of medicine yesterday, as well as the lack of raw materials plaguing the shops.

"So," he continued, tapping at his head, "I managed to pull an all-nighter to get an order for two hundred steel spears squared away…but I gotta come up with twenty swords, too, and I ain't even got one yet. There's just no material!"

"Why don't you just say you can't fill the order?" Kaido asked.

"Fool! You think I didn't, at first? But that damned minister Vester told me, 'So you're saying the great Kaijin, renowned across the entire kingdom, can't even fill a simple order like this one? Is that it?' In front of the king himself, no less! Can you believe that damned idiot?!"

In between the cursing and the screaming, I learned that Mildo, the taciturn third brother, had denied a request from Vester to build a house for him. The minister had taken it personally, badgering him about it to the point that Mildo had had to go into exile with Kaijin. Sounded like a stupid grudge to have.

So is this guy maybe buying up all the kingdom's raw materials so the shops can't sell anything? It sounds plausible to me.

"What's the difference between lances and swords?" I asked.

"I need special ore for the swords," the old guy spat out. "Magic ore. The spears are just simple steel spikes."

Without the right materials to work with, even a master artisan is merely a man. It must have been incredibly frustrating. The minister must've been waiting for him to show up, hat in hand, begging for mercy.

"And that's not the half of it. It takes a full day to complete even one of those swords. Even if I built an assembly line and streamlined everything I could, it'd still take me two weeks to make twenty..."

I thought to ask about the deadline but stopped. I could read the answer in his face anyway.

"I have until the end of this week." He groaned. "First thing next week, I'm charged with delivering them to the king. It's a task for the kingdom, and every shop has been asked to do the same. If I can't, they could strip my artisan's license from me..."

So five days left, it sounded like. And it seemed doubtful that much work would happen today, so four, basically? What a tough situation... *Wait, why am I here? None of this has anything to do with me.*

And...um, hang on, did he say "magic ore"? I have some of that, don't I? Not that it matters...

The next time I looked up, I realized that everyone was looking at me. *I don't like all these dudes staring at me, you know! Who do they think a slime is, anyway?*

Whatever. Time to fling a few serious favors around. They better help me get that goblin village going later!

"Heh-heh-heh… Ha-ha-ha-ha! Haaaaaaah-hah-hah-hah!! What a trivial issue! Old man… You think you could use *this*?"

Then, with a small *thud*, I hand-delivered a quantity of extracted ore on top of the work desk in front of me. Then I hopped on the sofa, lay back, and put my legs up (or felt like I did).

"…Wait. Whoaaa! That's magic ore!! And, my God, look at how pure it is!!"

Heh. Not magic ore, man. Already processed it for ya. That's a hunk of pure magisteel!
"C'mon, old man, your eyes giving out on you?" I asked. If they couldn't even see what this metal was, they couldn't have been worth much.

I'll sell the materials to you, but that's it. I'm running a business here, sort of.

"What…? No… It can't be! This entire piece is magisteel?!"

He finally noticed. His shock surprised me a bit.

"You… You'll let me have this? I mean, I'll pay the going price for it, of course!"

Heh-heh-heh. Gotcha!

"*Oooh*, about that…"

"Nggh, what do you want? I'll do anything I can for this!"

"Now that's what I wanted to hear! You heard what me and my team are up to, right? I need your help finding someone who'll travel to the village and give us some technical guidance."

"What? Is that all you need?"

"Pfft. I need some connections to clothing and weapon suppliers, too. And armor."

"If that's all it is, then of course!"

And so old man Kaijin and I forged a verbal contract for the hunk of magisteel. We agreed to iron out the details after his work was done. Judging by his reaction, I probably could've wrung him for a little more, but no point being too greedy. Whenever I tried that, it always blew up in my face. Even I learn from my mistakes sometimes.

Kaido took his leave after we all finished with dinner. *Guess the captain of the border guard can afford to skip work all afternoon. Nice of him to bring me here, though.*

The three dwarf brothers took turns thanking me profusely yet again. They felt a bit out of place, no doubt, and at fault for the government's toying around with Kaijin.

"So why not come along with us?" I asked. Their jaws dropped. Then they started discussing it with each other. To me, that sounded like the best thing for their predicament.

The next day…

Even though he had all the materials he needed, that deadline still looked impossible to me. Time to come out with it.

"You've got four days left, Kaijin. You think you can finish it up?"

"…No, to be honest. But I gotta!"

I didn't think a can-do attitude was going to help much. What I did know was that if something was impossible, it was simply impossible. It didn't become doable until all the right elements were in place.

...Sheesh. I already got my foot in the door. Might as well go all in.

"Well, I think I've got an idea. For starters, could you make just one sword for me? The best quality you can manage."

"What? But you're a complete amateur. What could you do?"

"I can't tell you. But you gotta believe me! If you don't, then go ahead. Keep going. You'll probably lose your license, but..."

"...So I can trust you? Because if I can't, you better not expect payment for that magisteel. I won't be able to take care of myself, much less cover you... You keep your promise, though, I swear I'll keep mine. I'll give you the best swordsmith this kingdom has!"

We have a deal. And promises are made to be kept.

Off we went into the workshop. I owed Kaijin one for letting me rest in his spare apprentice's chamber anyway, so I wanted to hold up my end of the bargain.

When we entered, we found the three brothers staring at the hunk of magisteel on the table, sighing to themselves as they turned it over in their hands, scrutinizing every surface. The chunk I'd spat out was about the size of a fist. Was it that rare? They sure acted that way.

"What are you talking about?" Kaijin exclaimed when I asked about it.

And according to his explanation—

Magic ore was a raw material that was refined to make magisteel. Even the base ore could rival gold in value, for a simple reason: It was both rare and useful for a variety of applications.

It all came down to the magicules that seemed to form nearly everything in this world—something that Earth seemed to do just fine without but that played a huge role over here.

On rare occasions, when a monster was defeated, it would drop an entire chunk of magicules, referred to as "magic stone." This was a sort of portable energy source, and it served as the fuel for something called "spirit engineering," an invention exclusive to this world. Magic stones came in levels of purity, and the purer ones were used as cores inside assorted products. Even ornaments could harness this energy for special effects. The resulting clothing and accessories could boost the wearer's abilities, grant them additional effects, and do any number of other things.

Now, the main difference between plain old ore and magical ore was that the latter could be obtained only in areas where higher-level monsters lurked. It required the combination of regular ore, a large concentration of magicules, and eons of time for the ore to absorb the magic and make the transformation—a sort of geological mutation.

Of course, any place with a lot of magic also tended to have a lot of monsters. Not the run-of-the-mill kind adventurers could kill for pocket change—you wouldn't find any magic ore around them. You'd have to travel to places with at least B-ranked monsters in them.

As a tangent, Kaijin finally gave me a full description of how the ranking system worked for monsters.

"Ohhh!" I said. "So I'd be, like, a B or so, maybe?"

"""......"""

I imagined everyone was thinking the same thing. Except for Gobta, who was a little slow. Let's leave him alone for now.

Regardless, the point was that magic ore didn't just pop up out of nowhere. What's more, the magisteel extracted from it took up 3, maybe 5 percent of its total mass. Even a fist-sized chunk of that steel was worth at least twenty times its weight in gold.

It also appeared that prices, in general, averaged out to near the same as they did in my old world. Gold was used as currency because it was worth a lot, just like back home. As a result, all the countries had adopted gold as a currency standard.

I kept the fact that I had a huge store of these magisteel hunks in my stomach a secret. Honestly, it was getting a little frightening. No way they could've known, but...what if they had? Or was that just my paranoid, lower-middle-class upbringing coming out?

Now, on to the real issue.

Magisteel was rare, certainly, but that wasn't what made it so valuable. That lay in how readily adaptable it was to serving as a conduit for magical force.

One could control magicules through the power of imagination, to some extent. My Magic Sense skill worked that way, but even Control Water worked by manipulating the ambient magic around me. Most monster skills harnessed it one way or another as well. I didn't know that much about magic spells, really, but I figured they worked on the same premise.

So what happened if a weapon was made of material infused with vast amounts of magic? Amazingly, it became a weapon that could mature!

How classic! Aw, man, now I want one! I almost said so out loud before stopping myself just in time. I mean, think about it—a sword that gradually molded itself to your ideal shape based on what you wanted from it. Depending on your own magical force, you might even be able to transform it midbattle! And since it was so compatible with magic, it'd help boost your skills, too.

Basically, unless you were really handy with a weapon, you were always going to be better off with a magically infused one. But what if—although this would take a lot of skill and money—you made a blade of pure magisteel and inserted a magic stone into it? Could you make, like, flame swords and blizzard swords and stuff?

My creative juices started flowing. My heart sang, demanding Kaijin make one right this minute. But I would have to be patient. *The next magic stone I get my hand on, though... For sure.*

After that quick lesson, Kaijin buckled down and went to work. I watched him as his would-be young apprentice. Gobta was probably sleeping somewhere, besides...

Swords, of course, came in a wide array of shapes and sizes. I, of course, pictured a Japanese-style katana as the strongest one out there—but even katanas came in all kinds of shapes. That was what made me so curious about the kind of sword he'd make.

Ten hours later, he was finished.

It looked, to me, like a plain old longsword. And—whoa, that was a lot of magisteel left. And here I was worried whether a fist-sized lump would be enough for even one. Turned out Kaijin couldn't even guess how much it'd cost to use 100 percent magisteel on everything. *I suppose not. No wonder nobody's come up with a flame swordor a blizzard sword or even a thunder sword. It'd cost too much. Makes sense.*

Instead, magisteel formed only the core of the weapon, and the rest of the blade was crafted from regular steel instead. That core was all it needed for its magic to work its way into the steel, eventually merging itself with the whole sword. That, he said, was why a weapon grew stronger as it was used over time. The blade would never rust or lose its shape—it could just use ambient magicules to regenerate itself.

Oddly enough, though, even these magic swords had their life spans. If they were bent too far or otherwise warped beyond recognition, the magic would leak out, leading to rapid weathering.

Kaijin showed me his freshly forged sword as he spoke. It was all so interesting to me. I took the weapon in hand as I marveled over it—all right, not in *hand*, but close enough. It was simple in make, straight as an arrow. No bells or whistles. It wasn't meant strictly for slicing like a katana, but the blade seemed suited to slashing.

But this was just a base. Over time, I supposed, the sword would adapt itself to whatever its user wanted from it. No wonder the forger kept things simple.

Okay.

So Kaijin and his team had crafted this lovely sword for me, as promised. Now it was my turn.

"Right!" I said. "Time for me to pull a little secret work for you. I'm sorry, but would you all mind leaving me alone here for now?"

There was no way I could let them see this. It would be too hard to explain, for one thing.

"Well, you have everything you need here, I suppose. But are you sure? I would be glad to help."

"I'll be fine, thank you! Just promise me you won't peek into this room for the next three days. Swear it!"

"All right. I'll trust you and wait..."

With that, Kaijin and his men left. Gobta, too, for some stupid reason. *What goes through his mind, day in and day out, that keeps him alive? I've got to wring it out of him someday.*

So our recipe today's for a longsword. Couldn't be simpler! First, take this completed sample...and swallow it up! Next, take the rest of the ingredients lined up here...and swallow them up, too! Munch, munch...*gulp!* Mix well in your stomach, and...

Notice. Analysis target: "longsword." Successful. Creating copy... Successful.

Repeat nineteen times. Bon appétit!
Easy, wasn't it?
Kids, don't try this at home!

And with that ridiculous mental commentary, I set to work.
Yikes... Each copy was taking, like, ten seconds.
190 seconds—three minutes and change—and I had nineteen swords scattered around the room. It had been maybe five minutes since I shooed Kaijin and the rest out of the room.

I mean, I figured I could do it, but it was just so easy! And people spent entire lifetimes crafting stuff like this. I started to feel as if I had done something shamelessly rude to them. This Predator is such a cheat code.

So now what? I told them not to open the door for three days. Am I supposed to just hole up in here until then? No... I can't just sit here like the blob that I am. Maybe I should come clean...

So I did. I threw the door open and stepped outside. The four dwarves immediately stood up, giving me worried looks. Gobta was...sleeping.

God, five minutes? Yep. That was when I decided I had to do something about him.

"Wh-what is it? Did something happen?"

"Are you short on something?"

"Or...or it didn't work, then?"

"Yeah, um...well, actually..." I sized up the dwarves, whose eyes were laden with self-torment. They hurt to look at.

But I just couldn't resist. I had to put on an act.

Why did I have to be so mean to people all the time? Not even my death and rebirth had cured me of that habit.

"...Ha-ha! Just kidding! They're all done, actually!"

""""......Whaaaa?!"""""

Guess I can't blame them.

✳

""""...Cheers!!"""""

We were at a kind of dwarven nightclub, holding a rather anticlimactic wrap-up party. The weapons were safely in the king's hands, and it was time to celebrate. I mean, I told them they didn't have to...

"Aw, come on! There's lots of beautiful ladies in there!"

"Yeah, yeah! Young ones, and older, too, if you like a little weathering on 'em! It's the perfect place for any gentleman!"

"......!!"

"C'mon, Rimuru! We can't go out without the big guy himself!"

It was four against one, so I had no choice.

Never a dull moment, huh?

The place was called the Night Butterfly.

Were the hosts really butterflies, then? *They'd better not turn out to be moths!*

...Not that I really cared. I was a gentleman. I'd try anything once, I thought as we strolled in.

"Ooh, welcome!"

""""Welcome, sirs!"""""

Phwoaarrrr!! The place was lined up and down with babes!! Whoaaa! Their ears were so long, too! *Is it hot in here, or is it just those elves? Dang!*

Ohhhh my Godddddd, *and their clothes are so* thin*!! It's like I can* *almost see through…but I can't… Dammit, and I got Magic Sense going at max force, too! They've got the boundaries of their clothing down pat, don't they? Is this meant to be some kind of…challenge? Nnnngh!!*

"Oooh, look at you, cutie!"

"Aww, I saw him first!!"

Eeep! Boing! Boiiing!

Th-there it is!!

My entire body is jiggling! And I can feel something soft jiggling against my back, too! Is this paradise, or what?!

"…Umm… I guess all that squirming means you're enjoying this, huh?"

Agh! Oh, no. I didn't mean to…

"Huh…? N…no, not *that* much."

Guess I shouldn't have expected the world, then. Nobody believes in me after all. But so be it. What do I care? I'm perched in the lap of a real-life elf! I can't believe this is actually happening!!

Ahh, I feel so bad for my dear, departed friend down there! If only he were still around! I'd be bouncing off the walls!

However, while we were enjoying ourselves…

"Well! If it isn't Kaijin! Goodness me, what are you doing, bringing this vulgar monster into a high-class establishment like this?"

Who's that guy? Looking to start a fight, it sounded like. Things quickly fell silent around us. Even the girls sneered at this visitor—they must not have liked him too much, although they were polite enough to keep the scoffs very discreet.

By dwarf standards, this one was quite tall and thin in stature, making him…well, an average human in size.

"Hey! Boss! You guys allowin' monsters in here these days?"

"N-no," an older female manager called out, "but it's just a little slime, so…"

"Uhh? It's still a monster! Ain't it? You sayin' a slime's not a monster anymore?!"

"I… No, sir, but…" The manager stuttered noncommittally,

trying to calm the man down, but the boor wasn't even paying attention. Clearly, he was after us.

"Oh, great," one of the girls sighed. "That's Vester, the minister."

Speak of the devil! Well, I'll be... He did seem like the kinda guy who refuses to let go of a grudge. I could see it on his face.

"Y'know what best suits a monster?" Vester bellowed. "This!" Then he emptied the contents of his water glass over me.

I wasn't exactly a fan of that kind of provocation, but I kept myself in check. This was a government minister—I couldn't let my short temper get Kaijin or the manager of this place in trouble. Wouldn't want them banned from the premises. *Just sit tight, let it pass, and—*

"Hey... You think you can just pick on us all you want?!"

With an audible kick at the table, Kaijin stood up.

"You think you can run around and make fun of my guest, Vester? You think I'm not gonna mind that? You *think*?!"

...Um? Hey, Kaijin, this is a top government official and stuff, isn't it? You sure you're on good footing here?

Vester, to his credit, was just as startled and stepped back.

I boinged back a bit in surprise, too, cushioned amply by the chest of the elf behind me.

...Not on purpose! I swear!

"How...how dare you speak to me like that, you...!" Vester sputtered, still in shock.

"Will you shut up already?!" Kaijin shouted, accentuating his point by launching a punch at the minister's face. A few moments later, he asked me, "Hey, Rimuru, you were lookin' for someone to help you, right? Would I be good enough, maybe?"

Good enough? More than. But...really? I supposed he'd quite literally just punched a one-way ticket out of the Dwarven Kingdom. Now he was making a verbal request.

"That's what I've been wanting to hear. It'll be great working with you, Kaijin!"

It would be. We could hammer out the details later. If Kaijin was willing to come over, I was more than willing to invite him. We didn't need no fancy contract! *We do what we want, when we want!*

Kaijin and I sealed the deal with an emphatic nod.

*　　*　　*

Just one thing... How were we gonna book it out of here? Maybe a little prudence wasn't such a bad idea after all. You create a lot of problems for yourself otherwise. All the bravado in the world wasn't going to solve them, was it?

*

So.

As anyone could imagine, punching a government minister in the face presented a number of issues.

"My brother, my brother," muttered Kaido, a few security officers behind him. "What did you do this time?"

He was on duty today—not even he could get away with skipping shifts all the time. Kaijin had given him an invite, but he'd refused...only to come to the nightclub anyway thanks to his brother's boorishness. Simply running would have been an easy enough plan for us, but chances were it'd be doomed from the start.

"Hmph! That fool!" As four knights dragged Kaijin away, he shouted and pointed a wild finger at the minister. "He practically spat in the face of Rimuru, my client and the best patron I've ever had! What's so bad about putting him in his place a little, huh?!"

Vester, for his part, hadn't overcome the shock yet. He was simply staring at us, blood still dribbling from his nose. It looked both pathetic and a little comical. Never saw it coming, I guess. The surprise probably kept it from even hurting.

"Brother," Kaido whispered with a sigh, "you don't put a government minister 'in his place' like *that*... Either way, you're all coming with me!" He nodded to his men, then took me aside for a moment. "Just stay calm, all right? I promise we'll treat you well."

I wasn't planning to do anything else, of course. Before I left, though, I sidled up to the manager of the place and tossed five gold pieces into her hand. "There's some for your trouble in there, too!" I said to the surprised matron. "We'll be back!"

It seemed like a decent place, after all. Wouldn't be nice if I never got to see the inside of it again.

So went my second arrest here in the Dwarven Kingdom…but I'm forgetting someone.

Gobta! He wasn't with us at the club. Instead, he was atoning for his sundry idiotic behavior by undergoing what I liked to call "bagworm hell." I'd thought about hanging him by his feet at first, but that just seemed like cruelty for cruelty's sake, so instead I'd tied him up with Sticky Thread and let him hang from the ceiling.

"Wait!" he'd whined. "This is so mean, sir! I want to come with you!"

I'd showed him no mercy this time. "Enough, you fool! I can't take any more of your blockheaded behavior! If you don't like it, summon your tempest wolf buddy and have *him* help you out!"

Not that he could do it, I figured as I shut the door behind me.

A goblin was one thing, but a hobgoblin could probably go without food or drink for about a week straight.

Still, if we were going to be held for a while, I'd have to break out and get him down sooner or later. For now, though, I filed it in the back of my mind.

Was I being mean to him, maybe? I thought I was, for a moment. But it was all right. He could deal.

The five us of were taken to the royal palace. Not that we were under very heavy guard. If anything, it seemed entirely voluntary.

We wound up having to spend around two days in the castle jail room. It wasn't so bad—the food looked decent, and we had all the comforts we needed in the place. It was less like a jail cell and more like an urban apartment shared by the five of us. We weren't treated too terribly, either.

"I just had to lose my temper, and now I've got all of you in here with me… I'm so sorry, guys!" Kaijin apologized.

But none of his dwarven friends minded too much, either.

"It's fine, Kaijin! No problem at all!"

"Yeah, don't worry about it, boss!"

"……"

"Besides, once we're released, we want to come with you, Kaijin!"

"Yeah, can we come with you, Rimuru?"

"……?"

I wasn't observant enough to tell what the third one wanted from me, but I got the gist well enough.

"Hah! Sure, we'll take care of all of you! You better be ready, though… Once we reach the village, you guys're gonna work!"

"Got it!"

We were already talking about life outside the big house. As prison terms went, it was pretty chill.

It was the night of our second day.

"By the way," it occurred to me to ask, "why did that minister have it in so badly for you, Kaijin? Was there some reason for it?"

Kaijin's expression immediately soured. With a sigh, he began to explain. It turned out he used to be a captain in the palace's royal knight corps—a leader of one of the seven armies making up the whole system. Three corps were devoted to behind-the-scenes work like engineering, supply, and emergency aid. Three more—heavy strikers, magic strikers, and magic support—played more of a starring role. The last one, and the most important, was the king's personal guard. Kaijin had been head of the engineering corps, and Vester had been his second-in-command.

"He was the son of a marquis," the dwarf moaned. "A noble title he bought with money. I think he must've been jealous of a commoner like me taking the head role. It was complicated, you know? It must've been humiliating to him, taking orders from someone below him. And I'll admit that I didn't care much about what other people thought about me. I was too busy trying to stay on the king's good side. That's when it happened."

The "magic-armor affair."

At the time, the engineering corps was seen as the lowest of the army's seven departments—barely producing any new technology for itself. Vester believed a kingdom rich in technology should have an appropriately famous corps of engineers, while Kaijin was more of a status-quo man when it came to research and development. Despite how intense their arguments got, they never managed to reach an agreement during their countless garrison meetings.

Along the way, the corps launched a so-called magic-armor soldier project with a team of elf engineers. Vester was hell-bent on making this project a success and boosting the corps's position in the military pecking order. Kaijin warned him that he was proceeding too quickly with it, but even then, Vester had little time for the advice of a common-born man.

In the end, thanks to Vester's arbitrary whims, an experiment went awry and led to a spirit-magic core running out of control—a very public failure and a bad setback for the project at an early stage.

Thus, despite some of the greatest minds of the world working on it, the magic-armor project ground to a halt. As head of the engineering corps, Kaijin wound up taking the heat for it, resigning from his position in the army. Not only did Vester make Kaijin the scapegoat; he even convinced his friends among the higher-ranked leaders to give false testimony against him. That, according to Kaijin at least, was the truth.

Once he finished, Kaijin let out a tired sigh.

I could understand his perspective. There must've been a lot of resentment built up over the years from that.

Still...man, Vester's just a total storybook villain, isn't he? They don't come easier to spot than that. As far as the minister was concerned, Kaijin could make a comeback in the military and threaten his position at any time. That kind of thing.

Didn't he deserve the death penalty, really? Maybe not, but...

"So," Kaijin concluded, "maybe he'll settle down a bit if I leave the country for a while."

He sounded a bit forlorn about it, but at least he had backup. The three brothers with us were just as aware of the truth, and there was no love lost for Vester among them, either. Hell, even I hated him now.

Still, Kaijin did sock a noble, so I kind of wondered whether they were just gonna release us and wave good-bye.

"I wouldn't worry about it," Kaijin reassured me. "I'm out of the army now, but I did make it up to the corps leader. As far as my social position goes, I'm just below baron. If it were strictly commoner versus nobleman in the courts, well, hanging might've entered the picture."

He accentuated that morbid fact with a hearty laugh.

Meanwhile, I just sat there. If things got rough, I'd hightail it outta here—but otherwise, I was happy being a good little slime until cooler heads prevailed.

✳

Our day in court arrived soon after, and the entire lot of us were brought in front of the monarch.

The Heroic King of the dwarves.

Now that I was seeing him in person, his stately aura was almost awe inspiring.

His Majesty Gazel Dwargo closed his eyes and sat deeply upon his throne. He was stocky, dwarflike in appearance, and his exposed armor-like muscles positively radiated energy. His skin was a deep, dark brown, and his black hair was pulled back on his head.

He exuded pure strength. My fight-or-flight instincts kicked in all the way for the first time in ages.

Two knights were stationed near him, one on each side. They were equally muscle-bound, no doubt, but they still looked wispy compared to their ruler. Seriously, this guy was a monster. I'd been planning to beat a hasty retreat if I needed to, but now... Not so much. The moment I was placed in front of him, my every nerve was wound taut.

It might have been the first time in this world that I actually sensed a clear danger to myself.

A man knelt in front of the king, checking over something with him. After receiving permission, he stood up and read the affidavit.

"We will now begin the trial! Silence, everyone!"

For the next hour, both sides presented their cases. As criminal suspects, we weren't allowed to speak—in the royal court, that right was reserved for those with a rank of earl or greater. Otherwise, you needed the king's express permission. If you did speak out of turn, that apparently proved your guilt on the spot and earned you a bonus contempt-of-court charge.

Whether you were innocent or not, that was the way this place worked. We were stuck having our representative speak for us. He had paid us a few visits during our two days in custody, discussing the nature of our case. Our kind-of lawyer, basically.

Could we trust him, though? Anxieties like that had a tendency to crop up for a reason...

"So there Sir Vester was," he continued, "sitting back at this club and enjoying an alcoholic beverage, when this gang pushed their way into the place and exposed him to dreadful violence! This is not the kind of behavior that should ever be forgiven!"

"Is that the truth?"

"It is, my liege! I heard it from Kaijin himself, and I also have written testimony from the owners of the club. There can be no mistaking the course of events that night!"

...Um, what? What did he just say? I thought he was on our side, and it took all of five minutes for him to go turncoat. That can't be good, can it?

I shot a look at Kaijin—his face turned bright red, then slowly began draining of color.

I'll bet. Our lawyer wasn't even bothering to make excuses for us.

It went without saying that representatives for the accused weren't allowed to lie in court. If they were found out, that would be another hanging. It was impossible to think any would-be lawyer would attempt it, barring extreme circumstances, and yet ours was doing it right in front of us.

"My liege!" Vester exclaimed, egging him on. "You have heard it for yourself! I beg of you to deal with these miscreants harshly!"

He flashed us a smile of supreme confidence.

Bastard. Maybe I should've hit him after all.

The king remained motionless, eyes closed. In his place, one of the guards beside him spoke.

"Order! I will now give the verdict! Kaijin, the mastermind behind this crime, is sentenced to twenty years of labor in the mines. His accomplices are sentenced to ten years of labor in the mines. With that, this court is hereby—"

"Wait," a deep, quiet voice interrupted.

The king opened his eyes and looked at Kaijin.

"It has been a while, Kaijin. Do you remain in good health?"

"...Yes, my liege!" came the instant reply. Presumably he had the right to speak now. "It gladdens me that you remain so as well!"

"Yes. Now, do you and your friends"—looking at us—"have any desire to return to us?"

The audience in the royal court murmured among themselves. It must have been an unusual development. Vester immediately blanched. Our traitorous representative, meanwhile, had developed a deathly pallor.

"I beg your forgiveness, my liege, but I have already found a master to serve! I have made my vow, and it has become my treasure. A treasure so fine that, indeed, not even the direct order of my liege could make me part with it!"

This clearly angered the audience. I could see the guards staring daggers into Kaijin's forehead. But he stood strong—chest puffed out, the picture of dignity.

The king, seeing this, closed his eyes again. "I...see."

Silence ruled for another moment.

"I have made my decision. Listen well to my sentence! Kaijin and his friends are hereby exiled from the kingdom. After midnight tonight, when the new day comes, they are officially no longer welcome in my lands. That is all. Begone at once!" Opening his eyes, the king made his proclamation in a loud voice.

Ah, the dignity of a born leader! His overwhelming presence sent shivers through my body. Although, being king around here seemed like a terribly lonely job to have.

So there we were, after the trial, back at Kaijin's shop. That little celebratory drink we wanted to get sure broke bad, didn't it? Now we had to pack up and leave for good.

Oh, wait, is Gobta all right? We're still only at day three with him, right? I was a tad nervous about that as I opened the door to his punishment room.

"Ooh! Welcome back, sir! Did you have fun? Gee, sure hope you take me with you next time!"

There he was, leaping up off the sofa to greet me! How did that happen…? He couldn't have gotten out of my spider silk that easy!

Taking another look, I realized that the cushion Gobta had been using on the sofa was actually a tempest wolf. Wait, seriously? He actually summoned the guy?

"Uh, Gobta, how'd you get that wolf in here?"

"Oh! Right! That! I just thought to myself, 'Hey, can you come on over, please?' And he did, sir!"

He made it sound so easy, the bastard. None of the other hobgoblins had managed the feat from such a long range before. Maybe his brain cells were all devoted to his natural talents instead of, you know, actual intelligence. It seemed crazy to me. I concluded that it must've been a coincidence.

I then realized that the sight of the tempest wolf had frozen the dwarves in their tracks. "What's wrong?" I asked. "We need to start packing, don't we?"

"W-wait a second!" the panicked Kaijin replied. "What on earth is a black direwolf doing in here?!"

"Yeah! You need to run! That's a B-ranked monster!"

And now they were panicking.

They looked so ridiculous, I was actually amused.

"Oh, he's fine! Really! No problem! He's like a big dog, really! We keep him indoors and everything!"

My attempts at calming everyone's nerves met stony silence.

Black direwolves, by the way, were a somewhat advanced version of regular direwolves. If they evolved in a more magic-oriented fashion, their fur would turn black. The coats of the tempest direwolves were black as well but with a uniquely colored sheen.

Direwolves weren't really supposed to evolve toward the "storm" element in the first place—that was just a side effect of the name I gave out.

In volcanic regions, direwolves would evolve with a fire element and become red direwolves. Near bodies of water, you would find blue direwolves. In the forests would be green direwolves. In other words, adopting elements was a fairly common evolutionary pattern for these guys. The magic-infused black ones, meanwhile, were apparently a notorious threat to any nearby humans and humanoids. The tempest element gave our wolf pack an ever-so-slight purplish shine to their black color, something you wouldn't notice if you weren't paying attention.

Sorry I spooked the dwarves, I guess. We didn't have the time for me to explain the whole story. *I'll just call him Gobta's pet for now and move on.*

After hurriedly pressing the dwarves to put on their best traveler's outfits, I pushed them out of the shop, went back in by myself, and proceeded to swallow up the entire contents of the building. Capacity-wise, I was still A-okay, but swallowing the building whole would probably have drawn a little too much attention, so I kept it at that.

Once our preparations for the journey were complete, we made our way to where Rigur and the other goblins were waiting.

●

The space was silent, a far cry from the loud arguing of a moment ago.

After the five accused had all but fled from the court, nobody in attendance dared move an inch. Vester nervously swallowed. The persistent silence of the king put both him and everyone else on edge.

Then Gazel shattered the stillness.

"Now, Vester. Do you have anything you wish to say?"

"A—a thousand pardons, my liege, but this is all a misunderstanding! It simply must be a mistake!"

Vester's voice was a nervous warble as he pleaded his case. The king regarded him coldly, betraying none of his emotions.

"A misunderstanding? If it is, then it has cost me one of my most faithful servants."

"How can you say such a thing, my liege?! You call what he offered to you 'faithfulness'? Why, he is simply a man off the street—"

"Vester. I see you are mistaken. Kaijin left my corps on his own volition. When I speak of a faithful servant I have lost...I refer to you."

The minister's heart raced. *I need to find an excuse...* But his mind was blank. The words refused to come to his lips. His thoughts were slow to form. *What did he just say? He referred to me? Then...*

"Let me ask you once again, Vester. Do you have anything you wish to say?"

Fear, pure fear, dominated Vester's head. The king had asked him a question. He needed to reply. But all his speech had abandoned him.

"I... My liege, I am afraid...I..."

"I had great expectations for you, Vester. I have been waiting for so long. Even during the magic-armor affair, I waited for you to finally speak the truth. And now I find that, yet again..."

The expression Gazel showed Vester could almost be described as one of kindness. The king's words pierced through the minister like the sharpest of swords.

"Look at these."

The king pointed out two items one of his attendants had produced. Vester, eyes hollow, looked at them. One was a sphere filled with a liquid that he had never seen before; the other was a single longsword.

"Do you know what these are?"

The liquid remained a mystery to Vester, but the longsword he remembered. Kaijin had brought it in.

"You may explain to him," the king ordered his attendant. The following speech took a fairly long time for Vester to fully understand.

The liquid was a life-regenerating elixir, a near-perfect extract of the juices of the hipokute herbs. A so-called "full" potion, named for its miraculous recovery properties.

Even with the best technology the dwarves had at their fingertips, the purest extract they could produce topped off at 98 percent.

That made it only as potent as a "high" potion. *This* liquid, meanwhile, was at 99 percent!

Vester's face twisted in shock. He had to know! *What did they do to produce such a level of—?* But before he could ask, the attendant had even more shocking news for him. The longsword had a core of magisteel that was already working its way through the rest of the blade.

Impossible. That process began only after a ten-year adaptation procedure! The shock set Vester's mind reeling. If this was true…!

"Both of these wonders were brought about by that slime," the king said. "And thanks to your behavior, we have lost our connection to such a creature. Do you have anything you wish to say?"

Now Vester realized the full extent of his king's rage. There was truly nothing he could say.

"I… I do not, my liege."

Tears began welling in his eyes. He knew it all too well now—his lord had abandoned him. All he wanted was to serve his king. To win his approval. That was it. *When did I go wrong? When I grew jealous of Kaijin, or before…?* He didn't know. All he knew was that he had betrayed the king's trust.

"I…see. In that case… Vester! I hereby forbid you from entering the palace. Do not let me see you before me again. I shall leave you with this: I have tired of you!"

Hearing his words, Vester stood up and bowed deeply to his lord. Then he left, setting off to pay his penance for his foolishness.

As he did, a guard ran forward and arrested the representative serving as Vester's accomplice.

The king watched them out of the corner of his eye. "My dark agent!" he shouted with some urgency. "Track the movements of that slime! Do not let it escape your notice. Ever!"

The emphatic order of the normally taciturn king gave pause to everyone in the chamber.

"By my life, my liege!" the dark agent said before disappearing.

The king thought to himself.
Who was *that slime?*

A type of monster, no doubt. Was that the level of monster being released, then?

His hero's instincts were giving him a feeling he couldn't ignore. Trusting it, he began to take action.

●

Rigur and gang were all safe at the edge of the forest.

Between this and that, we had spent a total of five days in the city—pretty much what we expected. Things didn't quite go according to plan, but we largely accomplished what we'd set out to do.

Too bad we didn't get to hit the Free Guild in town. It sounded kind of like an adventurer's club to me, the exact kind of place where an otherworlder or two might hang out. It would've been nice to check out all the gilt and armor the dwarves were known for, too. But oh well. We had a bunch of master craftsmen with us here. That was enough of a find. That, and I still had twenty gold pieces. Score.

I took the time to introduce Kaijin and his hapless friends to the goblins. We'd all be working together for a while to come, so I wanted to get off on the right foot. Come to think of it, I didn't see much in the way of casual racism from the dwarves—most of them, anyway. Given the demi-magical origins we all shared, I suppose it made sense. I could imagine us crossing their paths again someday.

We were now more or less ready to roll. The only problem was transport. Ranga, of course, was wagging his tail, as if me hopping on him was the pinnacle of his life. I explained to him that I needed his full fifteen-foot size for a bit so we could fit two out of the three brothers on his back.

Ranga was not a fan of this idea. His face instantly turned sullen as he wobbled backward and plopped his ass on the ground. He glowered at the newcomers as if to suggest he could just eat them instead and save everyone a lot of trouble.

The dwarves almost jumped out of their skin. Even when they first saw him, they'd wailed in perfect unison. """Gaahh! How could you ever…?!""" and so forth.

Either this was a well-practiced routine of theirs, or Ranga really did scare them that much. There had to be something I could do.

"Hang on, Ranga," I said. "I tried transforming into one of you guys earlier, and I'd like to test out how it works a bit. That's why I want you to let these dwarves on, all right?"

His head immediately shot up. "I understand, my master!"

Kaijin and Garm, eldest of the three brothers, would go on my back; Ranga would take Dold and Mildo. Once they were on, I'd spin some Sticky Thread to make sure they stayed on. These guys did nearly fifty at their peak. In this motorcycle-free world, the experience would probably make them pass out. Not that I knew whether I could handle that speed or whether I wanted to.

Now for me.

Mimic: Tempest Starwolf.

"Astounding! Your dazzling strength knows no bounds, my master!"

"Hah-hah-hah! Yeah, I'll bet! And you'll look like this someday soon, if you keep it up!"

"We will do our best to live up to your lofty expectations, my master!"

Ranga's eyes sparkled at this new mission in life. The rest of the tempest wolves grew equally excited. Always a good idea to motivate the troops a bit.

So I turned to Kaijin and Gharm to get them to hop on, and...

Well, that's weird. They're all unconscious and foaming at the mouth. What're these guys doing, anyway? Oh well. I knew that practice would come in handy! A little Sticky Thread off my back, and everyone was pulled up and put firmly in place. Success!

Fainted dwarves wouldn't make great traveling companions, but either way, we were off.

By the way, I intended to start off at a leisurely trot, only to find myself going over sixty miles per hour or so. Maybe it was for the better that my passengers weren't awake to see this. If they were, our acceleration would've made them lose their lunches.

I looked back at Dold and Mildo on Ranga's back. They had a

little more backbone…or I thought they did. Then I realized they were just unconscious with their eyes open. *My condolences.*

Putting the dwarves in the back of my mind, I proceeded down the path back home. At least they wouldn't bite their tongues or whatnot if they were unconscious. If I were them, I wouldn't want to wake up in the middle of this scream machine anyway. It'd be better for everyone if they stayed asleep until it was all over. *I'll feed 'em, of course, but…*

I really am *mean to people, aren't I? And speaking of which…*

"Rigur! Have you ever successfully summoned one of the black wolves before?"

"…I have not, Sir Rimuru, it embarrasses me to admit."

Hmm. He hadn't, and it was a point of frustration for the other goblins, too, not to mention their wolf partners. So why just Gobta?

"Really? Because I guess Gobta managed to."

"What? Gobta, is that true?"

"Y-yes! I gave the call, and he came over for me!"

There was a fighting spirit in everyone's (and every dog's) eyes now.

"…It's not impossible," Rigur reflected. "Gobta *is* strong enough to have done the Dwarven Kingdom journey round-trip on foot once!"

Oh, right… I thought he was a slobbering idiot, but apparently he was good in a pinch. He was an idiot, of course, but not useless. Surviving a four-month journey through the wilderness and foraging off the land wasn't something any old guy could do. He'd had to deal with monsters along the way, too, weak though they might have been.

I placed Gobta a few rungs higher in my internal totem pole. He'd probably tumble right back down soon enough.

We decided to make camp once night fell. I wasn't tired at all, but everyone else needed rest—I could test out my abilities in the meantime.

A tempest starwolf, to say the least, was physically gifted. I could practically feel the power pulsing inside me. Just a light jump, and I was way up in the sky; on land, I tore up any path I found with my rapid sprint. Add on some quick reflexes, and it looked like I had what it took to make good use of this form.

Most of my battles so far had involved me busting out a few Water Blades and ending it just like that. I hadn't thought about it much, but strength—and reflexes—were going to be a lot more important to me if things got hairy. On that front, the tempest starwolf seemed to have nearly everything I could want.

With the Sage's support, this wolf could probably insta-kill the black snake from back in that cave—no skills required. I'd learned in town that the lizard rated a B-minus in rank, and from there, I used the Sage's simulation skills to figure out how the rest stacked up against it.

It told me that the black snake wasn't even an A, and I could win against ten of those centipedes at once, so I'd be an A-minus or so? Sounds about right.

A tempest starwolf not under my control would be stronger than a black snake, though it probably couldn't take ten at once. Although there *was* that weird Dark Lightning skill to think about...

My instincts told me that one would pack a punch, so I'd test it out in slime form first. *That ought to temper it a little bit so I can observe it.*

The Dark Lightning I unleashed was... Let's call it "beyond belief." There was a flash, followed by a deafening roar of thunder. The large riverside boulder I chose as a target was gone, crumbled to pebbles. I could see the bolt crashing down faster than light... but witnessing its dreadful force for myself simply amazed me. Way beyond expectations.

Heh-heh-heh... Let's pretend that didn't happen! I made my decision instantly.

Right! I wasn't doing anything! Just a little lightning storm.

Let's leave it at that. Seal it away for later, like the snake's Poisonous Breath. It'd be better if I saved it until I knew how to temper the strength of my attacks a little. Besides, with all the internal magic that cost me, I'd better learn how to adjust things soon. No tossing *that* around willy-nilly. I could wind up running out of magic in the middle of battle.

Given the range of that lightning strike, though, it could make a good ace in the hole someday. The entire twenty-yard radius around the disintegrated boulder was now blazing hot and glassy. Something to think about.

Rigur, of course, had a few hobgobs there in short order to find out what was going on. I told them it was just a rogue thunderbolt. *Sorry for interrupting your sleep, guys.* I'd need to save the more dangerous experimentation for someplace where I could work in peace. Some soundproofing would be nice, too. Otherwise, it'd be hard to really flex my muscle.

Still, there was some more data to work with. I replayed the simulation in my mind. According to the results, a tempest starwolf out of my control could use Dark Lightning and probably kill ten black snakes at once. Which meant the attack was probably past A rank.

The guidepost for an A rating was being able to destroy a small town—"disaster" level, in other words. *Better avoid* that *transformation around urban areas.*

My experiments continued, albeit a lot more quietly, until morning.

The next day...

I let Rigur and his people handle breakfast. Goblin food was, well, pretty simple. Just heat and eat. Haute cuisine it wasn't, not that I could taste it. *If I ever pick up that sense again, I'll have to teach them the finer points, I guess. Food one can look forward to is one of the first steps toward an advanced culture.*

Could these goblins really acclimatize to "culture," though? I thought so. I had no idea how, but I wanted to test out everything I could. If we got tripped up over cooking, that would be a bad start.

The dwarves were up, still white as sheets.

"You all right?"

"Y...yes... Where are we?"

As they slowly shook out the cobwebs, they realized they were in unfamiliar territory. It unnerved them. I explained we were on our way to the village these goblins called home.

"Wh-what?! That would be a journey of some two months, normally! We won't have enough food unless we procure a cart at some nearby town!"

It's a little late to be surprised about that, isn't it? I wanted to say, but—thinking about it—I hadn't really explained much to them, had I? Things like how we got here and how fast we were going. We weren't in a hurry today, so I decided to take the time to explain in detail about what we were doing.

Breakfast happened to be served right then. It was just a few wild hares roasted whole, but it was more than enough stimulus for the dwarves' stomachs to start rumbling. *Guess they can keep food down, at least.*

As they ate, I reviewed our future plans. We would be at the village in another two days or so, I explained.

""""No...""""

They whispered in unison, realizing exactly how fast those wolves were taking them.

"Hey, don't worry!" I replied. "Once you get used to it, it's a breeze!"

It'd be nice if they *could* get used to it, but I figured we'd probably reach the end of the journey before then.

We set off back down the road.

Time to build a Thought Communication space for us. Now that I'd done it a few times, it came naturally to me. The dwarves picked up on it, too, which was a relief.

Thought Communication was a sort of high-level version of Telepathy, letting you build links and talk with multiple people at once. It also made things like strategy meetings easier for us. It remained effective across a range of half a mile or so, which was more than enough for my purposes.

On the second day, the dwarves seemed largely capable of remaining on their rides without passing out. The force of the wind kept them from opening their eyes, so I built a sort of visor for them all from silk. Kind of like a helmet replacement, I suppose, and it seemed to do the trick.

I also started noticing that I could control my Sticky Thread to some extent via Telepathy. Once you got used to controlling magicules, it was amazing what you could do with them. Sticky Thread probably wasn't the only thing I could apply that to, either. These little particles were the essence of magic.

Either way, the dwarves were getting into the swing of things, and their makeshift helmets were having the effect I wanted. I could talk with them now, and they were kind enough to teach me a thing or two about life in their kingdom as we rode on. The goblins were listening in as well, chiming in about their own experiences, and we had a nice, friendly confab for much of the day. *This should keep up in the village, too*, I hoped.

Dwarves, being partially sprites, were extraordinarily long-lived. Goblins, being partially magic-born, were notoriously short-lived. Evolution—or perhaps living conditions—had created a fairly large difference between the two.

I sometimes wondered if goblins were actually a step down the evolutionary ladder.

Hobgoblins, the next step up, seemed a bit like the monster equivalent of dwarves to me. Like they had gone back to their ancestral roots, in a way, with a lot more magic force at their disposal. I wouldn't know for sure, but I imagined the evolution did wonders for their life spans as well.

They still weren't the handiest, though, and there was a stark difference between monsters and fairies, but still...

Dwarves, for their part, were probably more closely related to monsters than, say, elves, another sprite race. Maybe that would help these two species get along, too.

As I suddenly remembered something else, I decided to bring it up.

"Kaijin. I know I'm a little late asking, but are you okay with this? You really respected that king, didn't you?"

"Oh, that? I did, yes. There isn't a dwarf alive who doesn't respect him. Imagine having the hero of your nightly fairy tales serving as your actual king!"

It was an interesting thing to consider—the mythical heroes of the past, still alive and kicking and protecting their people as king. That *would* help me build a pretty healthy respect, yeah. I'd want to support him—this ideal king, one who always did the right thing and never allowed room for mistakes.

I wondered how much he had to sacrifice to maintain that ideal in reality.

In a way, it was frightening. It took a lot of spirit, I'm sure, to be a leader like that. That was what made people believe in him.

…Was *I* ready for that? I had become, more or less, the master of this goblin village. *But what comes after that?*

"Well, let me ask you this, then, Kaijin. Why did you come with me? Wouldn't it have been the best thing for your life if you rejoined the king?"

"Gah-hah-hah-hah! Well! A lot more sensitive than I thought, eh, Rimuru? I did it because it looked like fun. It was just instinct, you know? Like, 'Hey, this guy's gonna go out and *do* something!' That's all the reason I needed, y'know?"

…*Yeah. Maybe. Fair enough. He's right!*

"Heh," I retorted. "Well, don't come crying to me later if it turns sour. I'm pretty well-known for being mean to people!"

It was true. I did practically nothing by myself. I entrusted everything to others. But I did want to help. To be relied on. I wanted to be the sort of person who could manage that.

"Oh, I know!" Kaijin replied.

I nodded, satisfied.

Two days later, we arrived at the village on time. Mission accomplished.

THE GIRL AND THE HERO

Tap, tap, tap...

Quiet steps echoed across the castle.

The demon lord had already fled, leaving his bastion behind him. I was the rear guard. A sacrificial lamb. He used me like a tool right up to the end, showing me not a sliver of emotion along the way. The only kindness he ever showed me, I think, was when he called me by name.

Did I hate him for that? I honestly wasn't sure. Was it the will of Ifrit, the high-level flame elemental, that made me serve him, or was it mine?

I still don't know. And I didn't mind being a sacrifice very much. Nothing seemed to matter anymore.

It appeared that this castle was some kind of experimental facility. Abandoning it, however, didn't seem to be any great loss in the demon lord's eyes. What confused me was his goal in leaving me here. I could have just withdrawn instead of engaging anyone who came, but he ordered me to stay.

Maybe he had some plan in mind, but his thoughts remained a mystery to me.

The one who arrived was a so-called hero.

She had long dark-silver hair tied behind her head, and her light equipment was colored a uniform shade of black. Her beauty rivaled the demon lord's. The only difference was that she was a woman. A young one.

The moment I laid eyes upon her, I knew it. I had no chance of winning. But I wanted to fight her to the end—not as a person, but as a magic-born with powers of flame. *It's the least I can do,* I thought, *to make up for the sin of living all this time.*

My sword of concentrated flame was easily caught by the hero's own. My weapon burned with intense heat, capable of ripping through anything, and her simple curved blade stopped it. It made me doubt my eyes. No doubt it was the power of the wielder more than her sword itself.

Thanks to the training I took under the demon lord's trusted black knight, I had gained some mastery of swordsmanship. It was nothing Ifrit ever learned. I remembered how the knight praised me, told me it was all my own talent at work.

As a magic-born, I was physically strong enough to be in the upper ranks of Leon's guard. Plus, I had mastered sword skills under the black knight's guidance. It was far more than Ifrit's power that made me such a close confidant of the demon lord.

And yet—nothing I did affected the hero. The strikes and slashes I had worked so endlessly to perfect were all effortlessly parried away. Gently turned aside before our blades could even clash in earnest.

Even when Ifrit's searing flames enveloped my entire body, the hero remained calm, shedding not a single drop of sweat. Just as I'd first thought, she was on a completely different plane of existence.

Then I felt Ifrit falling asleep in my body, a side effect of consuming too many magicules. It was impossible to keep fighting. I lost, incapable of landing a single blow. I collapsed to the floor, confident that I had returned the favor to the demon lord. I sort of wished I could live a while longer, but I doubted a hero would ever show mercy to a magic-born like me.

"Are you done?" I heard her say. "Why are you here?" It was a bit surprising. I was expecting death to come the next second. My head turned up to her. The hero was a hunter of evil, and I was her foe, a magic-born. If she cut me down right now, I would have nothing to complain about.

What whim of hers prompted these questions? Timidly, I opened my mouth. Then I told her about how I was summoned to this world, how I had lived up to now... What I had done.

It was selfish of me. I was a magic-born now. I had no right, no expectation, to be believed at all. But it was true—having someone take an interest in me and listen to my story made me happy. It left incontrovertible evidence that I had been alive all this time. I could throw out my chest and proclaim to the world that I had lived, even if it was just in someone's memory. That's what I wanted to do.

I doubted the hero would ever believe a magic-born's tale. But that was fine. If I just created a nook in her memory to occupy, that would work. And yet:

"It's all right now. You've been through so much."

She believed me.

Her words brought tears to my eyes. The next thing I knew, I was clinging to her, crying. For the first time since I came to this world, relief embraced me as I expressed my true feelings to someone.

*

I wound up coming under the hero's care.

Her face darkened at the sight of my burn scars. I was used to them; the way they spread across half my body was proof that I was alive.

The hero tried to use healing magic to do something about them. It didn't appear to work. Merging with Ifrit had stabilized my body to its current state, scars and all. She thought for a moment and then took a pretty mask out from a bag.

"You know," she said, "this mask helps boost your resistance to magic. You might be able to use it to keep Ifrit at bay inside you." She gave it a loving caress, then handed it to me.

The instant I put the Mask of Magic Resistance on, it immobilized Ifrit inside me and hid the burn scars across my body. And that wasn't all. With the will of Ifrit no longer dominating mine, all the oppressed emotions I felt over the years immediately welled out of me. The pangs of loneliness, the fear of becoming a magic-born. The deep shame of killing the first friend I ever made. The intense hatred I held for this unfair world. Putting on that mask helped me regain the emotions I had thought I had forsaken with my childhood.

The hero held me tight until I was able to calm down. I remember how scared I was after that for a while—so scared that I couldn't even talk to anyone except the hero. But she never complained. She treated me warmly. And little by little, she loosened the ropes around my heart, teaching me how to converse with others once more.

I accompanied the hero wherever she went, hiding myself in a full-body robe. I was always following her, scared she'd leave me behind. That was about when I was introduced to the Society of Adventurers. I was, as other people at the time put it, a silent girl, one who always covered her face in a mask. One who never ventured out past the hero's shadow. A useless piece of baggage.

One day, something happened to me at the society, which I had visited alongside the hero several times. A man, concerned after seeing how I joined her on all of her monster-slaying work, spoke up. "Is that child in the mask a girl?" he asked. "Don't you think she should stay here this time? This'll be a dangerous one."

All I could do was shiver at the idea. At the time, the hero was the only person on the planet I could muster the courage to trust. The hero meant everything to me, and I couldn't bear the thought of being separated from her. I was sure the grown-ups would kill me if they found out I was a magic-born. I had that much common sense, at least.

The hero gave me a thin smile. "It'll be all right," she said in a reassuring tone. "Everyone here's really nice, all right? You're a strong girl, too. It'll be fine."

I think that's what made me do it. I wanted to live up to the hero's expectations, and I knew this couldn't go on forever. Something about the way she spoke always seemed brimming with confidence, too. It made me believe whatever she said was true.

It was with a strange sense of calm, then, that I separated from her on that day.

In the waiting room next to the society's front desk, I began studying.

That was around when I learned that I was in the kingdom of Blumund. There were several other nations nearby, I found out, around the Forest of Jura. And that wasn't all. When they weren't handling society issues, the workers there taught me arithmetic, as well as several different writing systems.

I listened intently to the passing adventurers as they spoke about the neighboring nations. My knowledge of these other states and the balance of power between them was faint at first, but I still gained a working understanding. To someone like me, who had hardly seen the inside of a school, the society became my place of learning.

I studied magic, as well. The society played home to sorcerers, shamans, magicians, and enchanters, as well as many others who were versed in magic ways. I was lucky enough to build friendships with them, and they, in turn, taught me about the mysteries of the world.

There was much about what they said that seemed unfathomable me. But what I needed most of all was to learn how to deal with elemental spirits. Ifrit, a high-level elemental, was merged with me. Apparently, this allowed me to harness his abilities without the formality of forging a pact with him. But remember—I still had my Mask of Magic Resistance on.

Carefully, I attempted to find an inroad to Ifrit. Soon I discovered ways to manipulate his skills without exacting a burden upon my own body.

Somewhere along the line, I came to be known as the "Conqueror of Flames." I was an elementalist, gifted in the arts of fire and explosive magic, and I had grown to the point that no one worried about me joining the hero on adventures. In fact, she had fully accepted me now—not as a traveling companion, but as a full-fledged partner.

It made me so happy. I had worked hard for so long to help her out, to have the woman who'd saved my life recognize me for who I was. All the effort had paid off. Life was good.

Several years later, though, the hero went off on a journey. Without me.

I didn't know why. The hero must have had her motivations, much like I had mine. I intended to set off myself someday, so I had no right to complain about it.

Did she want to slay the demon lord I served? No, the truth was...

She had saved me, then left me. I needed to find out why, perhaps, and I wanted her to accept me once more. I wanted to show that I was alive, that I was human. It was exactly that kind of selfish hope that proved I had no right to stop her in her tracks.

I was already grown up, not some child naive in the ways of the world. The droplets slipping down from behind the mask must have been my imagination. I made myself believe it was true as I watched her leave.

*   *   *

Because I know I'll see you again...

The thought made me want to grow stronger than ever before.

*

I continued traveling after she left me, across many countries. I wanted to help people in their times of need, as she did.

Whether it was Ifrit's influence on me or not, my body had stopped growing at the age of sixteen or seventeen. One of the demon lord's curses, I thought, but it nonetheless served me well on the road.

A large number of adventurers were in the business of handling other people's dirty work—searching for rare plants in the forest, slaying monsters and harvesting them for useful materials, and so on. It was a line of work that stereotypically involved huge, lumbering frames and equally bulging muscles. Sheer strength bred respect and trust from others, since it meant one could hold one's own in a job that flirted with the line between life and death.

The Society of Adventurers attracted the kind of people who lived free lives and were never tied down by any one nation. If they were injured fighting a monster, they could expect no assistance from one government or another. Nations already had their armies of knights to protect them. They didn't need the aid of some dirty adventurer.

Sometimes a local lord would ask for their help rooting a monster out from their lands or villages, but there was no formal system in place for encouraging cooperation between nations and adventurers. It meant that nations could expand only into the range their armies could physically defend—small pockets of civilization in an otherwise wild land.

There would be times when towns fell under attack from powerful monsters. Three-headed snakes, winged lions, and such. Whenever these so-called calamities appeared near a settlement, they would cause as much consternation as a full-scale war.

Of course, one might expect governments to cooperate and create support systems that extended beyond national borders. And such agreements did exist, but such support always came after things were stable. In the meantime, it was seen as a country's own responsibility to defeat the monster in question.

This was why those with full rights as city-dwellers were granted special treatment, while the others had to make do with life in neighborhoods built in the hazardous areas around the walls. Such people eventually acclimated to a life of being pillaged and exploited. The stronger among them saw an adventurer's career as a way to protect themselves.

The wealth gap quickly grew between rich and poor. It was a dog-eat-dog world, one where the weak had no recourse. I wanted to protect them. Just like the hero, who'd offered me the salvation I'd so deeply hoped for. If I abandoned them, I would be no different from my demon lord.

So I worked as hard as I could to be an ally to the weak. And somewhere along the line, people started relying on me. Calling me a hero.

*

A dragon attacked the town, with enough force to equal an entire army. A calamity-level foe, absolutely. Blumund immediately declared a state of emergency and placed the nation on high alert. I was one of the many people they enlisted.

A calamity-class monster was usually discovered once every several years, but this one was different. No halfhearted strike would ever faze a dragon, and the nation's knight corps was too offensively weak to provide any support at all. I myself provided all the offense I could for the effort, but my sword could do little against such a foe, and I was hardly much of a threat.

If something wasn't done, it would ultimately lead to thousands of deaths. So I decided to call upon Ifrit, sleeping within my body this whole time.

The dragon's stone-melting breath enveloped my body—but because I'd merged with Ifrit, it felt like nothing more than a passing breeze. By the time it realized I was impervious to its breath—that I was a force to be feared—it was already too late. Waves of white-hot flame whipped out of my hands, binding the dragon before it could flee. In another few moments, it was burned alive.

I, on the other hand, was left in a coma for a week afterward. The effort had sapped my magical force. I was aging now, and I couldn't focus my spirit as well as I could in earlier years. As my spirit flagged, so did my magic. Ifrit, and my relationship with him, gave me more than enough magical energy to work with, but the vitality I needed to harness it was dying on me. I had failed to notice it draining, thanks to my body's lack of aging. I'd had Ifrit held down that whole time—no wonder I'd been using up so much of it.

All's well that ends well—the dragon was defeated, after all—but if I had taken one step further, I might have released an enraged Ifrit, a concept far more terrifying than any dragon. I recalled the past, my face tensed and pale. If I wasn't careful, I could very well incinerate the people I swore to protect.

It might be time, I thought, *to call it a day.* If I let myself grow any weaker, Ifrit could go berserk on me. Retirement was something I had to consider, sooner or later.

I talked the matter over with Heinz, one of the managers who ran things around the Society of Adventurers. "If that's what it is," he said, "I'd advise you to travel to the kingdom of Englesia. They're looking for teachers in basic battle techniques over there. There's lots of ex-adventurers out there, but if you can teach your skills to people, you'll never be hurting for a job."

He handed me a reference letter I could use.

"Thank you," I replied. "You've done so much for me."

"Ah, forget about it," he protested. "We're the ones who should be thanking you, Shizu! You've been a rock for all of us." He blushed. "Well, have a nice trip, I suppose. If you get some free time, come back and visit."

They all saw me off before I left for good. It made me feel as if I belonged to this place. As if I had for years. I couldn't believe how happy it made me.

So it was that, toward the end of my career, I made the switch from adventurer to instructor.

CHAPTER
4

THE
CONQUEROR
OF FLAMES

That Time I Got Reincarnated as a Slime

So there we were. Back at the goblin village. It had been only about two weeks, but I was seriously starting to miss it a little. Assuming you wanted to call it a village at all. It was more of an empty space with a fence around it.

While we were gone, a few simple tents had been pitched around the area. There were signs of progress, at least. I spotted a large iron pot situated over the remains of the central campfire. Goblin cuisine used to be all about spit-roasting—but now they'd added simmering to the mix!

This was a truly remarkable development. Where'd they get that thing? Taking a closer look, I realized it was fashioned from the shell of a big turtle. *Man, how much did they expand their hunting grounds while I was gone?* I was glad they'd kept their home base safe, at least.

The resident hobgoblins spotted our returning party quickly, greeting us with cheers and applause. I had rudely forgotten to bring souvenirs, but given the monster pelts and such I spotted drying here and there—proceeds from their hunting, no doubt—I was sure the dwarves would have everyone kitted up and clothed before long. *I'd like the goblins to make that stuff themselves later, but let's take it one step at a time.*

I tried looking around for Rigurd so I could introduce the dwarves to him. I didn't need to. He ran right up to me. I thought he was just excited to see us, but he had something bothering him instead.

"Welcome back!" he said before I could ask. "I hate to bother you so soon after returning, Sir Rimuru, but we have visitors..."

Visitors? ...But I don't remember having any friends.

I decided to let the dwarves show themselves around. They'd be living here for a while, and I was sure they were curious to see what it was like. I also stowed the tools I'd brought along in an empty tent, figuring the covering would at least offer some protection against the elements.

Leaving our new residents to Rigur, I had the elder guide me to our guests. He took me to one of the larger tents, which had been converted into a sort of meeting room. *Who could it be? I guess I'll find out*, I thought as I bounced in.

Once I passed under the flap, I stopped. Inside were a bunch of goblins—the regular kind. Several of them were well dressed, each one accompanied by a handful of servants. Some elders and their guards, maybe? Nobody was armed. Not that I minded that.

Before I could ask what was up, the goblins prostrated themselves on the floor.

""""It is an honor to meet you, O great master!"""" they all shouted in unison. """"Please, listen to our most earnest of hopes!""""

Great master? I guess they mean me, but really, that's going too far. They sure believed it, though. Their eyes couldn't have been more longing or resolute. There was no telling what they wanted, but I figured I'd hear them out.

"All right. Go ahead."

"Oh, thank you for your generosity!" one of the elders shouted. "All of us here wish to join your throngs of followers, sir!"

""""Please, grant us your magnanimous kindness!!"""" the others said as they remained on the floor, eyes turned to me, before bowing low.

Honestly, I didn't want to deal with this.

We're just getting started with the rebuilding process here, guys. I don't have time to waste on you!

I would've loved to simply shoo them off. But we did have a lack of manpower around here. And I could already picture the turf wars these guys would want to spring upon us sooner or later. Maybe it was best to take them in while we still could.

If they stab us in the back after that, we can just kill 'em all.

I wouldn't take kindly to traitors. Rose-colored glasses would just get in the way when you were leading a pack of monsters. You had to keep a cool head around them. That was part of the reason I was willing to take these goblins in—because I wanted to prove to myself that I meant business.

Once again, I reminded myself, *If these guys turn out to be traitors, I will personally kill every one of them.* It was amazing how I could think about killing people as if I were wondering where to go for lunch, though. It came as a surprise, but—hell—it beat hemming and hawing over every life decision I made. Kept it simple.

By the way, if these were just the envoys, how many goblins were we talking overall? I sighed. I might have a hell of a lot of names to think up soon.

The guards accompanying the goblin elders had gone back to their respective villages to report the news. So what did they have to say?

To sum up, their story went a bit like this...

It all began with the recent disruptions to the order around the forest. The other villages had de facto abandoned Rigurd's during the direwolf attack in part because they simply had no combat resources left to assign to the place.

All the intelligent races in this forest—the orcs, the lizardmen, and the ogres, too—were starting to step up and stake their claims on this wood. There had been smaller arguments along those lines before, but there was also a sort of silent agreement that nobody would let it get to armed conflict. With the forest's one and true overseer out of the picture, however, there were more than a few races out there ready to vent some steam.

Monsters, in general, had a tendency to puff up and engage in regular displays of power. Now every village in the forest was rapidly preparing itself to kick some ass. It was only a matter of time before something got the ball rolling. And goblins, the wimpiest kids on the block, were doomed to let most of these other races lay total waste to them.

This, naturally, alarmed most of the other goblin elders. The moment they got involved in this cross-forest turf war, it'd be over for them. So they held a conference, talked it over for several days, and were all too blockheaded to come up with any decent ideas.

Not that I would have expected them to...

News of the impending direwolf attack came in the midst of this, but their attention was focused elsewhere. Rigurd's village was left for dead and all but forgotten. Their talks continued, with no miracles in sight.

Just as the villages' food stocks were starting to run low, they heard word of yet another new forest menace—rumors of massive, dark beasts, piloted by people riding on their backs. They sped through the trees, as if traversing flat plains, and they utterly vanquished the more powerful monsters of the forest. Who were they? The concept made the goblins tremble with fear and surprise.

They were apparently...ex-goblins.

Opinions were split on how to handle this. Some suggested to travel to them immediately and beg for protection. Others found the tale too extraordinary to swallow, concerned that it might be a trap and refusing to believe that the ex-goblins would have no reason to trick them.

Trap or not, though, there was no guarantee this new race would accept them. Especially since they'd abandoned Rigurd's village. Forgiveness appeared a futile hope for many of the elders. Even goblins were capable of shame, it turned out.

In the end, realizing they had reached the far end of their intellect, the conference ended with a total lack of any concrete conclusion. So the side that sought our protection decided to travel over here.

Now it all made sense. Still, pretty selfish of them, wasn't it? We're talking about weak, stupid, helpless goblins, though, so

I should have known better. I'd already agreed to take them in, besides.

"Anyone who wants to come over, have at it," I told the goblin representatives. That was enough to send them back home for now.

＊

That was where my problems began.

As I looked over the teeming crowds of goblins, I thought to myself, *This is…kind of too many, isn't it?* Far too many to house within the village's space.

Why did this have to be my problem, anyway?

Over the past few days, we'd been stuck building axes, using them to chop down trees for wood, and so on. We hadn't even started on houses yet. There was just too much to work on.

Kaijin was handling wood duties, while the three dwarven brothers worked on processing the animal pelts into hobgoblin clothing. The looks they had been giving the females were less than savory. I figured it was best to set them on that job before anything else.

We were in the midst of this when the goblins showed up. Four tribes, about five hundred of 'em in total. The rest were still in the villages with the elders who opted to stay put.

Well, time for a move. It wouldn't make much difference workwise, assuming we did it right now. I checked my mental map of the area. Preferably I'd have liked something with nearby water and some cleared land suitable for farming. As I walked around, I realized that the most ideal location was…the area right nearby the cave I'd popped out of. Hmm.

I decided to ask Rigurd about the state of things over there. "It was regarded as a forbidden zone," he reported. "Unlike the forest, it was a veritable den of powerful monsters…"

"No problem there, then. I mean, I lived there."

"Y-you what?!"

"Like, I guess I was born around there, so…it oughta be fine."

"...You constantly impress me, Sir Rimuru. I am astounded."

Funny thing for him to say. What's so astounding about being born in a cave? If he was cool with it, then fine.

I then called for Mildo, youngest of the three brothers, and told him as much as I could about how architecture worked in the world I came from. Surveying and measurement in this world were actually fairly accurate, thanks to magic. That, plus the amateur-hour knowledge I brought to the table, helped us decide to hatch a surveying project for the local area.

The wolves didn't need it much, but for the goblins and dwarves a waste-management facility would be a necessity. I thought it'd be nice if we could set up a pseudo–septic system that could store waste and turn it into fertilizer. We'd need something to keep infectious diseases at bay, besides. That was another thing I added to Mildo's list.

Do goblins get sick, though? I wondered. The answer was yes—they were susceptible to disease like anyone else. Pretty wimpy monsters, if you asked me. Though given the kind of filth they lived in before I showed up, no wonder...

They lost a lot of people but made up for it with an abundance of babies. Simple math. Although that wasn't so much the case with hobgoblins—they gave birth to fewer offspring at a time, which was another reason I assumed their life spans were longer.

Either way, if we lost too many to illness, we wouldn't be able to keep our numbers up. I had zero knowledge of medicine; anything a potion couldn't handle was beyond me, and we didn't have any magic healers.

So while we were in a building frenzy, I decided we might as well go all the way with hygiene. Mildo, for his part, actually had considerable knowledge about waste systems like this. I must not have been the only otherworlder to talk about this with people.

This world, for its part, had something called "spirit engineering," a unique field of study that led to all sorts of weird discoveries. What it didn't offer, however, was a way to make fertilizer out of people's dumps. Mildo was amazed to hear the idea from me.

Regardless, though, after some deliberation, I named him head of building operations for our village and left everything up to him.

Another classic tossing-off of responsibility, if I do say so myself.

After having Rigurd assign a few people to Mildo's detail, I sent them all off to survey our potential new home. Ranga joined them, just in case. I didn't think monsters would go swarming out of the cave at them, but you never know. Ranga ought to have been able to handle whatever popped up, so better safe than sorry.

That took care of one issue, but I had something bigger on my plate—naming. Just thinking about it depressed me. I had the sinking feeling that by the time I got halfway through the five hundred or so goblins, I'd just be running through the alphabet. "Abcdef" would be a little hard to pronounce, though.

Still, I had to get started. It took around four days to get through them all, with a quick bit of sleep mode in between, and I really had to hand it to myself—I stuck it out to the end. Not quite as exhausting as last time, but not a process I wanted to repeat anytime soon.

I called the tribal elders over. They knelt down in their stately hobgob way. Rigurd was there, and following in his footsteps were three others I had just named: Rugurd, Regurd, and Rogurd.

Put all the leaders together, and yep! You've got all five vowels!

Ranga being the *a* was a coincidence.

So maybe it wasn't my best, but it was okay! They'd never know. Don't forget how much work I put into this.

I've always been very good at making that excuse.

That left one unnamed elder, and she was a woman. Something feminine sounding was best, I thought, so I picked Lilina. One advantage of everyone being hobgobs was that I could actually tell 'em apart by gender. Magic Sense could help me do that with the regular gobs, but to the naked eye, it was a challenge.

Could I turn "Lilina" into another name series, maybe? I thought about it but decided not to worry about the future too much. No time for it.

So here we were. A few hundred hobgobs. Maybe it was time we built a class system for them? With these numbers, I couldn't tell them "Let's all be pals and get along" and expect them to follow that. There needed to be a clear chain of command, especially given how much monsters valued strength.

"All right," I declared, "I'm giving all of you ranks!"

Rigurd received a nice upgrade to goblin king; the other four elders became goblin lords. The rest of the goblins in the village immediately bowed to them, which was a spine-tingling sight to see.

""""Y-yes, our lord!!"""" the elders parroted. The ensuing cheers were deafening. I had just inadvertently penned a new chapter in goblin history.

Kaijin was kind enough to bring along all the carpentry tools he needed. Garm and Dold were proving to be able commanders on the clothing-production front. We were building a miniature tower of wood lumber in an empty space in the village. Preparations were going along smoothly.

By the time I had evolved all the goblins and made sure I hadn't missed anyone, Mildo came back to the village. The surveying work was done without a hitch. All systems go. I looked over the different blocks in the village he'd planned out. It was really more of a town than a simple village. A new home for all of us.

After making sure everything was in place, we set off. It was our first step toward a new land. Toward a new nation for us!

The man's name was Fuze, and he was the guild master at the Free Guild branch in the kingdom of Blumund.

His competence at his post was unquestioned, and even before then, his prowess as an adventurer had brought him all the way to the rank of A-minus.

And as he'd promised the Baron of Veryard, he quickly set off to conduct an investigation of his own. What his assorted intelligence contacts told him, however, was that the Empire was currently making no moves at all. It might stay that way, of course—that was Fuze's hunch—but there was no room for error.

He continued to have his people watch the Empire. It wasn't his usual line of work, but for now, at least, he was willing to make an exception.

One day, he received word that another investigation team had made its return to his city. He went to his chambers and sat down very slowly and deliberately on the sofa in the reception room he always used for classified meetings. Across from him sat three people—two men and a woman, all B-ranked adventurers.

This group, he already knew well. There was Gido, a thief who excelled at reconnaissance. Kabal, meanwhile, was a master of defense. Being fighter class, he willingly served as a wall for the rest of his party, and he did his job well. He tended to crack jokes a lot, but he was no slouch. Finally, there was Elen, a sorceress whose skill set was geared toward the more unique types of magic. She had a wide variety of spells at her disposal, but her true skill lay in supernaturally enhanced movement. It was also worth noting that her careful planning always did wonders to boost her party's chance at survival.

That was the team Fuze had sent to examine the cave Veldora had once been sealed in. His first reaction upon seeing them was slight amazement that they were safe. That cave was more suited for people with B-plus ranks or higher, and if you took its master into account, tracking down an A-minus traveler or two was usually your safest bet. Even if Fuze himself ventured in—not that his guild responsibilities would ever let him these days—it would likely be quite a slog if he took it solo.

Regardless of their ranks, these were the people Fuze had sent to find out what was up with Veldora at the moment. He'd made the decision because of their uncanny knack for staying alive. The ability to avoid battle while gathering intelligence, in this case, was worth far more to him than employing a B-plus powerhouse.

If something had happened to them, though, Fuze would have had to take the heat as guild master. Sending people into areas they were unqualified for by rank was a clear violation of guild regulations. A branch head daring to try that would create controversy if the incident became public knowledge.

But this was the group Fuze had wanted, and nobody was happier to see them back now than him.

"Let's hear the report," he said, ever careful not to betray his emotions. No matter how appreciative he was inside, he made it a point not to offer them any reassuring words. The trio was used to this.

"It was awful, man!" Kabal blurted.

"I so need to take a bath...," Elen agreed.

"Yeah, the hardest part was tryin' to keep this pair from ripping each other apart, I'd say...," Gido commented.

Their debriefings almost always started like this. Their eyes, however, were deadly serious. *It probably was indeed awful*, Fuze thought.

The report began with a description of the monsters they'd found in the cave. After bluffing their way past the tempest serpent that served as the area's guardian, they'd proceeded past the sealing door. It had been clear early on that Veldora was gone, but they'd spent another week or so exploring the cave, just in case. The end result: definitely no guardian, or leader, to speak of inside.

But one thing had caught their attention the most.

"Here's the thing, though," Kabal said. "Once we were done with our examination and went out the door...the tempest serpent was gone."

"Right, yeah!" Elen exclaimed. "I couldn't activate Escape inside the door, so I spent all that time figuring out how we'd get away from it... I feel like such an idiot!"

"Yeah," said Gido. "I brought along an illusion and heat-generating trap, and I didn't even use 'em. At least it saved us some time, though. Gettin' past it on the way in was one thing, but gettin' *out* woulda been another."

What was the meaning of this? This tempest serpent had a tentative rating of A-minus. It was absolutely the strongest presence in the cave. Not even Fuze liked his chances much against it. It was the whole reason why he had fretted over this trio's chances of a successful trip.

Something had definitely happened over there. Fuze could tell that much. And he needed to know what.

"All right, guys. I'll let you rest for three days or so, but after that, I'll need you back in the forest again. Not inside the cave this time—you'll be examining the area around it instead. I want you to leave no stone unturned out there, all right? Be thorough. That is all."

"'That's all,' he says!"

"Three days? That's it?! Give us a week, at least!"

"Yeah, yeah… You know he's not gonna listen to us, guys."

Fuze didn't let the protests bother him. He had some new information to stew over. What could be going on in that forest…? He lost himself in thought for a moment…then opened his eyes, only to find three pairs of spiteful eyes staring at him. *These guys…* He sighed, then yelled at them as he always did.

"Why are you still here? Get out! Now!"

The trio hurriedly excused themselves.

Three days later, Kabal, Elen, and Gido were preparing for their forest trip.

"That was barely any time off…," Elen moaned.

"You said it, girl," Gido replied.

"Could you stop complaining for a moment, guys?" Kabal, the more-or-less leader, admonished with a lack of conviction that indicated his agreement. "You're just depressing me now."

They had few routes into the forest to choose from. The monsters had been growing incredibly active in recent days, to the point that not even the merchants were willing to send wagons into the forest. Hiring bodyguards was out of the question—they'd lose money on this job if they did. If they wanted to visit the forest, it'd have to be on foot for the time being. They would have had to walk at least a little, since the path to the "Sealed Cave" was too treacherous to navigate in a horse cart.

As a result, preparation would be key. Procuring several weeks' worth of preserved food was a challenge in itself, but without it, they stood every chance of starving to death before they even reached their destination. Elen's magic, at least, guaranteed them potable water whenever they needed.

When they were largely done and it was time to head off, a person approached them, speaking in a voice that was somewhere between young and old, male and female.

"Excuse me. If you are headed for the forest, would I be able to join you along the way?"

The mask the figure was wearing prevented any guess at the face behind it. It was an ornate, beautiful mask, but it bore no expression at all. There was something vaguely unsettling about the whole package, but...

"Fine by me."

"Wh-whoa! I'm the leader here, Elen! What's your problem?!"

"Ahh, you know her. Once she decides on something, there's no changin' her mind."

"Thank you."

Those words of gratitude were all the masked figure said before silently following behind them. Thus Kabal and his band found themselves with another companion as they ventured into the forest.

The sound of chopping trees and hammering echoed throughout the forest. Slowly, the new town and its houses were beginning to take shape. In our minds, at least. We were still busy laying out the water and septic system, so for now, it was still just a clearing.

This system took the direction of its flow from the river we were adjacent to. We planned to have a water-processing building eventually, although it was still under construction. That'd be where the river water was purified and distributed to people's houses.

On the septic end of things, we built a large chamber out of wood that we planned to bury in the ground. The wood's inside surfaces would be treated to improve their resistance to rotting, then reinforced with cement. That was what we were working on now. We'd lucked out and found some quicklime-type material off a nearby hill.

Meanwhile, another building outside of town would be our waste-processing facility, where we planned to make the fertilizer we wanted.

In addition to this, I was having the crew build a large temporary building, a sort of gymnasium they could sleep in during construction. It was rather slipshod since we had no intention of making it permanent, but it would do the job.

Outlining the assorted neighborhood divisions was going along well. The upper-class houses, including the one I'd stay in, would be built near the cave mouth. We'd have a line of homes meant for the tribal elders, with the other residences spread out around them.

We were doing this before anything else, so it was easy to lay out the town plan without getting things cluttered and mixed up. It was basically built in the shape of a cross, with a wide main street, making it easy for townspeople to work as a group if the need arose. We'd have to be careful not to create long lines of identical roads—that'd make it easy to get lost—but it wasn't too much of a concern.

The only real disadvantage to this setup was that it could be easy for enemies to move around in case of invasion—but if they actually made it to the center of town, it'd mean a dozen other things would have failed by then.

No point dwelling on that scenario. If we got wrecked, we could always just rebuild.

It was absolutely a good idea to name all the goblins and upgrade them into hobgoblins, though. It did wonders for their intelligence levels, and they were all astonishingly quick studies. Their strength was upgraded, too. The dwarves described regular goblins as straight-on F-ranked monsters, while hobgobs hovered between C and D for the most part. They felt more like people than they did before, to be sure. Depending on their weapons and armor, not to mention their classes and magical arts, there was a lot of room for growth.

On that note, I was seeing substantial variation in the hobgobs' sizes and strengths. The four goblin lords I'd just named, for one, all seemed more talented in life than the rank and file did. Rigurd the Goblin King, meanwhile...

"Oh, is that where you were, Sir Rimuru? I was searching for you!"

Who *was* this guy? He was practically a muscle-bound freak of nature at this point, huge in frame and almost the size of an ogre. "Hell, larger, even!" as Kaijin put it. That must've been the result of giving him a class in addition to a name, I supposed.

I swear, the biology of these monsters was a total mystery to me. I'd have to try assigning a few more titles to see what happened.

"What is it?"

"I've come to report to you, sir. We've captured a few suspicious individuals."

"Suspicious? A bunch of monsters, or?"

"No, sir, humans. We did not engage them, as you ordered."

"Humans? Why here?"

Whoa! Sweet! Better get on their good sides, fast! If it was those three idiots from the dwarven gate, I'd be happy to chop them up and feed them to our work crews, but...

"They were engaged in battle with a group of giant ants, it seems. Rigur and his security detail rescued them and took them here, but...apparently he suspects they are conducting an investigation of the local area. I thought I would come to you for advice..."

Hmm. Some country's checking out this place? I already knew from the dwarves that the Forest of Jura was considered neutral territory, unclaimed by any nation. It seemed plausible that this was an expeditionary force, trying to find some new territory to take for its own. This could be trouble, but there was no point fretting over it without hearing them out. I could think about what to do after that.

"All right. Take me to them!" I said as I hopped on Rigurd's shoulder.

Ranga being out on patrol made transport around our new town a bit of a pain. I could walk easily enough, but when I was by myself, my lack of height was an issue. I always resented the feeling of being looked down upon whenever I met anyone. Having people kneel to greet me just got in the way of actual work. I had a reputation to uphold, besides, and I didn't want to be under people all the time. Perhaps I worried about it too much, but I always thought it was better to avoid trouble before it started.

That was why I tended to travel around on a lot of shoulders these days.

So aboard Rigurd's shoulders, I made my way to see these adventurers. *Who are they?* I wondered before a conversation entered my (figurative) ears.

"Wh-whoa! Hey! I wanted that!"

"That's just mean, isn't it? I raised this meat myself!"

"Sir, I regret to inform you that I am not giving up this food!"

"Munch, munch."

Certainly seemed like some excitement.

"..."

Rigurd replied to my silent question. "M-my apologies, Sir Rimuru. It would seem the ants made off with most of their luggage... and even before then, they had not had a decent meal in some time, so I had some brought to them."

Hmm. That was kind of the goblin king, to be sure. "Oh, that's no problem," I replied. "In fact, good job noticing. Helping out someone in need is a nice thing, you know?"

I felt it was appropriate enough to praise him. He was gradually becoming more and more of a leader, no longer asking me about every little thing that cropped up. A good thing, I thought.

"Ha-ha! I will do my best to improve my rule and be less of a burden upon you, Sir Rimuru!"

But I wish he wouldn't be so formal with me all the time, I thought as we approached a simple tent. The hobgob guarding it opened the flap for us.

The moment we stepped in, I felt all eyes upon me. Four adventurers sat on the ground, their mouths full of assorted meats and vegetables. Their eyes were wide open as they gawked at me. It was a hilarious sight to see, although they probably didn't realize it.

Hmm? Have I seen them somewhere before? ...Oh, right. They were the adventurers I passed by in the cave, although one of them was new to me. I wondered how any kind of food got through the mask this figure had on.

"Munch, munch..."

They sat there for a moment, chewing. They sure were taking their time.

Fresh roasted meat...mmm. If only I had a sense of taste. Argh... Does anyone have some spare taste buds...?

Whoops, got a little distracted there. I turned my focus to the matter at hand.

Rigurd walked up to a tall seat on one side and placed me upon it. "My guests," he bellowed as he sat next to me, "I do hope you are comfortable here. Allow me to introduce you to our master, Sir Rimuru!"

I could hear them swallowing down their food. Then, in unison:

""""Huh? A slime?!""""

"Munch, munch."

All of them reacted with shock.

Well, I'm not sure about the last one, actually. Whatever.

"It is good to meet you. I am Rimuru, a slime. Not a bad slime, you know!"

I heard a sputtering sound from under the mask. With all the food that guy was chewing, the results probably weren't pretty.

Rude jerk.

Must've been a surprise to hear a slime speak. The other three looked equally surprised, but at least they didn't have their mouths full at the time.

So. Who were these visitors? Good guys, hopefully.

"Well, pardon us, I guess. I just didn't expect we'd be saved by a monster tribe."

"Oh! We're human adventurers, by the way, and this meat is really good! We've been running for the past three days, I think, so it's been hard to eat much of anything... Thank you so much!"

"Yeah, thanks. I sure didn't expect some hobgoblins to be building a village around here."

"Urrp... *Koff! Glug glug.*"

"Well," I said, "please, feel free to enjoy your meal, all of you. We can talk afterward."

I sort of wished the hobgobs had called me over after the humans

were done stuffing themselves, but they were still lacking in politeness here and there. I'm sure they were surprised, but something told me I'd need to hold a workshop on manners shortly anyway.

So I left the tent, not too interested in watching them eat on the floor, wondering about my good luck at obtaining these human guests (or prisoners, depending). On the way out, I told their guard to take them to my personal gate near the cave once mealtime was over.

"Don't worry about it," I reassured the crestfallen-looking Rigurd as we walked. "We can work on manners later." They were, after all, growing by leaps and bounds. I wasn't expecting every diplomatic effort to go perfectly with these hobgobs.

Settling down back in my tent, I began patiently waiting. Rigurd had one of his female assistants prepare some tea for us. It looked more palatable than the last beverage I'd tried from them, but I could only guess at the taste. Neat how evolution even affected areas like that.

Slowly, we were settling down into a truly cultured society. Something about that tea convinced me.

*

After a few more moments, the four adventurers popped in, immediately giving a hearty "Sorry 'bout that!" as they entered. The tent was a little cramped with all of them inside.

Once their goblin guide was gone, another one brought out some fresh tea for the group. There, see? Real service, out of nowhere. They must've picked it up from the dwarves—I knew they had been spending nights drinking with them, learning about their society and culture.

"Ah, good to see you again. My name is Rimuru, and I'm the leader of this little group. What brings you guys over here?"

I figured it was a valid enough question. They nodded at each other—must've expected this—and began to speak.

"I am glad to meet you, Rimuru. My name is Kabal, the leader of this band...more or less. This is Elen, and that's Gido over there.

We're adventurers, all ranked B—you know what that means, I imagine?"

"Hi! Elen here!"

"Gido, sir. A pleasure."

So they *were* a party. Being ranked B put them in the upper echelons, to be sure, but they would've faced a rough time in the cave, no? Maybe they were masters at hiding from monsters or something. And what about the other one in their ranks? I was sure there were only three of them in the cave.

"This, meanwhile, is Shizu, a temporary addition to our team for this mission."

"Shizu. Charmed."

It was hard to tell her gender or age strictly from her voice. But after honing my talents trying to differentiate goblins, I could tell right off—she was a woman. And, if my hunch was correct, maybe even Japanese? That was the impression I had.

The way she carried her teacup and the way she knelt just so, tops of her feet flat against the floor. That position, I thought, had to be rare in this realm, and her three companions certainly didn't bother—the men just sat cross-legged on the wolf-pelt rug over the ground, and Elen chose to keep her legs to one side instead.

Ah, well. It wouldn't be strange to have a culture somewhere on this planet that resembled Japan's. I'd pursue that train of thought later.

Although, it occurred to me—was it me, or were these adventurers being way too cavalier with their own safety right now? So far, they seemed to be enjoying their stay immensely—eating, drinking, and laughing with each other. This *was* a monster's den they'd wandered into. They knew that, right? Maybe they just had a screw loose, I dunno.

…*Oops. Got sidetracked. Time to continue the conversation.*

"You too, thanks. So…"

………

……

…

They were exceedingly forthright with their story, apparently not wary of my motives in the least. Their guild master had sent them to examine the area around the cave and check to see whether anything suspicious had taken place...but this mission was proving to stymie them.

"Yeah, that's the thing!" Kabal continued. "We're here looking for 'suspicious' things, but what the heck is 'suspicious' supposed to mean? We're clueless here!"

"Totally!" Elen chimed in. "I wish he could've said, like, 'Look for this or that or the other thing' instead of leaving it so vague!"

"We might be good scouts and all that, but we can't do everything, y'know?" Gido added.

And so they bad-mouthed their guild master without a care in the world. I almost felt sorry for the guy.

Along the way, this group had run smack into a large, suspicious-looking boulder with a hole in it. *This is it!* they must've thought, because they drew their swords and stabbed it a little bit...only to wake up an entire nest of giant ants. Brother. I didn't know what to say.

It was a miracle they were alive—they'd spent the next three days constantly on the run, losing all their possessions on the way, before making it here. I had to hand it to them for managing that, really.

"Well," I reflected, "I wouldn't say there's much 'suspicious' going on around here, no. The cave, mainly, I guess?"

Elen shook her head. "But we didn't find anything in there, no. Did you know the story behind that cave? There's supposed to be this big, evil dragon sealed inside, but we spent two weeks running up and down that cave, and nothing! Two weeks without a bath, and we got practically nothing for it..."

"Whoa, c'mon!" an unnerved Kabal barked back. "We can't go around revealing that much to them!"

"What do you care?" Gido countered. "She's the one who did it! It don't matter to me!"

The men completely panicked at Elen's unwitting revelation.

I already knew, of course, thanks to my last encounter with them. And these people liked a dip now and then, huh? Maybe I'd have to get a bathhouse built around here.

Moving on.

"So what were you looking for in that cave, exactly?"

It couldn't have been treasure, after all.

Kabal somberly shook his head in response. "Well, if she's said that much, no point hiding it. Like she said, rumor's been going around that the dragon in there's stopped responding..."

Hmm. Not that I could've known, but Veldora's disappearance must've put the humans in a tizzy. That vanishing act, despite his being safely sealed away, was huge news—I guess this was some crazy powerful dragon after all, although to me he'd just seemed like a nice guy who liked to chat sometimes.

Must've been a big deal, though, if people were sending out search parties. Was building this town near the cave mouth a mistake?

"We brought along a Reaction Stone, too, because they said the cave was practically bursting at the seams with magicules...but it wasn't anything near what we thought it'd be. I mean, the concentration's a little heavier than your typical cave, but nothing outside what's normal now. And that is pretty unusual, so at least we've got that to go back home with, but..."

"It's still packed with strong monsters, though, so I don't really wanna go back in again if I have the choice," Elen said. "No treasure to speak of, either, and no magic ore. All that monster hacking you gotta do, and there's no payoff for it at all!"

"Yeah," Gido added, "you might find some bandit gear if you look a bit, but nothin' worth goin' out of your way for."

Oops. No ore, huh? Well, what if I told you that there used to be loads of it...and I swallowed it all up? And what if I told you the magic had declined in there because I swallowed up Veldora, the guy generating all of it? That's all basically my fault, isn't it?

Oh well. What they didn't know couldn't hurt them.

We continued talking for a while. They had said too much anyway, as Kabal put it, so they might as well go all the way. These guys were a lot more good-natured than I gave them credit for at first.

And if the cave was no longer a location of interest, maybe we wouldn't be the center of attention after all. I was considering having the town moved as a worst-case scenario, but now I doubted it'd be necessary. No country had any legal right to this land, so it wasn't as if anyone could force us out.

Just in case, I decided to ask whether the guild would have any problems with us building a town here.

"It...oughta be fine, right?" Kabal said.

"Yeah," Elen agreed. "It's not the guild's problem in the first place. What about the local governments, though?"

"Ooh, that ain't for me to say," was Gido's opinion.

Of course, the guild wouldn't know what their host nations were thinking. Plus, if any of them took action, they'd have to prove their claim to the other nearby nations. It wouldn't be worth it.

Then, as I thought over this, I noticed that something was going on with Shizu, who'd been sitting there listening the whole time. Suddenly, she slumped to the floor, unconscious. We all immediately came up to her, trying to hold her up, when...

"Nhh... *Nraaaaahhhhhh!!*"

Things progressed quickly after that.

∗

Once Shizu's extended groan ended, the tent was visited by absolute silence.

Cracks were now appearing over her mask, mystical force wafting out from beneath. All of us could tell that something bad was happening.

"Summon magic?!" Elen shouted in surprise.

"Whoa, for real? Where the hell'd *that* come from? What rank is it?"

"...Umm, judging by the size of the magic circle, I'd have to guess B-plus or higher."

"Well, we can't just sit here, boss. We gotta stop it!"

So they *were* seasoned adventurers after all, when they needed to be. A few words exchanged, and they immediately leaped into action.

"Great Earth, place thy bonds over her! Mud Hand!"

"Urrrrrraaahhh! Knockdown!!"

First, Elen tied her down. Then Kabal landed a full-body blow. Gido played backup, ready to act the moment trouble appeared. Hmm. For B ranks, their teamwork was top-notch. Not a single wasted movement.

But all Shizu had to do was lift the top of her index finger up a bit, and that was enough to trigger a small explosion around her. So much for my tent—which I didn't mind that much, but what about those three? Were they hurt? There was a bit of a shock wave, but I was unscathed.

Kabal, who had landed a Knockdown on Shizu after Elen bound her, had sadly taken the full brunt of the explosion with his body. It had sent him flying. Gido was fine, however, and he'd sensed danger early enough that he'd pushed Elen aside to safety as well.

"You all right?"

"We're just fine, yeah!"

"Um, I'm kinda aching all over!" Elen protested. "They better give us some hazard pay for this!"

Kabal, for his part, was already on his feet. "Owww... Guys, could you worry about your leader at least a little?" He must've been made of some sturdy stuff.

"I knew Shizu was a magic user, but summoning, too...?"

"What'd she summon, anyway?"

"No, no," Gido cut in, "that ain't even the half of it. As far as I know, you can't launch magic without a chant during a summoning—"

Before he could finish, he stopped, looking at Shizu as if he couldn't believe his eyes. He had just hit upon an idea.

"Wait... No way... The Conqueror of Flames?"

Shizu was still casting a spell. Her entire body was glowing bright red, hovering in the air a little. Her mask remained prominent on her face as her long black hair spilled out of her robe. *What's she trying to do? She seemed strange to me a moment before all this happened...*

"Rigurd, get everyone out of town! Don't let anyone near here!" I shouted.

"But..."

"That's an order! Once they're evacuated, get Ranga here for me!"

"Yes, Sir Rimuru!"

The goblin king sped off.

I could tell neither he nor his race could do much against this. It'd be a waste of countless lives. And I didn't want Ranga as a fighting companion. I'd called for him simply because I'd considered the possibility that this was all an act on the adventurers' part to divert our attention. Their oddly loose lips made a lot more sense to me if they'd never intended to let us live from the start. That, or they really could have been that stupid, but...

If this *was* an act, they might try to stab me in the back while I was struggling with Shizu. That was what Ranga would be for. Maybe I was overthinking things, but you can never be too careful.

"Yo, Gido! What's that Conqueror of Flames thing?"

"Wasn't that a hero or something?" Elen chimed in first. "I think she was active around fifty or so years ago?"

Famous, then? I thought to myself. Then Shizu's mask fell off her face.

Flames shot upward.

Up in the sky, three flame salamanders appeared. It was a hell of a way for Shizu to reveal her face to us. Her black hair fanned outward with the shock wave, shining brilliantly against the inferno. She had a fleeting, transient beauty to her—but her eyes emitted a wicked shine, and the edges of her lips were twisted upward in what seemed to be an expression of utter joy at the carnage she had seen.

Something about it struck me as completely unnatural, in a way I couldn't describe very well. Then...

Launching unique skill "Deviant."

The voice of the world echoed around us. As it did, the beautiful young girl transformed into a giant of pure fire.

"No mistakin' it," Gido shouted. "That's the Conqueror of Flames, the master of Ifrit the titan... The strongest elementalist in the world!"

Ifrit, the fire titan. The lord of fire, capable of burning anything in his path. A level above any royalty, mortal or divine.

"Gahh! Ifrit? Isn't that spirit, like, above A rank and stuff?!" Kabal yelped.

"Oof... That's my first time seeing it," Elen said. "But...how could we ever beat *that*?!"

"Yeah, we can't," retorted Gido. "We're all gonna die here... Sure was a short life, I guess."

With his three flame salamanders by his side, the Conqueror of Flames surveyed his domain. No wonder the three of them were in such a panic. Even a single salamander boasted B-plus strength. But... What was the deal with Shizu? To me, it didn't seem as if she was controlling all this—more like Ifrit was controlling Shizu.

There was a shock wave as Shizu—or Ifrit—unleashed a torrent of magic force.

...That was weird. It wasn't aimed at anyone, not meant to kill—just a little show of violence, although there was nothing little about it. It didn't seem like the work of a free mind; the attack looked more as if it was preprogrammed by someone. Now there was no doubting it. This wasn't Shizu's will at work. Ifrit was supposed to be hers to handle, but now he was out of control.

Whether that theory was right or not didn't matter right now. The problem was the force behind those attacks. It was beyond lethal. Pale red shock waves rolled across the landscape, hot enough to instantly burn all the buildings we had under construction.

God dammit! We just got started, too!

The three adventurers tried using a Magic Barrier to block the attack, I guess, but it didn't even last a single shock wave. They weren't dead, but they weren't doing too well, either—conscious, but probably immobile by now.

"Guys, don't move!" I yelled at them. "You'll wind up getting targeted!"

They responded by bunching up together, launching both Magic Barrier and Aura Shield. *Guess this isn't an act.* They were seriously defending themselves. So much for the "let's kill all the monsters" theory.

Talk about force, though. The magic power Ifrit was releasing—with no casting time at all—was blowing searing-hot wind a good hundred feet in every direction around us. If I didn't fight these guys—Ifrit *and* those three flame salamanders—we were all going down. What a pain.

But it was strange.

Even in this predicament, I wasn't trembling with fear or anything. Maybe it was because I was a monster now. I mean, Veldora and that black snake kinda freaked me out at first, but both wound up being good experiences in the end.

"Hey. What're you trying to do?"

"..."

Pop!

An explosion went off behind me. I was guessing trying to talk this out with Ifrit wasn't going to work. He just answered my question with another white-hot strike in my direction.

This time, unlike that untargeted shock wave from before, he was clearly trying to kill me, and his beams of pure heat were vaporizing anything they touched on the way. The force behind them far outclassed that first release of magic power—but, hey, if they didn't hit me, no worries. I had already dodged those beams, and with my quick senses, I could see things coming at the speed of sound.

In a way, I was glad we weren't finished with the town yet. I probably should've been more concerned about the flame titan in front of me, but that was the thought that popped up anyway. Our tents and temporary outhouses were gone, but that wasn't any disaster.

We had already cut down the surrounding trees to expand the clearing; if we'd been in the forest, there probably would have been a massive wildfire by now. There's a silver lining for you. I was a bit concerned about the wood and other supplies we had piled up, but there wasn't much I could do for it now.

This giant had a hell of a lot of nerve, though! With that attitude of his, I was sure he saw me as nothing but an annoying little bug

218

in his way. He was dissing me, and that was more than enough to get on my bad side. Ifrit was my enemy, and I decided now was the time for a counterattack. I had my qualms about Shizu, the person Ifrit was probably feeding off of for all this, but if I didn't strike, this would never end.

Suppressing Ifrit was priority one; I could check up on Shizu later. For all I knew, maybe Shizu wasn't being controlled at all.

I shot a Water Blade at Ifrit's stomach. It evaporated right before reaching the flame giant; a spiraling plume of fire cut it off. *Hmm. Guess that won't work.* But I didn't have time to ponder it, because the salamanders had just reacted to my attack.

"Icicle Lance!!"

Elen's ice magic stabbed its way through one of them. As I took a peek at her, she was already fleeing back into her corner of the Magic Barrier.

It was a clever attempt. It looked as if the barrier was holding up well enough without much concentration on the caster's part. But it'd take more than an Icicle Lance to shoot down those salamanders.

One of them lunged straight toward the adventuring trio.

"You all right?!"

"I can do this!" Elen said. "Risking our lives is nothing new to us!"

"Oh, come on," Kabal groaned, "I thought I was the leader! Well, so be it. I'll take one of 'em down!"

"Yeah?" Gido retorted. "I ain't heard of a bandit fightin' an elemental spirit before. Guess we're all in this together, huh?"

It was hard to tell whether they really counted on each other or not.

If Kabal was that eager to "take one down," I might as well let him. If he died, though, that was gonna weigh on me.

"All right," I said. "You take him. But don't push it! If you get hurt, use these."

Skipping the explanation, I spat out a few recovery potions and threw them their way. Gido managed to scoop them up.

"Um… Rimuru? What are these?"

"Recovery potions! Pretty good ones, too, so if you're hurt, use 'em!"

We didn't have time for details. I went back on the move, and the three of them were too busy dealing with the flame salamander to talk. Even one would be a tough opponent for them. *Hope they hang on okay.*

The other two salamanders, meanwhile, had started making their way toward me. Ifrit himself was calmly advancing, too.

Now what?

Just as the thought occurred to me, Ranga finally arrived. I'd expected to have him keep watch over the adventurers, but no longer. He'd be serving as my mount instead.

"You called for me, my master!"

I hopped right on his back. At least I had some speed now. The salamanders were pretty quick up there, but not as quick as Ranga.

"I want you to focus on dodging them," I ordered. "You don't need to attack at all. I'll take care of that!"

"Understood!"

We had almost a wordless connection with each other. Ranga instantly understood what I wanted to do. Then we were off.

The two salamanders fired off straight jets of Fire Breath at us, like two flamethrowers in the sky. It was light work for Ranga to avoid them, rearing back and out of range of the heat. The fire looked powerful, and I didn't want to try my luck. If I'd still been a human, they probably would've turned me into a black divot on the ground.

I'd better take care of those two guys first before tackling Ifrit. So I tried out some Water Blades. Unlike the fire giant, the salamanders couldn't cut off the attack before it hit home. I managed to slice off a limb…but, ridiculously enough, the guy grew it right back again. It must've been made of fire like everything else. Just cutting it off wouldn't accomplish much. The black snake probably exuded more raw strength than these guys, but the salamanders' special powers would make them a tad trickier to defeat.

"…My master, physical attacks will not work against spiritual foes. Striking their elemental weakness or using magic will," Ranga explained.

Oh. Right. Hitting an elemental spirit with a sword wouldn't do much, would it?

What about launching a ton of water at it, then? My "stomach" had about that much in storage from the underground lake. Would that be enough to put the brakes on this guy?

Understood. It is possible to release a large amount of water. This will cause a steam explosion upon contact with the sala- mander, but is this all right?
Yes
No

Huh? A steam...explosion...? What...?

Understood. A flame salamander is formed from collected heat energy. Being doused in water will cause it to immediately vaporize, creating steam that envelops the salamander's body. It will also trigger a high-temperature, highly compressed wave of pressure, creating a series of explosions.

—And? Will that beat the salamander?

Understood. Pressure times volume equals water released times vapor constant...

Stopppppp! Give it to me in a way I can understand!

Understood. It will trigger a large explosion, and it is pos- sible that the salamander will be knocked out without a trace. However, the results will likely turn the local area into a vacant plot of land.

Oh, come on! What's the point, then? I'm not suicidal, man!
But if not that, then what? Water Blades do nothing practical against it...
"Icicle Lance!!"

I spotted the trio once more, doing their best to survive, with Elen casting magic in the center.

Wait a sec. Water Blades don't work, because they aren't magic, I suppose. So is magic all I need?

"Elen! Hit me with an Icicle Lance! Just one's fine!"

"Hahh?! Umm, that's kind of..."

"Just do it!"

The request gave her some pause, but after a second, she began chanting. After another moment, the freeze-magic Icicle Lance was launched.

"Don't complain about this to me later! Icicle Lance!!"

As she shouted out the spell, a pillar of ice shot my way. I could probably capture that magic with my Predator skill.

And if I could—

Report. Launching unique skill "Predator." Icicle Lance Predation and Analysis successful.

Great! Just as I thought.

Really, I half doubted it while it was being explained to me, but this Predator had to be some kind of rule-breaking skill. That magic probably packed a punch, but Predator absorbed it all, leaving me undamaged, and I even learned it to boot.

"Hehh?! What happened to my magic?!"

Sorry, Elen. Can't explain.

The Analysis wrapped up in an instant, and now I could cast the spell just by thinking about it. No chanting required—that was another nice side effect of Predator.

"Icicle Lance!"

Omitting the casting time, I fired some magic off toward the salamander. Then, at that moment, I understood—the theory behind magic, and how it all worked. My Water Blades didn't damage a salamander at all, even if they managed to slice right through the guy, but Elen's magic did the trick.

The reason was surprisingly simple. Casting magic wasn't about acting upon your surroundings with a phenomenon—it was more like picturing something, then creating it in real life.

I was, in a way, launching a bolt of energy that had the effect of robbing the target of its heat. That bolt happened to take the form of an energy-sapping ice pillar, but it wasn't the ice that made it work. It was the energy inside. Thus, it applied damage to a salamander, whose own energy took the form of heat and flame.

And the multiple ice pillars I'd just launched—too big, really, to be called "lances"—had just skewered the two flame salamanders. That, apparently, was all it took to rid them of all their magical force. They instantly vaporized, like a puff of smoke, and were no more.

"Yes! All done here. Let me help you guys—"

I figured I would help them out, since I'd had Elen waste a magic bolt on me—but I was too late.

"Ah, crap," Kabal said, "it's gonna blow itself up!" As the first line of defense, he launched an Aura Shield, but the salamander's self-sacrificing explosion was more than enough to blow it away. The three of them were all exposed to the intense heat as they soared backward into the air.

Flustered, I had Ranga run up to them. They were more badly burned than I'd thought. Conscious, yes, but no longer capable of moving—and Kabal, up in front, had taken the worst of it. If it hadn't been for his shield, the relatively defenseless Elen and Gido easily could've died.

"Dammit... Ranga, protect these guys. Get them somewhere safe!"

"But..."

The order gave him pause for a moment, but he fell silent, perhaps sensing the mystical force I was letting off. His wild instincts told him that no back talk would be permitted, no doubt.

"This is an order! Do it! They've got recovery potions on them, so get them to a safe place and heal them."

"As you say. May you fight well!"

"Don't worry. Ifrit's all mine!"

That must have convinced Ranga well enough. He nodded, gathered all three of them up in his mouth, and—giving me one more look of respect—sped off. He might have had the wrong idea about my intentions, but either way, all I had left was Ifrit. Now I could fight without reservation. Forget about getting anyone else involved in this.

Let's get this farce over with, I thought as I stared the fire giant down.

The flames whirled violently in the air. Ifrit, before my eyes, had split himself up. Now I had multiple giants blocking my escape routes. He had some tricky talents, but I wasn't too concerned.

My detection skills could accurately tell where the fire was going. Even if the multiple Ifrits all launched attacks at the same time, I could easily determine their fire's danger level from the temperature and take suitable action. I already knew that they weren't all at the same level.

I sincerely doubted that Ifrit could hit me with any kind of effective attack. But at the same time, nothing I had was successful against Ifrit. Those flames were rough. The ground was turning into magma amid the ridiculously high temperatures. No way I could just walk across that, not unless I wanted a class change to "burnt slime."

Now what...?

Paralyzing Breath and Poisonous Breath were effective only up to thirty feet away. My breath attacks needed to be launched within that distance of Ifrit himself, which wasn't gonna happen. I needed an attack that kept me at a safe distance while dealing a decisive blow to him. The only thing that came to mind was my new toy, Icicle Lance.

"Take this! Icicle Lance!!"

I launched several icicles' worth at the Ifrit clones and successfully vaporized a few of them. Vaporizing with ice sounds a bit odd, but with the clouds of water vapor after the attacks struck home, that was the best way to describe it. I started getting into this little target-shooting game, knocking down the clones one by one with my lances.

But—

By the time I thought *Oh, crap!* it was already too late. The moment I felt it, I was already surrounded. A wide-range barrier to trap me? One of Ifrit's intrinsics?

In an instant, there was a magic circle painted on the ground, no chanting required to cast it. I forgot I wasn't the only one who could do that. He had transformed his own body into gas and turned a hundred-yard radius into a searing-hot ocean of flame. Probably one of Ifrit's high-level ranged attacks, and even worse, the area was brimming with energy from the Ifrit clones I had defeated.

"Flare Circle!"

I heard a voice that I couldn't quite decipher. Man, woman, young, old? Hard to tell.

There was...no escape. I was at the mercy of my enemy's spell. Ifrit made me attack those clones on purpose. They were both a distraction and a way to charge up his energy.

I mentally prepared myself for death.

Dahh... I didn't think I had let my guard down, but I could've handled that better. And I played right into the enemy's hands, too! Totally awful.

Maybe I shouldn't have been so self-centered. We should've all taken him on at once. Or maybe I could've taken my black wolf form, confused him with my speed, and then lunged at him, taking whatever burns I got. Or maybe a round of Dark Lightning would've done the trick. Sitting tight and seeing how things turned out? Not good.

Certain other regrets also entered my mind...

Still, I knew my senses were ultrafast, but it sure was taking a while for the damage to arrive. Not that I minded a painless death, if it had to be that way...

Seriously, wasn't this going kind of slowly?

Was he just screwing with me?

Weird... I should've been swallowed up by the flames a while ago.

Hmmm...?

＊

...Understood. The effects of "Resist Temperature" have successfully canceled flame-based attacks automatically.

I detected at least a bit of "You forgot all about Resist Temperature, didn't you?" sarcasm to the voice.

Who asked you to speak up right now, you pile of junk?!

Yeah. I thought I got a "..." in response to that little outburst.

Hopefully that was just my imagination. The Sage had been completely faithful to me before now. It wasn't even self-aware. It'd be stupid to think otherwise.

Ha-ha-ha. I'm just being silly. I'm sure of it!

Now, then.

Wait. It cancels flame-based attacks? So...

Dude, I have this in the bag, don't I? Like, this is all part of the plan. I pretend that I'm on the ropes, then I turn the tables. Let's go with that.

Right. Time to finish up, then.

"What was that?" I shouted as I silently unraveled my Sticky Thread across Ifrit's body. He was done for. My Analysis already showed that he was using Shizu for his body's core. I couldn't have tied up a pure spirit beast like the salamanders with this string, but one with a physical core was a different story.

Next, I'd combine the Sticky Thread with some Steel Thread to get the benefits of both. Another product of my experimentation—and as a bonus, it adopted the same immunities I had, so it wouldn't get burned up.

Checkmate. I know I sneered at you earlier, but you were probably sneering at me, too. Let's call it even. You're free to hate me for this if you like.

"I'm up next, right?"

Ifrit, in a panic, struggled to free himself. I expected that. But my "Sticky Steel Thread" was never going to let him. I took my sweet time, casually approaching.

It was time to land the final strike. On Ifrit, the monster that had probably taken Shizu's body over.

No need for too much haste. I walked up to this flailing creature, who was trying to throw every attack he could to stop me. Sadly for him, flames didn't work on me.

Then...

Use unique skill "Predator"?
> *Yes*
> *No*

That'll be a big ol' yes, please.

A flash of bright light covered the area, then suddenly vanished. All that was left was a lone old woman and me.

●

Was this a dream?

My mother's hand, cold.

Her cold eyes, gazing at me.

A warm smile and a pile of pure white ash.

All these memories did was torment me. I didn't want to remember them—

But that was the path I walked.

If I hadn't run into the hero, I doubt my soul could ever have been saved... But I was too awkward, too unskilled, to wind up like her. With so many people relying on me, too...

It was just that—

It had been several years since I'd retired from the adventurer life. I was a full-fledged teacher, leading the next generation of our trade as I helped out the society with its work.

The Society of Adventurers, a group that crossed borders and had grown beyond the control of any single government, had built its headquarters in the kingdom of Englesia. I was no longer an adventurer, but if there was anything I could do for them, I wanted to help them with it. It had been the society, after all, that had given me a home of sorts when I had nowhere else to go.

There, I had a chance to teach a number of talented students: A young man with eyes that beamed with complete purity. A girl, her gaze tinged with hopelessness. More otherworlders, I assumed, just like me.

The two of them were exact opposites in so many ways. Yuuki was a bright, optimistic boy, while Hinata was insular and reserved, as if she carried all the darkness in the world with her.

Bandits had attacked her when she came here. At the time, I had thought that she would warm up and come around as the days passed. The bandits met their fates at the hands of some other assailant, which saved Hinata's life, but I'm sure the incident must have scarred her.

I saw a bit of myself in the girl, after all. I had an affinity for her. It was apparently one-sided.

"Thank you for everything you've taught me," she said. "There is nothing else I can learn from you. I doubt we will meet again." Then she turned around and left.

I thought it might have been best to chase after her, but I couldn't will myself to leave town. The society was building a new shared-assistance program with Englesia, a new organizational structure originally proposed by Yuuki. As a former hero, I was put in the position of representing the society in the requisite negotiations. It was something I wanted to see succeed, considering how it would define the society's future direction.

So in the end, all I could do was see her off. "If you ever get lost," I called to her, "I want you to rely on me."

After agonizing over it, I decided to support Yuuki over Hinata. The girl had walked a similar path to mine, but she was always far more strong willed than I was. I figured that I should believe in her. That her iron will could clear the darkness in her soul and transform her into a great woman.

It was no great surprise when I learned, a mere few years later, that she had risen to an important position in the Church. I felt a little proud, a little lonely…and just a tad anxious.

Hinata isn't feeling lonesome, is she? Is she doing all right with her life?

The questions overwhelmed me, but I figured I had no right

to ask them. I once had the chance to grasp her hand, and I had refused it.

All I could do was pray for Hinata's continued safety.

Yuuki, on the other hand, was far more dynamic.

It was Yuuki who built the current system for the Society of Adventurers, now renamed the Free Guild. Thanks to him, the guild was able to build a successful cooperative relationship with nations across the world. He had forged new treaties with governments, earning the guild positions in their topmost of councils. His efforts had made the organization more powerful than ever.

I should have expected nothing less. Until then, every nation had been focused solely on protecting its own borders. When the Free Guild began taking on monster-dispatch duties, it lightened the loads of every other government in the world. And that wasn't all. Adventurers—people who traveled the world, never beholden to any single country—were obligated to file reports on their journeys. The Free Guild then collated these reports to gain a grasp of how monsters were distributed worldwide. Danger levels were assigned to every region, allowing people to travel in relative peace.

The system had one other major effect. Knowing where and when to expect monsters made it possible to quickly detect anomalies—letting people discover and report on monsters not seen before or eliminate hordes in short order if they grew too numerous.

Whenever a monster that normally didn't appear in a certain region suddenly menaced a nearby town, the guild was also obliged to send an expeditionary force to figure out the cause. Getting to the root of it early on let the guild and local governments assemble a dispatch corps far more efficiently than before.

Having this kind of organization made people's lives both safer and more comfortable. Mankind found itself expanding its cities, and the overall population has grown rapidly in recent years. The institution of rankings assigned to monsters did much to reduce the number of deaths as well.

For someone charged with training new recruits, nothing could have made me happier. Thanks to Yuuki, the Free Guild was now an organization that neither the nations of the world nor its people could do without.

Yuuki, for his part, just laughed it off. "I was just imitating what I saw in this video game I played," he said. "Though, of course, you can do anything you want in a game. You can have monsters that say, 'I'm not a bad slime, you know'…or even have them join your party!"

He was always a joker like that. Monsters becoming your friends? That sort of thing could happen only in your dreams.

The world I was born in had almost been razed to the ground by war. Had it recovered to the point where it could create people like him—people who never seemed to have a care in the world?

He explained to me that these "video games" were children's toys that let you experience a full story yourself…so if Japan had recovered enough to give children dreams to play with, it must have become a wonderful place.

So I listened to Yuuki's stories, thinking to myself about a home I could never go back to.

I continued to serve as a support for Yuuki after that—advising him from the rear, never appearing in the forefront. The Free Guild continued to grow and became an outfit used by nearly everyone. It embraced a philosophy of rescuing the weak, accessible to everyone equally.

Then Yuuki, my very own student, became the guild's grand master, its highest position, the one who organized and oversaw the guild masters of each branch. Given everything he had done for them, I should have expected it. His efforts were the catalyst that allowed people to live at peace for a change. He had done everything he needed to. I felt the satisfaction of a job well done.

So I decided, then, to go on a journey. A journey to take care of some regrets.

I kept having dreams of the past, back when I was still a magic-born. It was getting hard to contain Ifrit's will. Perhaps I was approaching the end of my natural life. I knew my Mask of Magic Resistance was still working as well as ever, so the reason seemed obvious.

Once I realized that, I concluded that I had best leave town as soon as possible. I couldn't know when Ifrit would finally fall out of control, and I had no idea how my death would affect Ifrit himself.

Plus, I wanted to retaliate against my demon lord. Just once, I wanted to have my say with him.

So I decided to set off on my journey.

When I told Yuuki about my plans, he silently nodded, saying nothing about them. Hopefully he was willing to forgive this one final act of selfishness. *Maybe*, I thought to myself, *this is how the hero felt, too.*

I made my way to Blumund. Heinz was retired by now, since his son Fuze had taken over the guild master's role in his place. We got to meet up and chat a little about old times. He had a lot to say, which I was glad for.

Remarkably, he reported that Veldora had disappeared. The guild was conducting a frantic investigation to find the cause. "I don't know too many details," Heinz told me with a snicker. "They don't tell an old pensioner like me too much. I can tell it's troubling my son, though."

He must have trusted Fuze well to speak of him like that, I thought. I had gone on several monster-hunting operations together with the boy, and I remembered him doing a fine job supporting me. Now he was out of the front lines and following in his father's managerial footsteps. He must have inherited all of Heinz's natural talent.

"Thank you," I said. "You've been very kind to me."

I shouldn't get in their way. After my polite response, I stood up.

Was Veldora's disappearance meant to be some divine message to us? Either way, I was headed for the forest.

"You stay safe, too, Shizu! I think there's an expedition leaving here tomorrow, actually," he muttered, almost to himself. "If you're hitting the forest, you might as well join them for a while."

He didn't try to stop me. He was always an awkward fellow, and this was how he preferred to show kindness.

"Ah, Heinz, I should have expected nothing less. I suppose I'll owe you to the very end, then."

"You owe me nothing, Shizu. And no talking about the 'very end' yet! I'd like another look at you sometime."

I could feel the warmth behind his words. "True. I'll be back."

I bowed low and left.

The next day, I managed to run into the expedition Heinz mentioned to me. It consisted of three adventurers, and as he'd told me, they were a bright, inviting group. I genuinely appreciated joining such kind people for my last journey, though their excessive carelessness did baffle me.

There was, to say the least, a lot of trouble along our way through the Forest of Jura. I was impressed, in a way, that they had attained a ranking of B at all. They had the battle technique such a rank implied, but if I had to sum up everything about their team in a word, it would be "nonsensical."

Our journey continued on nonetheless, right up until they jammed a sword into a giant ant nest. I was horrified. This happened not a moment after I told them it was a bad idea, too. Never in my life did I imagine they would try something like that.

My flames could've torched those giant ants instantly, I imagine. But by the time I realized how hard it was to control my power, I had already started to feel my body deteriorate. It remained physically young thanks to Ifrit's presence, but as my power over him dwindled, it rapidly began aging. Or, I suppose I should say it went back to the age it should always have been.

Would Ifrit be released once my body gave in? Or would he crumble and fall apart with me? I would have no idea what would happen until it did. That was why I had set off.

And why I hesitated to pull out my fire.

We were lucky enough to be rescued by a passing patrol, saving us from any further trouble. But this patrol was one of the fishiest things I had ever seen.

Being saved by monsters? Nothing like that had ever happened to me before.

These were hobgoblins riding upon magical wolves. It would have been one thing if they understood a few broken words of human speech, but these were intelligent creatures, and they had tamed what was clearly a high-level monster species. This was absolutely the kind of "suspicious event" this adventuring trio had been sent out to investigate, I thought.

My destination, meanwhile, was the castle of the demon lord Leon. His domain occupied the lands just beyond the forest. I should have chosen that moment to take my leave of their party. But...I don't know. I suppose I just wanted to see, along with these adventurers, what kind of home these monsters had made for themselves.

It was a strange place indeed, this town our rescuers lived in. It was no dank lair or stinking, filthy den. A "town" was the only way to describe it.

The shock I felt was beyond comprehension. This wasn't some rude shelter, some glorified hole in a mountain. It was a proper town, one they had built for themselves from scratch.

It was under construction, I should probably add. It had been surveyed and laid out, and building materials had been placed in each section, ready to be converted into houses. There were no buildings yet; the monsters were still living out of neat rows of tents. But they had even started their work by focusing on the underground infrastructure. I had never heard of anything like it on this planet.

It was a bizarre settlement.

But it was bursting with energy. The residents, despite being monsters, truly seemed to enjoy working on it. Most of them were hobgoblins, but they seemed to share their lands with the black direwolves. A tad different from the ones I was familiar with, and I didn't think it was my imagination.

The leader of the hobgoblins spoke very fluently to me. I imagine he was the most intelligent among them. He even prepared food for us. Remarkably, though, he turned out not to be the leader at all. Instead, he was joined by a slime—one who lay back in his lofty throne, acting as if he were king of the world. It might be odd to say a slime could "lie back" on anything, perhaps, but that really was the sense he exuded.

This slime was the strangest thing of all—for he, in fact, was the leader of all these monsters.

It was hilarious.

I couldn't help but do a spit take as he spoke. "I'm not a bad slime" was how he chose to describe himself! Just like Yuuki's "video game." I began to wonder whether it was a coincidence.

Still, there was something inviting about the space this slime created. The strange creature somehow made me recall memories of my own hometown. My heart felt full. Now I was glad I'd decided to step away from my intended path. This meeting, I thought, was fate at work. And yet—

The hours we spent enjoying ourselves came to a sudden halt. My life was about to expire. I had yet to reach my destination—to fulfill my goal—but here it was.

Ifrit had been waiting for this moment. I could feel his will taking over mine. *It's happening... I'm going to ruin all of this, too...*

If only, one last time, I could just—

The titan manifested himself, all but laughing at my folly.

My consciousness faded away.

I went to see how she was. She didn't have long. In fact, she might never regain consciousness. Still, I wanted to take care of her to the end, this fellow otherworlder human.

The wounded adventurers all pulled through, thankfully, whining incessantly about how it'd take more than hazard pay to atone for getting burned half to death.

"Hey, what's the deal with this?" Elen asked. "I don't see any burn scars or anything... Like, my skin's as soft and shiny as a baby!"

"Dang," Kabal added. "I didn't think I'd be able to move for another week or so, too."

"Yeah, count me surprised. That's some potion he had there!"

They were right. That potion had made all of them good as new.

"You know, though… This probably means they'll turn down our request for hazard pay, doesn't it?" Elen moaned.

"Yep. Nobody's gonna believe us…," Kabal replied.

"Yeah, I s'pose so. Beats bein' laid up for good, though!" Gido commented.

It never took long for this trio to start bickering with one another over their own self-interested quibbles. I wondered if they ever really had a thought about anybody besides themselves. They didn't have anything against monsters, at least.

"You know," I suggested, "once things calm down a little, maybe I could go visit your town."

"Oh, if that's the case, I could give the guild master a message for you!"

Just what I wanted to hear. Kabal had made my day. I looked up to adventurers, kind of. I didn't have any sort of ID papers, though, and I didn't even know whether they'd let monsters join the registry, but…it could be fun.

So Kabal promised me that I could just say the name "Rimuru" and the guild master would hear about it soon enough. Nice guy. I was in such high spirits that I decided to give them a farewell gift—a few pieces of equipment, freshly made by the dwarven brothers. They were all test models, made with materials they had procured themselves, but the quality was respectable.

Spider robe:	A robe of pure white, woven with spider silk.
Scale mail:	Heavy armor made from the shell of a lizard. Far lighter than appearances indicate.
Hard-leather armor:	Made from the skins of local monsters. Magical resistance included.

I also tossed in some food and ten recovery potions for good measure.

"Ooh! Look at this robe! It's so light, and I can't believe how sturdy it is! And pretty, too!"

"Whoa! I've always wanted some real scale mail! This… Waaaait a second, did Master Garm make this?! This'll be like a family treasure to me!"

"Yeah, are you sure we can have these? This is almost too nice for the likes of me. I mean, real direwolf fur?"

It was a miniature celebration for a little while. But—I mean, the fire had torched all their equipment, and I doubted their salary would let them replace it all that easily. It wasn't exactly my fault, but I had to feel a little sympathy for them. The equipment was all prototypes, crafted before the dwarves could move on to mass production, but it was decent enough.

Besides, look how happy they are. I was confident they'd remember to pass my name on. They were calling me "boss" with the rest of them, too.

The three of them had their qualms about what happened to Shizu, but not enough to keep them from setting off again after three days of rest. They had a report to file and a looming deadline. If anything, three days was a generous amount of time to worry over a woman who'd essentially shoehorned herself into their traveling party uninvited.

Still, I promised them all that I'd take care of her, and that was enough to put their minds at ease.

✳

A week passed before Shizu woke up again.

"Is this…? Oh. I…apologize."

Despite the transformation, she still retained all her memories.

"I was dreaming," she told me. "Dreaming about the past. The city I lived in… A place I can never return to."

Japan?

"Tell me, slime. What is your name?"

Hmm. Maybe her suddenly elderliness was affecting her memory after all. I knew I had introduced myself in her presence. "Rimuru, ma'am," I replied.

Shizu closed her eyes, as if thinking over something. "Could you maybe tell me your real name?" she said.

She must've known all along. I hesitated for a moment.

"Hmph," I offered. "You aren't long for this world anyway. I'll tell you. It's Satoru Mikami."

My real name. A name I figured I wouldn't be using again.

"Ah. From my land, are you...? I had thought you might be. I sensed it from you." She fell silent for a moment. "I had heard from my students, as well. The city's much better now? Prettier? The last time I was there, there was nothing but fire all around me."

"Yeah. I could show you, if you'd like."

I used Thought Communication to do exactly that. Fairly useful thing to have at a time like this. I liked it.

"Ahh..." The sight made Shizu shed a tear. "Listen, slime...or I should say Satoru, I suppose. I have a request for you. Would you mind listening to it?"

"What kind of request?"

Nothing particularly doable, I was sure. But I did promise to take care of her to the end. She deserved to be heard out.

"I want you to eat me..."

Um? What did this old lady just say?

"You consumed the curse...that was placed on me, did you not...? I'm so glad to be rid of it..." Her voice grew quiet. "I wish I had the chance—I doubt I could've ever done it, but I wish I could've had the chance to confront the person who placed it on me, one more time... So I have just one request for you—would you let me sleep inside you?"

Something about her eyes, the resolve that she just couldn't relinquish, grabbed at me. It seemed so absurd, so cruel...

"I have to tell you—I have nothing but spite for this world. But I couldn't bring myself to hate it, still. It's the same as how I feel toward that man... Perhaps I can't help but think of him when I look around me. That's why I... I don't want to be taken into the earth here. So please... I was hoping you could eat me instead..."

Hmm. Well, that's easy enough.

Fulfilling her request would bind me, no doubt, and give me a curse of my own. I would be charged with taking on her despair and hatred.

Was there any need to waver on that, though? If I wanted her to see the afterlife with her mind at peace—the answer was obvious.

"All right. I'll be happy to take on your feelings. And what was the name of this man...the one who hurt you?"

At the question, Shizu opened her eyes, scrunched up her burn-scarred face, and shed a few more tears. "Leon Cromwell," she said. "One of the strongest demon lords."

She looked at me with pleading eyes.

"I promise!" I declared. "By my name as Satoru Mikami, or Rimuru Tempest, or whatever works best for you, I promise I'll make Leon Cromwell know everything you feel about him. I'll make him regret every moment!"

"Thank you," she whispered, and then she closed her eyes, her breath turning shallow as she slept.

Use unique skill "Predator"?
     Yes
     No

—*Here's hoping you'll find some peace inside me, then.*

Yes, I thought to myself, in a sort of prayer to her—a hope that her dreams inside would remain happy forever. With no more rude awakenings.

●

Tap, tap, tap, tap...

She looked up, her face bearing the innocence of youth. Relief spread across it as a smile emerged on her face.

Well, there you are! Don't leave me alone like that again, all right?

But the figure shook its head before pointing at something far away. The girl turned toward it, her expression suddenly clouded with doubtful sadness.

There she found—

Mom!!

A burst of happiness rushed through her entire body as she rushed toward her mother. The figure watched her trot off for a moment—then disappeared, as if nothing had ever occupied the space at all. Perhaps it was just an illusion crafted by the girl's memories.

Thus, the girl was reunited with her mother.
It marked the end of what had been a long, long journey.

THE INHERITED FORM

That Time I Got Reincarnated as a Slime

Shizu was gone now—gone, after giving me one final goal to strive for.

Up to now, I had largely taken things as they'd arrived, fighting to keep my head above water. Now, though, I had a motivation to gather some intel on this "demon lord" guy. It was a job I readily accepted, but it was also a promise. And I'm a man who keeps his promises.

Besides, I wasn't empty-handed. She left me with a few new abilities—the unique skill Deviant and the extra skill Control Flame.

Oh, right. I ate Ifrit, too, didn't I?

He wasn't much of a match for me, but it turned out he was a tough character—rated beyond an A, in fact. No way some snake or wolf could handle him, to be sure, given that none of their attacks could even faze him. It took a lot to make it past an A, and now I could see why.

There was still a lot of research to be done on my abilities. But! Before that! There was something even more important I needed to check up on.

That's right—transforming into an actual person!

I ventured inside the new tent the hobgobs had set up for me, making doubly sure to have all visitors turned away before I closed the door.

Heh-heh-heh… Hah-hah… Ah-ha-ha-ha-hah! Three levels of laughing, and then…

"…*Transform!*"

It wasn't accompanied by any cool sound effects, but I executed Mimic: Human on myself nonetheless. But…

…*Huh? Whoa, whoa, whoa.*

There was none of the usual black smoke I was expecting. *What the heck?* I thought, as I realized that my field of vision was only a little higher than usual.

I had grown arms and legs, and my usual light-blue shade had morphed into a flesh tone.

Hmmmm? I wasn't sure what had happened, but something told me it wasn't what I had planned. I didn't have a mirror on hand, which was a pain. But—

I kinda didn't want to admit it, but I actually was familiar with this form after all. It was from a long time ago, maybe thirty years or so.

This was how the world looked to me back when I was still bumbling around in elementary school.

Hang on a sec. I was too excited to notice at first, but there was one key difference.

It wasn't there.

My should-have-been newly born manhood, that is, which I was expecting to see down below. It wasn't there! What the hell? I internally shuddered as I took another close look at my crotch. It only confirmed the worst. It was smooth as the hypothetical baby's bottom.

Thinking back, this wasn't something I had bothered to check up on when transforming into other monster types. But I supposed it made sense. If I never had to eliminate waste from my body, what use would I have for the associated organs? And if I didn't need to reproduce—I was still fuzzy on that, but if I didn't, then why bother with genitals at all?

That was just who I was now, was all. It was strangely convincing, even as it drove me into a deep sense of mourning.

Suddenly, I was taken by an urge to touch the top of my head. I felt soft hair up there. It made me breathe a sigh of relief. At least I wasn't shaped like a space alien! *That's a step forward! And, come to think of it, I was a giant ball of fur in wolf form. I don't even want to imagine what that'd look like without hair. Nope. That's a dangerous line of thought.*

Really, though, I thought I'd keep a cooler head than this. Why was I letting myself get in such a panic? I'd just have to accept the truth about what happened down there. It was hard to swallow, but at least I wasn't a slime any longer.

Too bad I can't check up on my whole body, I thought. *What about the Replication skill I just picked up from Ifrit?* Seemed like a nice idea. Good job, me. I didn't know if it'd work, but it was worth a shot.

Black mist darted out of my body, forming a human figure in front of me. Looked like it was a success after all. It was completed in an instant, only to reveal—

—Oh, crap. Bad news.

First off, my appearance. The hair was a silvery gray with a light tinge of blue to it, topping off a pair of wide-open eyes and a charming, young… Feminine? Masculine? The lack of genitals made it fairly irrelevant, but in terms of appearance, I looked closer to a girl than a boy. This was probably thanks to Shizu; there were no features that I could identify as my own.

But it wasn't a perfect recreation of Shizu's genes, either. The hair color was one thing, but the golden eyes were quite another. Veldora had gold eyes, too, which was a common trait among the higher monsters, perhaps. And hang on, didn't Ranga's eyes go from a blood red to gold as well? Although they also changed depending on his excitement level. Still, maybe they changed because of my influence on him as his name giver.

Either way, nothing about this form was from me. In this world, the only thing that was truly mine was my soul, it seemed. This was mostly Shizu, and *man*, she must've been one darling little girl… My skin was tremendously smooth, too, with none of the rubbery bounciness of my slime form.

So this cute girl was just standing there in front of me, butt

naked. Not that there was anything that really required hiding, but it still presented certain ethical issues. If the police existed here, which they didn't, I'd be in serious trouble.

But that face was cute. I had to hand it to Shizu. She was blessed with a lot of gifts. I wasn't too hideous when I was young, either, but nobody would ever describe me as beautiful, no matter how much I padded my memories.

I really have to thank her, I thought to myself as I wrapped a blanket around my body, taking the time to hand one to my doppelgänger. Now I really needed to figure out some clothing.

Right. Back to the main topic—the real reason I thought *Oh, crap* at first. That all came down to this human form's abilities.

Something I hadn't considered with this replica of mine before actually conjuring it was that my enhanced thought processes allowed me a complete, real-time link with my copy. It and I were both "me" in a way—there were no appreciable differences between us. If anything, Ifrit's Replication skills couldn't hold a candle to mine—his copies were clearly imitations, but mine wasn't at all.

All right. Almost not at all. One big difference was my copy's capacity for magicules—it held only whatever I cast upon it when creating it, although I was free to "install" more inside if I wanted to. I had a fair amount of magic to work with, so depending on the application, I could probably do a lot with it. The other issue was that, while Ifrit could generate ten or so copies without breaking a sweat, my Replication skills were so intricate and detail oriented that a single copy was the best I could manage.

Still, I could make a copy of myself with all the same attack and defense abilities. Any foe who ran into this skill would think I was cheating.

The third and final "oh, crap" reason: the way it seemed so breezily natural to me, taking this form. That was something I noticed when I realized no dark mist had surrounded my body.

Take my black wolf form, for instance.

I definitely used the mist to create that form, although it made for weaker results compared to my slime self.

It was hard to notice thanks to the limited movement available to a form without limbs, but a slime's cells were powerful things—each one could serve as a muscle cell or a brain cell or a nerve cell. See the streamlining effect this makes? Seeing things with the eyes, relaying the information to the nervous system, bringing it to the brain—I could skip all of that. Even without the Sage's upgrading effects, my reaction speed was far above the average person's.

Transforming with the black mist, however, created a slight time lag between thinking something and moving my body in reaction to it. That, I figured, was what made the replication "inferior," if anything, to the real thing.

As for this mist-free human transformation?

You guessed it—it had the exact same reaction speed as my regular slime form. No wonder it felt so natural. Having limbs also improved my mobility immensely. Even in child form, it was so much easier to get around than as a slime, although it tired me out more quickly.

The biggest thing, though, was that the lack of black-mist usage meant turning human cost me zero magic. Talk about convenient! I figured I'd be taking this form for most of my future activity.

It was time to try something else. I gave an order to my replica—and it was a totally smooth process, just like moving my own body. Black mist welled around it…and the copy began maturing! A trim figure; long, flowing gray hair; and an androgynous sort of appearance. Perfect! I could then mold this figure to look more feminine or masculine—go all macho, or obese, or in the prime of my life, or elderly.

As I soon discovered, I could transform into all kinds of figures—using magic to cover for anything I didn't have, just like with monster transformations. That might be a good way to give me some more strength as a human. It hurt my reaction times, but the bigger I was, the more powerful it'd make me. Speed was the most important element of any battle, I knew, but striking a good balance was something I could experiment with in the days to come.

And so Satoru Mikami, an average middle-aged man living a perfectly unexceptional life, came to enjoy his unexpected reincarnation as a slime. After acquiring the form and the emotions of a certain woman, he also gained a mission in his new life.

And before long, this single slime named Rimuru would play a central role in some of the most tumultuous times this world had ever seen.

Rimuru Tempest

Race
Slime
(transformable into human)

Protection
Crest of the Storm

Title
Leader of the Monsters

Magic
Elemental Magic: Icicle Lance

Intrinsic skills:
Absorb Self-Regeneration Dissolve

Unique Skills
Great Sage Deviant Predator

Extra Skills
Control Flame Magic Sense Control Water

Acquired Skills
Black snake: Poisonous Breath, Sense Heat Source
Centipede: Paralyzing Breath Spider: Steel Thread, Sticky Thread
Bat: Ultrasonic Wave Lizard: Body Armor
Black wolf: Coercion, Shadow Motion, Dark Lightning, Thought Communication, Keen Smell
Fire titan: Flame Transform, Ranged Barrier, Replication

Tolerance
Cancel Flame Attack Cancel Pain Resist Electricity
Resist Temperature Resist Melee Attack Resist Paralysis

After adopting several abilities from monsters, thanks to Predator, he consumed Ifrit and increased his power exponentially. Has now adopted the powers and memories of the Conqueror of Flames, Shizue Izawa, as well as her form as a child. With his newly acquired Deviant skill, he plans to develop various new abilities as well.

Shizue Izawa

Race → Fire-elemental magic-born

Protection → Demon lord's blessing

Title → Conqueror of Flames

Magic →
- Elemental Magic
- Spirit Magic
- Summon Magic: Ifrit

Unique Skills → Deviant

Extra Skills → Control Flame | Explosive Flame | Heat Wave | Magic Sense

Tolerance → Cancel Flame Attack | Resist Melee Attack

A girl whose body was assimilated by Ifrit. Actual age unknown, although she appears to be in her late teens and can harness a wide variety of abilities. As Conqueror of Flames, she can freely wield and manipulate fire, although her sword skills are also world class. Her Deviant unique skill is said to itself create a large number of skills.

SIDE STORY

GOBTA'S BIG ADVENTURE

That Time I Got Reincarnated as a Slime

This is a tale from back when Gobta was just another goblin in the horde.

The sky stretched blue across the heavens, a refreshing breeze flowing in the air.

And the humans advancing on him like always. Today, as lively as ever, Gobta was under pursuit.

"Halt, you! Speed's about the only thing you've got, is it?!"

"How dare you vandalize our fields again! I'm gonna kill you this time!"

The humans, eyes red with rage, were closing in on Gobta.

So he sprinted at full speed. It'd be bad for him, probably, if he let himself get caught. He could only imagine it, since he hadn't been captured yet, but none of his friends had ever come back alive from such an encounter, so all Gobta could do was imagine the terrifying results.

He could've just kept his hands off the fields and gardens, of course. But Gobta and the other goblins didn't quite grasp the concept of agriculture. All they saw was an open field with lots of fruits and vegetables growing in it. It was human territory, and they knew from experience that getting found would lead to a chase, but nothing could overcome their hunger.

So Gobta escaped down a narrow trail beaten into the earth by the local creatures, chewing the sweet flesh of a melon the whole way. The trail was barely visible at all, the sort of thing only a small goblin could successfully navigate. There would be no entry for the larger humans, who could only stop at a distance and lob insults at him instead.

He breathed a sigh of relief at his good thinking. *Finding an escape route's a basic move, it is!* he thought.

Upon arriving back at the village, Gobta found a group of the older goblin elders gathered around and discussing something. They were joined by a few kobold merchants who were in town.

"As I told you, these are too valuable for us to be able to trade elsewhere..."

"But that means this magical equipment will simply go to waste. Are you sure you can offer nothing for them?"

"If they were somewhat smaller, we would be able to wield them ourselves, but..."

"Hmm. I see. Indeed, these are too large for us to handle, either."

Eavesdropping as he passed by, Gobta figured they were trying to sell some magical something-or-others to the kobolds. Human equipment, barring shortswords and daggers, was too large for goblins.

Armor, too, was out of the question. Clothing made out of things like hard leather could be taken apart and used in piecemeal fashion, but metallic pieces were too much to work with. None of the goblins had that kind of knowledge.

Magic items were a big unknown. Even touching them, they feared, would break them and make them worthless. If not even the kobolds wanted them, it was a classic case of pearls before swine.

"How about this, then?" one kobold suggested to the goblins as they scratched their heads. "If you are willing to travel to the Dwarven Kingdom, they should be able to take these items from you. They would be willing to accept it as payment for dwarven hardware and the like, and they will gladly deliver your purchases to you as well. It will be a fair distance from here, mind...but as long as you travel upstream along the river, it is impossible to lose your way."

This led to a clamor among the assembled goblin elders. "The Dwarven Kingdom?!" one bellowed. "That is an impossible distance! I have only heard rumors of that foreign land!"

"How long would it take to travel to such a distant place?"

"Yes! And who would embark on the journey? Our young are our most valuable workers; we cannot afford to spare a single one!"

Nothin' I need to worry about! Gobta thought as he blithely ambled by, paying little attention to the seemingly never-ending bickering.

Fate had different plans.

"Hold on," the village elder said, stopping him. "You look like you have little occupying your time. Could I ask a favor?"

Gobta immediately froze. Something told him this favor wouldn't be much to his liking.

"Look at this knife," the elder continued. "Don't you think it's a wonderful piece? If you do this favor for us, I'll be happy to give it to you!"

The gleam of the blade was more than enough to grab Gobta's attention.

"Say what you will, sir! I'll handle whatever you need!" he blurted, immediately forgetting his earlier sense of foreboding. But perhaps that was unavoidable. The silvery gleam on this knife was the product of the magic imbued inside. It immediately robbed Gobta of the ability to engage in critical thought. His mouth had moved before his brain did.

Ah!

But it was already too late.

"You will, then? You will travel to the Dwarven Kingdom for us?"

"Huh? Me?!"

"May we count on you for this?"

Now the elders surrounded Gobta, identical smiles on their faces. The sight of their stern eyes above their upturned lips forced Gobta to nod meekly in response.

*   *   *

It was said that the average goblin's life span was no more than a fifth of a human's. Their lineage could be traced back to the ancient fairy-affiliated races, allegedly, but given their current degenerate monster selves, it was a tenuous link at best. Even the longest-lived were lucky to see their twentieth birthday, and most racked up only a decade or so before shuffling off. The age of three, when goblins were ready for reproductive activity, was seen as the start of their adulthood, with full maturity at age five.

They were not very strong creatures, and as a result, their species made up the difference through explosive numbers of offspring. Relatively few survived to adulthood, however, making the cruelty of nature all the more obvious. Only about half of all goblin children reached full maturity, and of those, less than half ever saw that fifth birthday.

It was simply the lot they were given, and considering these short lives, goblins did not have the habit of acquiring language skills. They could speak words, yes, but this was done strictly to communicate their intentions to each other and nothing more. There was no concept of gaining knowledge and imparting it to the next generation, nor any habit of stockpiling resources to improve their living conditions.

This was exactly why the goblins saw no use for magical items apart from selling them in exchange for their daily needs, along with any decent armor they could get their grubby paws on.

The lack of intelligence among even the elders meant that they truly had no idea what a journey to the Dwarven Kingdom would entail. The round-trip would take several months—a hefty part of a goblin's life span—and he would have to risk everything he held dear. Yet nobody in the goblin village considered it to be a terribly important mission. To the elders and other mature adults, they were simply taking a rough-sounding assignment and giving it to a child with nothing better to do. They held no ill will toward him—nor, really, the arithmetic skills needed to appreciate the scope of this quest. It was just how it was.

And so, with only a few moments of hesitation, Gobta's journey to the Dwarven Kingdom was set in stone.

✳

Why is everyone so mean? Gobta whined to himself.

He had a valid point. He was a goblin child, still not fully grown, and they were strapping a load the size of a mountain on his back and sending him off on some grand quest. He had heard from the kobolds that it'd be a two-month walk by itself, but with all this baggage? It was hard even putting one foot in front of the other.

But no point complaining about it. Gobta started to think. Then he had an idea.

Why don't I put all this junk in a box and pull it behind me?

This, unfortunately, didn't work. The box refused to move. Gobta scratched his head some more. Then he remembered the really big box he saw once, near a human settlement, with a horse pulling it around.

Oh yeah, that one had some round things on it, didn't it...?

What he was remembering was a cart, and the "round things" were wheels, although he didn't have the words for them in his vocabulary. So Gobta foraged around for something that would work in their place. What he found was a pair of abandoned circular shields.

This oughta do it!

Things proceeded commendably quickly from there. He took a straight club, then used his shiny new magical knife to whittle it down to size. Then he put a couple of holes in the box with his belongings and ran the stick through the both of them. He jammed the twin shields onto both ends of this makeshift axle and bound them in place with some handy vines he'd found. A couple extra pieces of wood for handles, and voilà—an instant pull-wagon.

With a few rags piled on top to keep things from falling off—and a few more from the village to keep warm in the evenings—he was set. The elder was kind enough to provide some food and water, too.

So Gobta left the village. Long, sentimental good-byes were never really the goblins' style anyway.

∗

I'm hungry...

A week later, Gobta was staggering forward in a state of near-total exhaustion. The food on his wagon, which he'd sort of assumed would last him the rest of his life, had disappeared by day five. There was still some water left, but not much, probably.

The wagon, meanwhile, kept getting stuck on tree roots and such, sapping Gobta's strength. Traversing on foot with his energy running low, Gobta and his journey were in jeopardy. He had now walked for two days without any food.

As his steps grew increasingly unsteady, Gobta struggled to pull his wagon along, but...

I can't...

He plopped down at the base of a large tree on the side of the path. In an amazing stroke of luck, the moment he settled down, he spotted a mushroom sprouting up from the ground. If he had examined it for a little longer, he probably would have noticed its tremendously poisonous-looking color, but the hunger was starting to cloud his vision.

Ooh, a mushroom! I could fight for three years with this!

He lunged at the mushroom, wolfing it down raw without much of a second thought.

Yet again, though, Gobta's sheer luck saved the day. The particular type of mushroom he chose was dangerously poisonous, but only if heat was applied to it—grilling, boiling, whatever. The juices of its meat would then transform into a lethal compound, something Gobta had no idea about as he inadvertently chose the safest way to enjoy it.

Having a full stomach did wonders for Gobta's spirits. He filled his leather skin from a pool of water inside a cavity in the tree, then decided to take a rest, not too interested in traveling any farther that day.

His wagon was set to break apart at any moment, but luckily there were some useful vines nearby he used to lash it back together, as well as some handy sap from the tree to fill in the assorted holes and crevices that had appeared. The bark from the tree did wonders to patch up the largest breaks in the box, too.

With that vital work complete, Gobta slept the rest of the night, relieving his fatigue. He woke up the next morning, surprisingly chipper considering how yesterday had gone, and began foraging, picking up some edible-looking nuts and wild strawberries—and spotting some more of the mushrooms from the previous day.

"I've never seen such a dangerous-looking mushroom!" he exclaimed to himself. "Not even I could eat something like that." So he left them behind, picking a duller-looking mushroom to take along in his pocket. Given all the brightly colored, poisonous-looking mushrooms in the area, he figured (in his hazy memory) that this must've been the one he'd eaten.

Man, was I lucky to find this winner among all the poison ones!

So he foraged around a little more before deciding to set off. It was still before morning, and he didn't have the foresight to stockpile food a little more before departing—so instead he slowed down, searching for more edibles along the way.

*

A month after he departed his home village, Gobta finally arrived at the large river he was told to look out for. The flowing water was beautiful and almost totally transparent. The occasional glints of sunlight he spotted within must have been fish, he reasoned.

It appeared calm on the surface, probably because it was so wide he couldn't even see the other side, but just a little below, the current looked as if it would give even a decent swimmer a run for their money.

The sheer size of the river made Gobta's eyes widen in surprise. He was familiar with creeks and the like, and he loved playing in them, but this was a whole other level of grandness. He had seen nothing like it before. The sight was unimaginable, and it was little wonder that it amazed him.

"Hyaaahhhh! This is so great!!" he shouted. The sight of the flowing water never got old to him. He sat there the entire day, just watching it go by, until night fell.

The next morning, fully satisfied at the view he had taken in, Gobta set off early. Only when he was about to start walking did he notice an important issue.

"Huh? They said to follow my left hand once I reached the river," he whispered, not expecting an answer. "But if I turn around, it's going in the opposite direction...?"

He was right. He knew he had put a mark on his left hand so he'd remember which one it was when it came time to tackle that important issue. The only problem: It turned out his left hand would point in different directions whenever he moved. Follow his left hand *where*? That was the hard part.

In the end, he decided to pick up a tree branch he found at the side of the river, let it fall to the ground, and travel the way it pointed. The fact that it wound up facing the correct way was another testament to Gobta's astounding luck. He followed the branch's lead, not doubting it for a moment, and the trip went problem-free from there.

Just when the journey was starting to bore him a little with its simplicity, Gobta saw some shallows in the river up ahead. It was a watering hole for the forest animals nearby, although none of them seemed to be fighting each other. They were avoiding confrontation at this spot—a sort of instinctual, unwritten law of nature, perhaps. Carnivore and herbivore were here together, one of the few places in the wild world where you'd ever see it.

That rule, however, was reserved for the animal kingdom. Humans and monsters didn't adhere to it. Neither did Gobta. What's more, since most monsters that hunted animals tended to be nocturnal, the animals lowered their guards when it was still light out.

What a chance! My first meat in ages!

Gobta's eyes began twinkling as he watched the creatures. Large, slow animals enjoyed the feeling of water on their backs; nimbler predators took a drink and quickly left the premises. There were even smaller birds and hares and such, drinking on the far edges to avoid the others.

His eyes swam as he took in all the options. Then he found a wild hare—a slower-looking one, fat and juicy to his eyes. The perfect size for someone like Gobta. Anything larger would've been too dangerous.

Approaching his target, Gobta stopped after a short distance and carefully observed his surroundings.

All right. So far, so good.

He grinned to himself, slowly closing in as he gathered a few stones from the ground. In a moment, he was within what he felt was comfortable throwing range. His stealth skills, honed by a long career of raiding vegetable gardens, paid off for him.

"Yah!"

Brimming with confidence, Gobta launched a stone at the hare. His unerring aim gave him a clean hit, and the animal fell into the watering hole. The others around it immediately darted off. Gobta didn't care. He was already salivating by the time he picked up the body.

Then, a problem occurred.

"Groooooooooar!!"

With a mighty wail, a magical beast appeared from between the trees. It was standing majestically atop a small cliff, and slowly its eyes turned toward Gobta.

This was a blade tiger, the so-called king of this dense forest. It enjoyed a rank of B, pretty well ensuring that an F-ranked goblin stood no chance.

This beast was here for the animals around the watering hole, just like Gobta was—but thanks to Gobta taking action first, all the animals had scattered, leaving the blade tiger with nothing. Nothing, that is, except Gobta himself. And his catch, of course, but that wouldn't be nearly enough to sate this monster.

"Gehh! Are you after me?!"

The blade tiger leaped from its perch, unfazed by the height of the cliff, and landed in front of Gobta without a sound. It made him flinch, but his instincts told him that running was pointless.

As it was, there was no escaping a fate that ended in the tiger's maw. What should he do?

Gobta thought as hard as he could. Then...

If this is how it is, I'll have to struggle as much as I can!

Steeling himself, Gobta readied himself against the blade tiger. There weren't many options at his disposal. His left hand still had a stone in it, but against a blade tiger, that wouldn't accomplish much.

Maybe that *would work...*

He suddenly recalled the knife given to him before his departure. Maybe it could wound the creature? And maybe, if he was lucky, that'd buy him enough time to escape. Once he made that conclusion, there was no time to waste. There was nothing else at his disposal, so he decided to believe in his chances and keep resisting until the end.

First, Gobta lobbed the stone. The knife was his real ticket out of here, but if the tiger dodged it, he was dead. So he used the stone first to distract the beast. The blade tiger easily leaped out of its way, and Gobta, anticipating where his adversary would land, removed the knife from his pocket and prepared to hurl it toward—

Um, this is a mushroom...?

It took a few moments for him to realize that it was no knife he was about to throw at the blade tiger. But he was already in motion, unable to stop, and away the mushroom went. He was kind of planning to eat that later. The one dull-colored mushroom he could find in a grove full of poisonous ones. He'd meant it for a snack and then promptly forgot about it.

But then something beyond Gobta's imagination took place. It turned out that this mushroom was a rare poisonous type, one containing spores that were loaded with lethal venom. Gobta had been walking around with that in his pocket the whole time, and then he'd thrown it at a magical beast.

The blade tiger glanced at the mushroom hurtling toward its face, then opened its mouth. It used its Voice Cannon skill in an attempt to vaporize it—which proved to be a mistake. The pulverized mushroom immediately released all its spores, which floated on the breeze and landed all over the tiger's body. It fell to the ground, twitching, racked from head to toe with pain; the spores had entered its eyes, ears, and mouth and were relentlessly punishing its senses.

For the first time since birth, the blade tiger was experiencing a truly indescribable level of pain. Gobta wasn't very smart, but he was smart enough to take advantage of the situation.

Whoa! I don't know what happened, but this is my big chance!

A greater adventurer would have closed in to stab the final blow. Not Gobta. Quickly, he planned his escape, making sure to pick up his hare before he left.

Reaching his battered old wagon, he tossed the bunny corpse on top of the load and ran away at full speed. He kept going as long as his breath would let him, until he finally made it to what seemed to be a safe place.

He breathed a sigh of relief, having escaped what had been the greatest danger ever to occur in his life.

Being freed from certain death immediately reminded Gobta that he was hungry. He recalled the hare in his possession, but not even he was simple enough to let his guard down here. He decided to move over to the riverbed, which would give him a good view of his entire surroundings, and used some stones and dead sticks to fashion a serviceable outdoor stove.

The danger of the past few moments was now firmly behind him as Gobta's thoughts turned to his appetite. He drained the carcass of blood, bristling with anticipation, and skinned and gutted the animal.

Before long, it was arranged on a stick atop the fire. Now all he had to do was rotate the stick around and make sure the surface was fully cooked. It was a simple recipe, combined with some berry juice squeezed over the carcass, and it took only a few moments to wrap up.

"This is great! This is *so* great!"

Gobta chewed on the meat, not minding the oils dripping down on him. There was nothing more delicious than the first meal after staring death in the face. In Gobta's case, after living off wild strawberries and assorted nuts for the past X number of days, the first meat he could remember tasted as though he had ascended to heaven. Nothing could have made him happier.

As far as he was concerned, the fear he'd felt before the blade tiger was all in the past. His brain had already processed it as just another incident in his life. It was the first time Gobta had gotten to eat his fill in a while. This he did, with gusto.

"Right!" he said. "I have a feeling tomorrow's gonna be a great day!"

To Gobta, the past might as well have been a faraway oblivion. All that really mattered was the next day.

$$*$$

The blade tiger run-in turned out to be the last major trouble Gobta encountered for the next month of traveling.

The hazy mountains that had seemed so far away long ago now loomed so large that the peaks were no longer visible, even if he looked straight up. The buttes above him had been weathered down by the rain to form a beautiful, powerful-looking, sheer wall. Everything was a new sight to Gobta, and everything grabbed his interest.

But he didn't have the time to leisurely take in the sights. He was almost out of food again. He was already in lands more or less under the protection of the dwarven king, mostly grasslands outside the Forest of Jura. He tried to collect as much as he could before he took up the mountain road, but not only would there be no replenishing his stockpiles—those stockpiles were starting to look pretty meager.

The breathtaking views around him helped Gobta forget about his hunger, but it was now time to face reality. And that wasn't the only problem. Gobta wasn't the only one on the road to the Dwarven Kingdom. As a neutral trade hub, it played host to all kinds of different species—not just magic-born creatures and people but also humans.

As Gobta discovered, most travelers along this route preferred to stick to large groups if at all possible. All races were guaranteed safety in the kingdom, as a rule, but security forces could reach only so far in the borderlands. People needed to and were expected to fend for themselves. That was common sense to the merchants, but Gobta neither knew nor cared about any of that.

This was why, while he was distracted over the food issue, he ran into a wholly different kind of problem. Just as he was thinking about how he'd better find some real nourishment soon, he heard a voice.

"Yo," it said, "what's a lone goblin doin' here cartin' valuables around, eh?"

Gobta didn't understand him. Goblins communicated with each other using a method not terribly far from the Thought Communication skill. A few broken words of human speech were the best they could handle.

He was, however, still sensitive to the malice behind the statement. He hadn't noticed the human's approach, and looking up at him, Gobta could already sense the danger.

Uh-oh... This can't be good.

Gobta grabbed at the handles on his wagon, preparing to run away at full speed. But...

"Ohhh no you don't!"

Another human appeared in front of him—a fighter in metallic armor. The other man, wearing lighter gear, peered inside the wagon and let out an appreciative whistle.

"Whoa! I wasn't expecting much, but these're *magic* items, aren't they? Boy, are we lucky today! All we gotta do is kill this little guy, and we've already earned the money for our shopping trip!"

"Oh? I was expecting just a little spending cash, but what a stroke of luck. Can't wait to see the faces on those bastards who were too lazy to join us!"

Gobta ignored the exchange as he thought about what to do next. Running into this unexpected trouble so close to the Dwarven Kingdom surprised him—but there was no time to ponder his fate. He calmed his beating heart as he searched for a decent solution.

What should I do?! If this keeps up, they'll take all of it. And I think my life might be in danger, too...

As he thought about it, it was clear these men might be after more than some magic doodads. Only then did Gobta realize the extent of the danger.

Soon he realized he was right. Blocking his path of retreat, the men began attacking him. Considering Gobta's childlike size, it wasn't a fair fight. The men were fully armored and boasting the strength of rank-D adventurers. Gobta didn't stand a chance. Without a stroke of luck equivalent to the one that helped him survive the blade tiger, it would be the end of the road for him.

But once again, the goddess of fortune smiled.

"What are you people doing over there?"

Gobta and his attackers turned around to find a goblina staring them down—a fighter, judging by her muddy red hair. They could see a kobold merchant caravan behind her—she must have been a bodyguard.

The men took a moment to size up their chances. They numbered two, and they'd potentially be taking on an entire caravan led by a professional warrior. Hobgoblins of either gender were high-level creatures capable of language, far more intelligent than their goblin relatives. In terms of skill, meanwhile, the men were still rank amateurs.

This was no match a sane man would take. And even if they just wanted to make off with this doltish goblin's baggage, it was too late for that.

"Pfft," the armored one said. "We'll let you go this time!"

"Best be glad to still be breathing, worm!"

And then they left, leaving Gobta miraculously alive yet again.

✳

Gobta must have been so elated at this stroke of fortune that he lost consciousness, because the next thing he knew, the clattering of the horse wagon had started to rouse him. The bruises the men had landed on him stung enough to wake him up fully.

"Oh, are you up?"

He looked up to find the red-haired goblina at his side—almost human in appearance, unlike the apish goblins. A single glance made Gobta her prisoner. He instantly forgot all about his injuries and immediately fell in love with the woman.

"An angel. An angelic woman from heaven! Please! I want you to birth my children!"

When it came to romance, goblins never took things slow. The rest of the wagon's occupants took it as a joke.

"Bah-hah-hah-hah! Nice one, kid!"

"Oh-ho! You heard him!"

"Silence, you two!" the goblina snapped. "Stop with the chitchat and stay on alert!"

The sarcasm flew straight over the head of Gobta, his burning eyes still fixated upon his new ideal. Reality, unfortunately, was not as kind.

"Look," the woman said, "cowards like you just aren't my type. Letting yourself be bullied by humans *that* weak? I'd never let a man like that into my life! I'd at least like someone who could rescue me, if need be."

Thus Gobta's first romance ended several seconds after it began. The physical pain returned.

"N-no… I can't believe it…"

Then he fainted again, the sense of loss too much to bear.

The kobold caravan wound up taking him all the way to the Dwarven Kingdom, at least, which saved him the trouble of being killed by roadside scavengers at night…

His first love didn't quite work out, but at least his first quest did.

Thanks to his newfound kobold connections, Gobta was quickly taken to a dwarven shop willing to purchase his luggage. The employees were a bit surprised to find magical weapons underneath the stained rags covering his wagon, but the rest of the transaction was handled with trademark dwarven customer service.

The dwarves here were so accustomed to dealing with monsters that they could even communicate with them to some extent. One of the staff pointed at Gobta's hips.

"Hey, are you selling that?"

He looked down to find his knife resting against his hip.

Oh! I had it along my side, not in my pocket!

No wonder he had plucked out a mushroom instead.

"No, this is mine," Gobta replied. "Not selling."

The dwarf nodded. "It's a good piece," he said, "but its magical force has almost run out. It'd only work one or more two times, I imagine. Do you know how to use it?"

"No, but...is this a magic weapon?"

"It is. It's called a Flame Knife. It's made of silver, but it's been imbued with magical force. It was originally made as self-protection for human nobles. I could teach you the incantation if you like, but don't expect it to last long when you use it."

"Really?!"

"Really. Just take good care of it. It's a dagger of Dwarven Kingdom make, after all!"

So the good-natured dwarf gave Gobta the correct spell to use, apparently deciding that the idea of a goblin with magic dwarven weapons was amusing enough to warrant giving some help.

Gobta's business here was now over. He had accepted items instead of money for his load, but there'd be no need to cart it all back—the cost of shipping was factored into the deal the dwarves gave him. Gobta's terms: as many kitchen knives, large pots, and other everyday goods as could fit in his wagon. He also arranged for some breastplates, knives, and other pieces suitable for goblin use.

He brought it all to the transfer station for registration and shipment. They gave him a magic-infused tube that, once he placed it where he wanted it, would transmit his items right to that point. It would work only once, of course. Inexpensive purchases like Gobta's could also be sent by Heavenly Transport, but that was available only for short distances, and besides, Gobta didn't have the language to express exactly where he lived. For him, even though it added to the price, magical transfer was the only option.

Gobta didn't hesitate to take the offer, not exactly champing at the bit to pull a full wagon all the way back home as well. It'd save him from more potential raiders and unburden him to boot. The decision would prove to be the correct one later on.

After he was done at the transfer station, Gobta returned to the seller from before, hoping to express his thanks to the dwarf who had referred him. "Hello!" he said. "They're going to transfer my purchases for me. Thanks!"

"Oh, you again? Well, wonderful. Oh, and you can have this back. We can't sell this piece."

The dwarf gave him a thick coat made of the animal pelts Gobta had been using as a blanket. He had taken several more wild hares, saving their skins for later sale; the coat was made from all of them, offering the wearer shelter from the cold. The dwarf had offered to return them, but he must have crafted the item specially for Gobta.

"Huh? Are you sure?"

"Mm-hmm. Besides, if we took all those pelts, what would you sleep on at night? You need to prepare well before setting off on a journey, you know." Then the dwarf took out a well-used backpack. "Take this, too. Instead of giving you your change in money, I put some dried food in there. It should last you a week or so. Safe travels."

"Really?" Gobta said, astonished at the dwarf's kindness. "I thank you!"

"Ah, don't worry about it. I actually made that knife you have, you see, and I wouldn't want to leave its owner in the lurch. I'll be praying that you make it home safely."

Then the dwarf stepped away, off to handle another customer. Gobta nodded at him one more time, although he doubted his new friend noticed.

He's right… If I left here empty-handed, I wouldn't even make it to the forest. What a kind dwarf that was!

Putting on the coat, then the backpack over that, Gobta left the shop. His mission was complete, but he wasn't about to set off that quickly. "I've made it this far," he whispered to himself. "It's all right if I see the sights a little, right?"

The Dwarven Kingdom was built inside a large, natural cave, preventing Gobta from seeing the sun directly. Thanks to some clever engineering that allowed natural sunlight to enter the city's living spaces, however, it was more than bright enough to see by. At night, the fluorescent moss that covered the cave's walls provided about as much light as a full moon.

One issue was how people handled fire. The kingdom wasn't an enclosed space, but the cave made it easy for clouds of thick smoke to form, making ventilation a priority. As a result, whether indoors or "outdoors," the use of fire was restricted, with firemen required to be on hand at all times near workshops, kitchens, and any other workplace that handled flame.

Which meant that cooking food was allowed only in certain places, always indoors.

Usually, if he was uncomfortable, he could just douse himself in some water. But Gobta had just wrapped up a long journey. To be blunt, he was rank. It was to be expected, given goblins' lack of regular bathing habits. He didn't stand out too much in the shops near the entrance, which were packed with freshly arrived adventurers just as smelly as he was, but things were different in the lodging quarters. There was ventilation, yes, but Gobta's natural smell was more than enough to alarm the people around him.

In the merchant areas, passersby and visiting merchants visibly crinkled their noses. It was enough to make even Gobta feel socially awkward.

I don't really like it here… Maybe I should leave sooner rather than later.

Feeling ashamed, Gobta decided to head home.

That was the right decision to make. For one thing, he had no money and no way of eating while he toured the city. He didn't even understand the concept of money, for that matter, which was why he had just wrapped up a huge bartering session with that dwarf. There was no way around it.

So Gobta decided to wrap up his little tourist jaunt and get back on the road—and then he saw it. A store festooned with beautiful, eye-catching decor, filled with goddess-like women chatting with each other. The goblina bodyguard from the caravan had seemed divine to him before, but these women were different. They had long, flowing blond hair, their long ears poking out from below. They were elves, particularly fairylike members of the sprite races.

Concepts like beauty and ugliness would normally be dependent on the race or species one belonged to. There were no absolutes. However, when it came to goblins, their likes and dislikes were closer to people's than not. It was a relic from their fairy heritage, and while their looks had retrogressed more than a little over the years, they were still magical in nature. It was to the point that some particularly senseless goblins would even attack people with procreation purposes in mind.

So lovely! I wish I could make friends with a pretty elf girl sometime, too!

Gobta wanted it to happen. And he knew that getting stronger was the only way to do it. Just as that caravan guard had said, if he was stronger, beautiful women would like him—that was how his thought process worked.

It was with that new goal in life that Gobta spent his single night in the Dwarven Kingdom. It seemed foolish to depart for the wilds at night, so he camped out in the park near the main gate instead. The cave at least prevented him from getting rained on, and the coat that nice dwarf had made for him kept the cold at bay. It was a more comfortable night than he'd expected, and Gobta awoke bursting with energy.

The fountain in the park apparently used spring water as its source, allowing passersby to drink from it. Gobta took his skin out from the backpack, filled it up, and set off, leaving the Dwarven Kingdom behind him.

*

Someone spoke to him right after he passed through the gate.

"Oh, is that you, kid? Is your work done here?"

Gobta looked up to find a kobold merchant. Two hobgoblin fighters were behind him, along with the goblina with the muddy red hair.

"Oh, it's you!" Gobta exclaimed.

The caravan was also just about on its way. Richer merchants would spend several nights in the city, enjoying the assorted entertainment options it offered, but the smaller-time caravans didn't have that luxury. Get in, do your business, get home, and relax with your own kind—that was how they normally worked.

The kobolds invited Gobta onto their caravan after greeting him.

"We're taking the same route, aren't we? We have room, so why not join us? Just provide us some protection if any bandits or magic beasts show up," their leader said with a grin. He was expecting nothing from Gobta, of course—this was just a polite excuse to get him on the wagon. Gobta, completely insensitive to sarcasm, laughed with him, a little proud to be offered such a role.

The group proceeded along the river path, blessed with an uneventful journey as they pressed through the grasslands and plunged into the Forest of Jura. Gobta had ample wild birds to hunt wherever they rested, a decent supply of nuts and fruit to gather—and he did his part, pooling his resources with the caravan's.

"You've got a real talent for this, don't you?" the leader said, a tad astonished. "Look at all the food you've tracked down for us..."

"Indeed," another kobold interjected, "you must know the Forest of Jura like the back of your hand. In the woods, you're a lot more help than I'd ever expect."

"Quite true. I had no idea you had this kind of talent!"

Gobta, his latest catch in one hand and a spare stone in the other, couldn't hide his joy at this. Nobody ever praised him this much in the village. He enjoyed it.

One day, they came across those poisonous-looking, brightly colored mushrooms again—just like the one Gobta had inadvertently eaten to quell his hunger.

You can't eat these... But hang on. Huh? Those normal-looking mushrooms over there look kind of dangerous, too. Was that really the one I ate?

There was a spark of self-doubt in his mind—but those mushrooms were too colorful, and too bloodred and foreboding as well, to be considered edible at all. Even Gobta, who was rapidly letting all the praise get to his head, was a little iffy about trying it.

"Um, those plain ones? You can't eat those," the goblina told him. "Those are known as firespores, and they're deadly. The stronger ones even explode if you expose them to fire, spreading poison all over the area. I won't stop you if you want to try, but don't expect to survive."

Gobta nodded appreciatively. Of course he did. No way would he ever eat anything so dangerous.

Ignoring the firespores, Gobta and his friends focused on gathering nuts and fruits instead. In addition to the group he was in, there were others by the river, replenishing their water supply, as well as cooking the food they'd found.

Just as they all had finished their jobs and were about ready to prepare dinner—

"Grooooooar!!"

—they heard a terrifying, earth-shattering roar. A magical beast appeared, exuding rage as it eyed the caravan. It was that blade tiger again, the B-ranked beast that Gobta had inadvertently defeated a few months back. The poison spores had damaged it, but it had been lucky enough to be near a lake that must have helped it recover. It was still as angry as ever, though, more than angry enough to convince the low-ranked goblin that had once escaped it that all was lost now.

The beast, proud by nature, had sworn it would avenge the slight upon its reputation. With another roar, it used Voice Cannon to cleanly blow one of the guards away. The single blast made it all too clear how powerful the blade tiger was—even the stoutest of hobgoblins would face grave injuries after taking the brunt of it. If it weren't for the full-plate armor protecting him, he would have died instantly.

"My brother!"

Another hobgoblin let out a yelp of surprise, but he was too petrified to move. All he could do was hold an unsteady ax in his hands and keep a watchful eye on the blade tiger. No one could blame him. Hobgoblins were ranked C or so. They weren't made to take on a tiger like this.

"Don't prod him," the female guard quietly warned. "This guy's dangerous. It'd take ten of us to have at least a chance of taking on a blade tiger. Merchants! We need to give up our goods and slowly step away from the area."

She knew that angering a blade tiger would do nothing but make the situation even more treacherous. She at least wanted her clients to survive the encounter. While the tiger was feasting on their horses, they could at least attempt an escape—if they were lucky, they might even make it.

But that hope was quickly dashed. The blade tiger didn't want a meal. It wanted revenge. It eyed the rest of the guards slowly, seeking out the goblin it really wanted. Then it snarled at the kobolds slowly edging away from their encampment. The merchants fell to the ground, understanding they'd be allowed no mercy.

"Well, this is it," one of the guards muttered. "It's not gonna let us go."

"What should we do, miss? We can't win this?"

"Guess we gotta charge it. Merchants! Once we're on our way, I want all of you to run like hell! And don't bunch up, either, unless you want to die."

The guards were ready to sacrifice their lives for the sake of their clients, using themselves as bait to let them survive. Despair filled the air around them, but one among them failed to read the mood. That was Gobta, of course, who took the blade tiger's roar as nothing less than his big chance.

It's that tiger, isn't it?! The guy I chased off with that mushroom? Even I could beat him!

It would have been a fatal mistake for anyone else, but Gobta was the only one in the camp not completely stricken by terror. He leaped forward as the blade tiger let out another sinister snarl.

"You fool!" the female bodyguard shouted. "What could you ever do?!"

"You can leave this to me!" Gobta shouted back with a smile. Then he dashed into the forest. The blade tiger immediately gave chase, ignoring everybody else.

The rest of the group were left dumbfounded, if only for a moment.

"That idiot... How could he be so reckless...?"

The seemingly selfless move shook the guards to the core, but they knew they couldn't let this chance go unheeded.

"Everyone! Get out of here now! We'll hold that thing off here!"

"But..."

"Don't worry. This is our job. If we can get away from that monster, we'll send a flare up to signal you."

"He's right. We're not intending to die here, either. I'd kinda like to see you guys again, all right?"

With that, the guards piled the merchants into the wagon. Gobta wouldn't give them much time to work with, but if the guards stayed behind, that would open up a chance for the merchants to get out safely. They waited for the wagon to set off, then plunged into the forest where Gobta left them.

Meanwhile—

Ahhh! This is scary! This is so scary!!

Now the sight of the blade tiger catching up to him was getting a bit unnerving. It deserved every bit of its B rank when it came to speed, and soon it was right on Gobta's heels.

Maybe I shouldn't have tried to act all cool back there—

There was no point regretting it now. Gobta was too busy trying to widen the gap to care. But even as his chances of being cornered grew by the second, another brilliant idea entered his mind.

Maybe if I use this—

Gobta stopped, standing his ground, and took something out from his pocket. With a defiant grin, he threw it straight at the blade tiger. The creature stopped, more surprised at the sudden end to this chase than at the object hurtling toward its head. This would normally be when the blade tiger used Voice Cannon, its mightiest weapon, to pulverize whatever was in front of it. But the memory of its past errors made the tiger hesitate.

It was intelligent enough not to repeat the same mistake twice—but what would normally be an advantageous trait spelled doom for it. Instead of Voice Cannon, the blade tiger figured it would bite down on the incoming object to stop it. With its reflexes, it would be an easy thing to do.

But the moment the object was between its teeth, Gobta shouted: "Unseal!!"

Before the blade tiger could understand it, the incantation took effect. Just as Gobta had hoped, the magical tube provided to him by the transfer office did exactly what it was made to do—unfurling all the pots, pans, weapons, and even his wagon inside the tiger's mouth.

This had exactly the effect Gobta had been hoping for—it ripped the blade tiger's jaw off its head.

"All right!" Gobta shouted in joy. But that wasn't the end of his plan. He still had one final weapon on hand—his Flame Knife. Considering a blade tiger's performance in battle, merely losing its lower jaw wouldn't be enough to send it down for the count. That was why Gobta figured his pride and joy—his one magic weapon—would be what it took.

Then Gobta noticed the (slightly bloodied) items strewn on the forest floor.

But if I burn this here, I'm going to burn my stuff, too, aren't I? Maybe I should try to lure him deeper in.

Once again faced with an agony it had never known, the confused blade tiger was starting to lose its ability to make rational decisions. Gobta's fleeing enraged it. It could no longer consider its adversary's schemes or ultimate goals. Instead, it followed instinct and gave chase again.

The pain was intense, but it was the humiliating loss of Voice Cannon that made it especially furious. All that filled its mind was a consuming desire to kill Gobta for good.

After creating a measure of distance between him and the tiger, the small goblin dove into a dense thicket. This reduced the blade tiger's advantage and further widened the gap between Gobta and his pursuer.

Turning around, Gobta focused on the blade tiger. Just as he'd thought, it was making a beeline for him.

Okay! I can't miss from here!

Caught up in the dense underbrush, the tiger found itself robbed of its mobility. A straight throw, Gobta figured, was all he needed to hit home—and he had magic to trigger, too. Not even a magical beast would crawl home from that in good shape.

With Voice Cannon gone, the blade tiger had nothing to block with. Gobta knew it. So he threw the Flame Knife.

"Fire!" he shouted, the word the dwarf had taught him. That activated the knife. Flames encompassed it as it zoomed toward the blade tiger. A magic weapon like this would normally be nothing to a B-ranked magical beast, but the tiger was on its guard. Fatally so, as it came to be.

Using one of the bladelike fangs on its upper jaw, the blade tiger deflected the flame-infused knife. Gobta gasped in despair...but that was exactly what he needed. The Flame Knife bounced off the tooth, hurtled downward, and thrust itself into the ground. There, as it happened, grew a mushroom with certain special qualities. A kind that spat out lethal poison when exposed to heat. One that was fully mature, ripe, and packed with spores.

The firespore exploded in all directions around it, triggering cascading explosions across the area. The blade tiger was right in the thick of it, with no escape, its body exposed to every one of the searing spores. It had deflected a strike that would've been merely a flesh wound at best, only to expose itself to devastating damage instead.

Too tired to take another step, Gobta was greeted by some familiar voices.

"Wow, nice one! We'll handle the rest!"

"Dang, kid... You're one hell of a fighter after all, huh? That'll learn me!"

The guards could handle a blade tiger this injured well enough. Soon, it was all over. Gobta was victorious.

✳

It was now time for them to take their own paths—Gobta deeper into the wood, the caravan back along the river to the demon lord's lands.

"I broke my treasure in the battle," Gobta whined, "and I'll have to pull that wagon all the way back home, too..." The smile on his face, however, indicated he wasn't especially torn up over it.

"Well, thanks to that, you saved us all," the head merchant said. "We really need to thank you again."

Gobta grinned sheepishly at them.

"You know," the goblina guard stammered, "I—I think I could—"

"I'm gonna get stronger, miss! I'm gonna beat another magical beast just like that—all by myself! So I can save your life sometime!"

"Huh? Um... Yeah. Yeah, exactly. Keep it up!"

Gobta had stopped her before she could finish the sentence. Which was probably a good thing. It likely gave Gobta all the encouragement he needed to keep striving for loftier heights, besides.

Thus the two of them parted ways. Gobta's love would have to remain unrequited, maybe for his whole life.

Pulling the wagon behind him, Gobta walked deeper into the forest. The guards and merchants watched as he did.

"You know," the female guard whispered to herself, "I wouldn't mind bearing children, if they were his."

"Not too late, miss!" one of her friends said with a laugh.

"No, it's fine. He's probably different from the likes of us anyway. He's *got* something, you know? He has to. Otherwise he never could've survived any of this."

"Maybe so, maybe so... You're right, I think."

They stood there until Gobta finally disappeared from sight.

AFTERWORD

Hello there! Fuse here. First of all, I'd like to thank you for picking up this book.

This volume is a heavily revised, rewritten, and expanded version of a story originally released on the web. This work, as I'm sure some of you know, is still being released on syosetu.com, a Japanese-language website for online novelists and storytellers. The side story and other extra material in this particular book are all original to this volume, crafted for followers of the web version to enjoy.

If this is a completely new tale to you, I'd like to suggest that you check out the web version as well. The main plot is the same between both versions, but you'll also find a fair number of differences here and there, so I imagine it could be fun to compare the two for yourself.

This is the first time I've ever written an afterword, and figuring out what I should write in it has made me slightly nervous. As a result, I suppose I should write a word or two of thanks to the original forces that brought this book to life.

First, thanks go out as always to the people that read and supported this story on the web. Your reviews and thoughts gave me a great deal of strength.

Thank you, Mitz Vah, who provided the wonderful illustrations for this book and gave so much life and motion to all the story's many characters. I'm sure I'll be making lots more selfish requests to you going forward, but I hope you'll be willing to put up with it.

Thank you, Mr. I, the editor who first approached me about making a print edition. If it weren't for his passion, this volume never would've been released.

Finally, thank you to everyone who purchased this book. If you read through *That Time I Got Reincarnated as a Slime* and liked it, nothing could make me happier.

With that, I hope to continue having you read my stories. Thanks again, everyone!

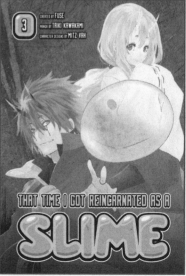